ROGUE JUSTICE

By John R. Monteith

BRAVESHIP BOOKS

Table of Contents

CHAPTER 1

Dmitry Volkov straightened his back beside the navigation table and questioned the definition of victory.

For the moment, survival sufficed.

"Any chance our weapon will hit?" he asked in Russian.

"Impossible," the sonar operator said. "The Israeli torpedo has a better chance of hitting us than vice versa."

"Very well," Volkov said. "Our shot was reactive garbage, but I doubt the Israeli shot was much better aimed."

"Not much. You're on the proper course to evade, and eight knots is adequate to make it pass safely behind us."

Volkov's heart rate slowed.

"You've turned off our phantom noise?" he asked.

"Of course. I did so the moment I heard the hostile weapon."

Volkov had hesitated to play the recorded propulsion sounds of an Egyptian *Type-209* submarine from his *Scorpène*-class submarine's sonar system, but his mission parameters demanded that he attempt to convince the Israeli Navy of increased Egyptian naval activity.

After transiting the Suez Canal, leaving Port Said, and crossing Egypt's twelve-mile boundary into international waters, he'd transformed his ship, the *Wraith*, into the acoustic equivalent of an artificially loud Egyptian submarine to bait an Israeli vessel.

Now that one had shot a torpedo at him, he considered a significant tactical goal achieved by making the Israeli Navy suspicious that its southern neighbors were sending submarines to challenge their superiority off the coasts of the Gaza Strip and Sinai Peninsula.

"Good," Volkov said. "I'm glad that step is behind us and that accursed signal generator is off."

"I understand, but I think that piping out an abnormally loud signal strength may have had an unexpected benefit. It convinced the Israelis that we were closer than we really were. That threw off their targeting."

"Perhaps. Or perhaps their torpedo attack was designed to be no more than a warning to their neighbors to remember who possesses the stronger undersea fleet."

The sonar operator showed increased interest in the conversation as he turned his head towards Volkov and lowered an earmuff to his jaw to better hear his commander.

"That's an interesting theory, but we may never know."

"I'm sure we'll never know" Volkov said. "And, thankfully, I'll also never have to broadcast my position to a hostile submarine again. That was disquieting."

"There was never any real danger in that shot. You'd think we'd all be used to running from torpedoes by now, anyway."

"I fear you've lost your sense of reason, Anatoly. I hope that running from torpedoes never becomes a habit. We can tempt fate only so many times."

"That's not what I meant," Anatoly said.

"What did you mean, then?"

"I mean if we have to keep running from torpedoes, nobody's better at it than us."

"That much I can concede," Volkov said. "And we evaded yet another, but now we have an angry adversary."

He recalled that Egypt had offered to delay any military escalation while diplomats sought peaceful resolutions to the Israeli prime minister's threats of expansion.

The southwesterly presence and violent response of the *Dolphin*-class submarine against his faked Egyptian vessel proved the Israeli Navy's doubt of that offer. The attack also verified Volkov's intelligence declaring the naval forces as supporting the Israeli prime minister's policies of reclaiming the lands gained long ago in the Six-Day War.

One errant hostile torpedo told him that fifty-one years had healed nothing.

Though split among dissenting factions of its military, government, and public opinion, Israel followed its prime minister's push to reclaim lands it had won in past wars. Some feared disobeying their nation's leader for the risk of his retribution. Others feared his warmongering for the risk of collateral damage.

Grateful to avoid becoming the first naval statistic counted in that collateral damage, Volkov represented the inception of the effort to prevent aggressive political speech from growing into unchecked military tension and the rekindling of war.

"We need to maintain eight knots for ten minutes," Anatoly said. "I still can't hear the Israeli submarine yet."

"I don't expect that you'll hear it ten minutes from now either, when we slow."

"No, Dmitry. It must be too far away."

Volkov turned his thoughts towards his special weapons and glanced at the gray-bearded mechanical technician seated at the panel that controlled his ship's propulsion, depth, and steering.

"Tell the trainer to get his dolphins ready," he said.

The gray beard lifted a sound-powered phone to his cheek.

"He's getting them loaded into the tube," he said.

Volkov looked at the display on the navigation table and watched the icon of an Israeli torpedo drift behind his vessel. He realized that a lucky steering command sent up the hostile torpedo's guidance wire could prove deadly, but he trusted fate to protect him from such misery.

While glaring downward at raw sonar data on a screen-within-screen view, he pondered his mission.

He understood why the Israeli prime minister sought expansion. Though the Sinai Peninsula presented few immediate problems to his nation, three conquered but non-annexed areas provided continual unrest.

Covering an area one-fourth that of Israel proper, the West Bank fell under a blend of Israeli governance, Palestinian governance, and mixed rule depending on the block-by-block location. Despite tensions, the strange mélange of culture and religion functioned, although the United Nations exacerbated the pressure by condemning anything the prime minister ordered that resembled permanent Israeli settlements.

The Gaza Strip, walled and blockaded while under Palestine's Hamas rule, was worse. And the Golan Heights, which provided crucial water to Israel, offered another front that included spillover problems from the failed nation of Syria and from Lebanese Hezbollah militants.

Volkov understood why the prime minister felt compelled to push his military influence deeper into the dangerous regions surrounding his nation.

But he understood why people would resist. Backlash, desperation, violence. Diplomacy was imperfect, but it had held the disparate people in neighboring and intertwining lands together in some semblance of a functioning existence.

"It's hard to choose a side," he said.

"Excuse me?" the gray beard asked.

"Nothing. I was just thinking out loud."

"About the problems in Israel?"

"Well, yes," Volkov said. "It seems so desperate from every angle. The only thing that gives me any hope is the position of the Israeli Military Intelligence Directorate, which makes perfect sense to me and is the one we're supporting."

He glanced at a young man wearing the green uniform of an Israeli Army Captain, who nodded his concurrence. Some factions of the military resisted the prime minister, and the intelligence officer rode Volkov's ship as a gesture of trust, a measure of oversite, and as a conduit to possible real-time information. He also proved useful as a backup translator.

"The situation in Israel has always been unstable," the gray beard said. "The Six-Day War more than doubled their land, most of which they gave back, but they kept their military presence in the Golan Heights, West Bank, and Gaza Strip."

Volkov raised an eyebrow.

"I didn't know you were a student of history."

"I'm not. I'm just an old man with a memory."

"You certainly don't remember nineteen sixty-seven."

"No, but I remember the aftermath in the seventies, including another short war. You can't expect peace when two peoples have deeply rooted disagreements about their worldviews and about who owns the land."

"So, should we give up and go home?" Volkov asked. "You make lasting peace sound hopeless."

"It is."

Volkov scolded his veteran.

"Don't tell me you consider this mission folly."

"Of course, I don't. I'm here to stop aggressions. I also hope that my participation helps get supplies to women and children who would otherwise suffer without."

The comment reminded Volkov of his second fringe role in as many missions with his mercenary teammates. Though working in the same sea as his comrades, he felt unsure if they accepted him as an equal.

Having assumed he'd been undergoing a rite of passage in their prior mission, he'd accepted being a distraction in distant waters. But now he wanted to fight where his skills could harmonize with those of his elite colleagues to create profound outcomes.

He stuffed the doubt inside his gut and forced himself to focus on the positive. Lifting his chin, he summoned a lively tone.

"Don't be so negative," he said. "You're talking like a jaded pessimist. We might actually contribute to an enduring peace."

"I disagree, Dmitry," the gray beard said. "If there were a path to lasting peace in these lands, humanity would've found it by now. People like us can only right the wrongs within our grasp."

"Yes, I'll agree to righting wrongs we can change. Let's get back to such business if that torpedo's a concern I can consider a matter of history."

After glancing at his display, he deemed himself safe and aimed his voice at his sonar guru.

"Does your hearing align with the solution in the system?"

"Yes, Dmitry," Anatoly said. "We're free of the torpedo."

"You should inform our fleet command," the gray beard said.

"Spoken like a true son of the Russian Navy," Volkov said. "Was it only six short months ago we were fighting for our homeland against our present employer?"

"Roughly," the gray beard said. "Time's flown by so quickly. I've seen more real action since then than in my entire Russian career."

"Perhaps you are indeed our historian by virtue of age. You've lived our history, and you remember it."

"Fleet command, Dmitry?"

"Right. Our employer is our fleet commander. Bring us to periscope depth and prepare for a satellite video and data link with Pierre Renard."

Volkov turned and stepped upon the *Wraith's* elevated conning platform. The deck tilted as the submarine rocked in the swells, and he extended his hands to balance his descent into a bulkhead-mounted foldout chair.

The video feed appeared.

He tapped keys and lifted his chin towards the upper monitor where crow's feet framed the piercing blue eyes of his French employer. Sharp features under silvery hair faced him.

Leaning on the polished rail encircling the conning platform, one of the *Wraith's* translators awaited orders. Volkov obliged, speaking in small phrases and letting the familiar two-way translations become a background drone.

"I just exchanged inaccurate torpedo shots with a vessel I couldn't detect," he said. "The hostile torpedo was a SeaHake, which suggests an Israeli submarine."

"Very good," Renard said in English, which the translator regurgitated in Russian. "Were you augmented?"

"Yes. Per plan, I was simulating an Egyptian *Type-209*."

"Excellent," Renard said. "You've managed to complicate the perspective of the Israeli Navy."

Volkov frowned at his boss.

"I can't help but think this ruse as an Egyptian submarine was doomed from inception. Won't the Israelis figure out that I just took the *Wraith* through the Suez Canal? Won't they also have spies watching the berthing of each Egyptian submarine?"

"Yes and yes. They'll surely know that our three-ship fleet is in the Mediterranean. They'll also note that two Egyptian submarines are deployed, which happen to be conducting exercises to the west beyond Israeli detection. Therefore, the sum of all this subterfuge will be uncertainty in the Israeli Navy's perspective, which is to our advantage."

Volkov attempted to measure his employer's comfort level in micromanagement.

"I intend to give chase to the submarine that attacked me."

"Interesting," Renard said. "For what goal?"

"I would use a slow-kill weapon to reduce the Israeli submarine order of battle by one."

"I see. But by using our custom slow-kill warhead, you'd reveal my fleet's involvement against them, and you'd unravel the subterfuge of Egyptian involvement."

"I know, but you certainly wouldn't have me use a heavyweight torpedo?"

"I hope and trust that you'll never use a heavyweight torpedo–or an anti-ship missile, for that matter–against Israel."

Volkov suspected Israel had been Renard's past client, but such information lived in the untold stories he hoped to someday hear as he gained his boss' confidence.

"That's good to know," he said. "What's your opinion on my proposed aggression?"

"I agree with it. I'll allow you the engagement. Let's see how you do against Israel's best. I trust you'll use your dolphins?"

"Yes. I have no other advantage."

"Very well. I'd wish you luck, but that's not my way. I prefer to ask my commanders to remain charmed. I hope the good fortune that surrounded you in the Black Sea and in the Arabian Sea continues for you now."

Volkov tested his learning by answering Renard in English.

Prior to the Frenchman's call to arms against the Israelis, he and much of his crew had immersed themselves in English language training.

"Thank you, Pierre," he said. "I will do well."

The *Wraith's* commander ordered his ship deep and then passed behind the backs of technical experts seated at consoles of the ship's Subtics tactical system. He looked at his executive officer, a man in his late twenties who'd been a junior officer on a Russian *Kilo*-class submarine, and told him to take charge of the bridge.

Volkov reached the torpedo room where a man as lithe and graceful as the animals he trained hovered over a makeshift aquarium in the compartment's center passageway.

"Vasily?" Volkov asked.

The trainer kept his hand on a broached dorsal fin as he looked up and forced an uncertain smile.

"I think they're getting used to their cramped tank. They appear to have adapted since our last mission."

"My crew's still fond of them, too, despite having to crawl around them. I assume you've already loaded Andrei?"

"He's in tube three."

Volkov glanced at the opened breach door on the middle of three stacked starboard torpedo tubes. He saw four sailors squeezing around spare weapons to maneuver a tarp attached to an overhead block and tackle system towards the centerline tank.

"Dmitry, please," the trainer said.

"Oh, right."

At the trainer's spurring, Volkov stepped back and let the sailors load the second bottlenose dolphin onto the tarp. With practiced skill, the men lowered the canvas under the floating animal and worked beast and cradle together.

They hoisted Mikhail and swiveled him towards the waiting tube, exposing a blue harness wrapped forward of his dorsal fin that carried a camera, a sonic communications transceiver, and a small explosive device. The animal began to wiggle, exposing long rows of small teeth, and he fluttered his tongue while releasing a staccato screech.

"Relax, Mikhail," the trainer said.

"Was Andrei calmer when you moved him?" Volkov asked.

"Yes, as always. Mikhail's still so emotional."

"Such is his nature."

"Slide him behind Andrei," the trainer said.

Two sailors pushed the dolphin's fluke as two others slipped the tarp from under the animal.

"Close the breach," the trainer said. "Good. Now equalize pressure. Slowly. Now flood the tube and start the clock. No more than four minutes. They can't hold their breath forever."

With the tube flooded, Volkov ordered the muzzle door opened.

"And once again my babies go into combat," the trainer said.

Back in the control room, Volkov stood over his sonar leader's shoulder.

"Hail them for a response. Minimum transmit power."

Anatoly called up the screen of recorded dolphin sounds and pressed the icon that invoked the chirps and whistles the cetacean duo would recognize as a request for an immediate response.

"They responded immediately," Anatoly said. "Range, two hundred and fifty yards, based upon the roundtrip speed of sound."

"Send them to six o'clock relative to our position."

"I've sent them a command to swim at six o'clock relative to our position of twelve o'clock, and they've acknowledged."

"Let's see what they see," Volkov said. "Query them for any submerged contacts."

"I'm ready to query them for the bearing to a contact."

"Transmit the query."

An exchange of chirps and whistles.

"They have nothing," Anatoly said.

"Understandable. This acoustic environment is noisy for them, and that Israeli submarine is far away."

"I recommend you turn and follow them, Dmitry. This may take a few hours before they swim within detection range."

"Right. I'll mirror their course but lag their speed by two knots to let them move ahead."

Four hours later, Volkov sipped tea from a porcelain cup to delay his creeping fatigue. The trainer sat beside the sonar guru, his preferred spot in the control room when his dolphins worked.

As he feared the Israeli submarine had retreated to its home waters, the *Wraith's* commander heard the control room's loudspeakers pump out unsolicited cetacean noises.

"What is it?" he asked.

"They say they have a submerged contact at five o'clock," Anatoly said.

"Excellent," Volkov said. "Query for the range."

After an exchange of chirps and whistles, the sonar expert offered an inquisitive look over his shoulder.

"It's medium range."

"Medium? That's unusual."

"Maybe I can explain," Anatoly said. "I've been modeling dolphin echolocation frequencies. In these waters, the temperatures are high and the background noise is really high. The dolphins will be limited in how far they can detect submarines."

"So be it. Set the range of the Israeli submarine at five miles from the dolphins and get an update on their position relative to us."

After three range checks to peg the cetaceans' location, icons on his screen shifted, and Volkov sensed an advantage forming over his adversary.

"Dare to risk a long-range shot?" Anatoly asked.

"No, the chance of hitting is questionable, and I have a better idea. I'd rather use the dolphins' explosive charges. It's a subtler approach and consumes fewer resources."

"Meaning we have more spare dolphin explosives aboard than torpedoes?"

"Not quite, but we should correct that since the dolphins' explosives take up much less space than torpedoes and are laughably cheaper. Remind me to have Pierre send us more spares with the *Goliath*."

"You can have the dolphins plant their charges on the Israeli submarine now," Anatoly said. "But I can't guarantee that you're close enough for your detonation command to reach."

Volkov recalled that the detonation signal mimicked crackling shrimp noise, a sound beyond the dolphins' ability to emanate. After his prior mission, he'd asked the trainer to condition his animals to detonate the explosives themselves, but they'd lacked the time to learn. The *Wraith's* sonar system would be required to set off the cetaceans' warheads.

Beside the sonar expert, the trainer displayed his habitual agitation as his children neared danger. But he surprised Volkov by remaining silent as the icon of the dolphins drifted closer to that of the Israeli vessel.

Then another unsolicited chirp arrived.

"They're within a mile of the target," Anatoly said.

"That's sooner than expected," Volkov said. "The Israelis are moving aggressively in our direction."

"They wasted no time turning around after evading our torpedo. I still can't hear them yet, though."

"You will soon. Give control of the dolphin communications to the trainer."

Anatoly acknowledged and tapped images on his screen.

"I've passed control of the dolphins to the trainer."

"I have control of my babies," the trainer said.

"Prepare the dolphins for explosives deployment."

Volkov envisioned one dolphin sliding its snout into the strap of the bomb attached forward of the dorsal fin of its partner while a chirp announced the completion of each animal's arming.

"They're ready to lay explosives," the trainer said.

"Very well, deploy the explosives."

Five minutes later, a chirp came.

"The explosives are applied to the Israeli submarine, and the dolphins have swum to a safe distance for detonation."

"Detonate."

The trainer tapped buttons on the console, and prerecorded shrimp-like sounds rang from the *Wraith*.

"Nothing," Anatoly said. "I hear no response."

"We're too far away for this level of background noise," Volkov said. "Vasily, increase power to one-half."

"I've increased power to half power."

"Detonate."

The two pops reminded Volkov of assassin bullets.

"Detonations are confirmed," Anatoly said. "I hear flooding. Now acceleration."

"Any high-pressure emergency air?"

"No, Dmitry. The ship is merely driving upward smartly."

"That's a cool bastard of a commander. After two instant geysers springing through the top of my control room, I'm not sure I'd be so calm."

"Now I hear hull popping as the ship makes for the surface."

"My babies succeeded again," the trainer said.

"Indeed, they did," Volkov said. "Bring them home."

"Andrei has confirmed the order," the trainer said. "They're coming back."

As he fought to suppress the rising smugness of victory, Volkov watched his sonar expert raise his finger and bow his head.

"What is it, Anatoly?"

As the question lingered unanswered, the *Wraith's* commander folded his arms and waited.

"Torpedo in the water," Anatoly said.

"Did our victim shoot at us?"

"No. It's from a different bearing. Zero-four-four."

"Is it drifting?"

"Slightly right."

Volkov recognized the danger of a surprise weapon and knew to place it on the edge of his submarine's baffles.

"Left ten-degrees rudder, steer course two-eight-four. Make

turns for twelve knots."

As the deck tilted into the turn, Volkov stood over his sonar expert's shoulder and watched the noise floor rise on his display as flowing water weakened the ship's hearing.

"Can you hear the torpedo?" he asked.

"Yes, the seeker is active. It's another SeaHake."

"You're kidding," Volkov said.

"No, Dmitry. There's a second Israeli submarine nearby."

In tense silence, Volkov watched the lines of bearing to the hostile torpedo drift behind him. But he needed them to drift faster.

"Increase speed to sixteen knots."

The deck shuddered with speed.

"We're at sixteen knots," the gray beard said. "Time on the battery at this speed is fifty-one minutes."

"What do you hear, Anatoly?"

"We need to maintain this speed, but we'll evade."

Volkov exhaled and shifted his mind to evaluation mode. He wanted to understand how he'd been ambushed.

"I never launched a torpedo," he said. "There's no way we could have been heard by any submarine, unless... damn."

"Dmitry?" Anatoly asked.

"The Israelis have studied current events, and I fear they've had access to privileged information. They know that we mimic biologic sounds to communicate with dolphins."

"How can you be sure?"

"You'll have to verify this by listening to our self-recordings of our generated sounds, but I'm sure you'll conclude that the only targeting data we gave the shooter was our dolphin and shrimp signals."

"That would ruin our greatest advantage," Anatoly said.

"I'm afraid that advantage is already at risk. In fact, let's be sure that cool bastard of a commander doesn't dare believe that he can repair two small holes at sea. Prepare the weapon in tube one for a one-third deployment of bomblets and aim it at the surfaced submarine."

"One third?" Anatoly asked.

"Yes. I don't want to sink the ship–just make sure our adversary returns to port and stays there for a long time."

The sonar guru interacted with the technician beside him, who tapped the icons to prepare the weapon.

"This will all but end our charade as an Egyptian vessel when we reveal our slow-kill weapon," Anatoly said.

"I suspect that ruse ended when Andrei and Mikhail announced their presence, and we've added circumstantial evidence if you count our synthetic biological transmissions. The Israelis have figured out who we are, or they will have done so by the end of the day."

"I understand, Dmitry. Tube one is ready."

"Very well," Volkov said. "Shoot tube one."

CHAPTER 2

Terrance Cahill strolled along the causeway above the dry dock and stopped at the railing overlooking his submersible combat-transport ship, *Goliath*. The catamaran's nearest hull appeared familiar, but farther away, overhead lights illuminated the alien-looking left half of his ship.

Questions rattled his mind faster than he could sort them, but he focused on the one that irked his sense of symmetry. The *Goliath* appeared stunted in its port, forward section.

"Tell me again why you've attached a stubby corvette-sized bow to the front of me port hull," he said.

The man beside him withdrew a Marlboro from his mouth and blew smoke.

"Because a stubby corvette-sized bow section was all I could acquire on short notice. You left the proper frigate-shaped bow section on the bottom of the Aegean Sea three months ago, if I remember correctly."

"Better the bow section than the entire ship," Cahill said.

"If you'd stop running my property into hostile weapons, we wouldn't have to worry about replacement parts. I believe that's twice now you've had relations with torpedoes that forced me to dip into my capital asset account."

"With all due respect, Mister Renard, you can press your dry old French lips hard against me bare hairy Australian arse."

His companion aimed eyes of steel blue at him and broke out in a smile.

"No need for vulgarity. I was merely jesting. I assumed you'd know that, but perhaps I hit a nerve?"

"Don't worry about it, mate."

Cahill felt a discomforting silence until his boss broke it.

"Unfortunately, your reaction is giving me cause for worry," Renard said. "You meant your comment about me kissing your buttocks as a joke, but I noted a hint of frustration."

Cahill shut his eyes as a waking recurrence of his repeated nightmares played in his head. A torpedo erupted, a wall of infinite water pounded him, and he drowned.

His awareness returned to Renard.

"I don't want to talk about it."

"In time, you must."

He grunted, left the Frenchman's comment unanswered, and posed one of his own.

"Ugly as it is, what do the simulations say about me new bow section?"

"Of course, with less volume, you'll have less buoyancy when submerged. You'll have to compensate symmetrically by holding more water in your forward starboard trim tanks."

"Right, mate. But what about top speeds surfaced and submerged? What about the risks of oscillations with the new hydrodynamics?"

"I admit the Taiwanese were unable, or unwilling rather, to commit to a simulation of hydrodynamic performance."

Cahill glanced around the covered wharf. The shipyard workers seemed lithe and short for Southern France, reminding him that Renard's primary workforce consisted of Taiwanese personnel, regardless of his location. The more he learned about his French boss, the more he understood how the secrets he shared with the renegade Chinese province guaranteed ongoing mutual trust.

"That's a pity," Cahill said. "The Taiwanese have been providing solid engineering to your fleet for years. I assume that if they can't run a simulation, then a simulation can't be run."

"Indeed," Renard said. "Rather, it could be run, but it's not worth the time and effort."

Cahill gave the Frenchman a sideways glance.

"You mean it's not worth your money."

"Admittedly, no."

"It's unlike you to leave your investments to chance."

"I wouldn't trust the simulations until they were proven against reality for such a strange thing as an undersized bow section. So I decided not to bother. Also, you already proved you can manage the *Goliath* without a bow section at all. Your maneuvering of the ship in the Aegean after losing your port bow was commendable."

A fresh snapshot of the recurring nightmare flashed across Cahill's mental view, and then reality returned.

"A feat I hope to never repeat."

A phone chimed in the Frenchman's pocket, and he reached into his blazer to lift the cellular device to his cheek.

"This is Pierre. No, I've not met them in person. You can match their faces to their photographs as well as I. Good. Give them badges and let them into the dry dock area. I'll meet them at the north entrance."

"Me Israeli Mossad guests?" Cahill asked.

"Not Mossad. That's for external affairs, and their problem–our opportunity–is due to an internal disagreement within the Israeli machine. Your riders are Aman, military intelligence."

"With all the mistrust and problems around Israel, you can't blame me for getting it confused."

"Confused indeed," Renard said. "And in the event that your Aman riders get confused about their priorities underway, you have the four Legionnaires I rented to protect you."

Cahill appreciated the security force and recalled that the four men who'd joined his crew a month earlier were respectable students in learning their jobs tending to the propulsion equipment. They would monitor gauges and clean machines underway to blend in and earn their keep.

"And you trust them, these Legionnaires?" he asked.

"Indeed. Their battalion officer is the son of a very close friend I've known since my years at *l'Ecole Navale*."

"Right, then let's meet our Aman riders."

"Agreed," Renard said. "Let's not keep them waiting. They'll be our allies only as long as it suits them. Best to begin this short relationship on a positive note."

Cahill kept pace beside the Frenchman while bringing the guardhouse into view. A Taiwanese security team buzzed around a half-dozen Caucasians, checking for metallic objects, harmful chemicals, and explosives. While gyrating through the inspections, the visitors revealed the taut bodies of soldiers, but one physique caught the Australian's attention.

She was built like an athlete with flat, shoulder-length brown hair, pert breasts, and a strong build with the hard, muscular lines of a swimmer. Then the Israeli lady turned, exposing firm, round buttocks, and Cahill noticed his heartbeat accelerating.

"Pierre?"

"Yes."

"You're putting a Sheila on me ship?"

"Is that a problem? Women haven't been considered curses aboard seagoing vessels for a long time."

"Right. It's just that…"

"What?"

He suffered tunnel vision as he watched her slide her green fatigue uniform over her tank top tee shirt.

"Well, she's a she, and an attractive one at that."

"I assure you, Major Dahan is competent enough to lead her team and maintain a professional relationship with you and your crew. I implore you to return her the same courtesy."

His heart fluttering, Cahill tried to regain control of his breathing. Seeing the Israeli woman had sent his hormones into hyper-drive, and he feared the distraction.

He lied to his boss.

"Will do, mate," he said. "It's no concern at all."

Renard approached her and introduced himself, and Cahill held his breath as the Frenchman aimed her attention at him.

"This is Terrance Cahill, former commanding officer of Her Majesty's Australian Ship *Rankin*, and now the commander of the *Goliath*, the flagship of my fleet."

Cahill inhaled and extended his hands to hers. He felt electrified as her soft hands rendered a firm grip, and he melted in her eyes.

"Terry, please. Call me 'Terry'."

"Major Ariella Dahan," she said.

Warmth billowed throughout him as her voice struck with beauty and strength. He judged her capable of nursing a child in one arm while snapping a man's neck with the other.

"Call her 'Major Dahan'," Renard said. "Although we abandoned formal ranks in our fleet, she and her team are Israeli military. Remember to honor that."

The reminder helped center Cahill.

"Of course," he said. "I would have it no other way. Let's get on with the introductions and get you familiar with me ship."

After a quick and quiet walk from the guard house, Cahill led Renard and the Israeli soldiers down serrated steps into the dry dock basin. Concrete walls reflected the echoes of steel-toed boots as the group descended to the bottom.

From behind and below its starboard hull, the combat transport ship appeared a magnificent beast.

Cahill adjusted his hardhat and then pointed upward.

"The ship is a marvel of reuse of existing designs with minimal customizations. Both screws and rudders are from the French *Scorpène*-class submarine, but you can see that the shafts are extended deeper into the water with a sunken stern area. This allows the screws to avoid cavitation while we're surfaced and to give extra buoyancy carrying the weight of our cargo."

"Mister Renard had it built to triple the speed of transport of his submarines to operational theaters, but the ship alone has proven itself as a tactical asset," Dahan said.

"She knows of our work in Greece and Russia," Renard said.

"The whole world knows of your work in Greece and Russia," Dahan said. "Your missions make too great an impact for Renard's mercenary fleet to remain a secret, and this is why we knew to call upon you."

"Renard's Mercenary Fleet," the Frenchman said. "Is that what people call it?"

Dahan shrugged.

"Yes," she said. "At least in my intelligence circles."

"I'm chuffed," the Frenchman said. "Renard's Mercenary Fleet–RMF. Welcome to the RMF *Goliath*."

"Me boss' swollen ego aside, I'll take this notoriety as a compliment," Cahill said.

"It's up to you how to take it," Dahan said.

The comment's brusqueness reminded Cahill of Israeli directness as he led them between two of the thick wooden blocks that cradled the ship's underbelly. He assembled the entourage midway between the hulls.

"The railguns are hydraulically raised and lowered into each weapons bay, which mark the highest points of the ship. Of course, that's also where we run our masts and antennas, and we mount our phased array radar panels, there, and there."

He pointed at either side and then turned forward.

"Above us is the aftermost lateral support beam that connects the halves of the catamaran. It's also the largest beam since it holds the stern planes, which are those huge wings above us. It's also the only path the crew can take between the port and starboard hulls."

"So, it's a crawlspace," Dahan said.

"Real tight and hardly used," Cahill said. "In fact, we essentially have two crews and two subcultures aboard the ship. Let's keep moving forward."

He showed his future riders the repetitive crossmembers that held the halves together and supported the central bed that could hold the weight of two submarines. Hydraulic arms were retracted to either hull, ready to grab and stabilize the *Goliath's* cargo.

"We're passing the sections that hold the MESMA units," Cahill said. "Those are the French-designed air-independent power plants that can be added to *Scorpène* submarines. The submarines use one each, whereas we use six total, three per side."

"We had estimated six to eight," Dahan said.

"I had considered eight, but the increase would have given

25

only an extra knot of submerged speed," Renard said. "I deemed it unworthy of the cost given that the ship can make thirty-four knots surfaced."

"On the gas turbines," Dahan said.

"Yes," Cahill said. "To my knowledge, we're the only ship designed to submerge that can also run on the surface at destroyer speeds. Much of that speed is thanks to our bows, which are normally cuts of steel designed for *Lafayette*-class frigates."

"Or *Kang Ding*-class frigates, rather," Renard said. "Same design, different production facility. Much as I respect French ingenuity, I must admit that the Taiwanese are my preferred hardware vendor."

"Regardless, this time, I have some alien corvette-like thingy on me port bow," Cahill said.

"That thingy is actually the best replacement component I could find on short notice." Renard said. "And yes, it's from a decommissioned corvette that was in processing for scrap."

"So, it's true that you took a torpedo hit in the Aegean Sea," Dahan said. "That explains the ugly bow on the port hull."

"Ugly?" Cahill asked. "I still find it a beautiful ship despite that temporary stubby bow."

Where he might have expected a perfunctory apology for the insult, Cahill knew better with Israelis.

"You called her an 'it'," Dahan said. "Aren't ships referred to as women?"

"That habit has fallen from use," Cahill said. "I don't have a good reason, but it might have to do with the growing number of women on crews. I personally find it archaic because no matter how attractive a hunk of metal is, it pales beside the beauty of a real woman."

As he smiled, her unreadable stare stymied him. Unsure if she welcomed the flirtation, ignored it, or pondered the proper krav maga strike to silence him, he welcomed the Frenchman's rescuing.

"Let's take a look at the domed bridge before we get everyone aboard and flood the dock," Renard said.

After slow, uncertain steps, Cahill felt his employer's hand on his shoulder as he chuckled in his ear.

"Remind me before I would ever teach you the art of negotiation to first coach you in subtlety," Renard said. "It was a noble effort, but ill-timed and ill-placed."

"Sorry, mate. I just haven't had me eye on a Sheila for years. She's a beaut, and she caught me off guard."

After a return climb up the basin's stairway, a crossing of the brow that bridged the pier to the back of his starboard hull, and a memorized walk through the cargo ship's innards, Cahill made his way to his familiar watch post.

Standing atop his ship restored his dignity, and he looked through the windows that interlaced steel bars stabilized. Water inundated the dock, and the *Goliath's* commander watched ripples lap the underside of the port hull.

Liam Walker, his executive officer and a former sailor from an *Anzac*-class frigate, lifted his eyes from a status screen.

"I don't like that makeshift port bow section, Terry. Not at all, I don't."

"Likewise, mate, but it beats no bow at all. We tried that by accident already, and it was miserable."

"Forgive me for complaining, but I don't like our Israeli riders either," Walker said. "This is the first time we've had so many strangers aboard, and I really don't like that they're military types."

"You can't get involved in a civil war without getting chummy with fighters from one of the sides."

"Good point. And I get the sense you wouldn't mind getting chummy with their officer."

Cahill frowned at his executive officer.

"What's that supposed to mean?"

"You can't take your eyes off Major Dahan."

"Am I leering at her? Is it that obvious?"

"Sorry, mate," Walker said. "I wish it were that simple. You're not leering, you're adoring. I think you're suffering from an acute bout of infatuation."

The revelation hit hard, and vulnerability diffused through-out his chest and limbs like a poison mist.

"Bloody hell, Liam. I'm screwed."

With ironic timing, her voice issued from the loudspeaker.

"This is Major Dahan. I request permission to join you on the bridge, Mister Cahill."

He panicked.

"I don't know what to do. I don't want her near me while I gather meself, but I can't be rude."

"Shall I handle it?" Walker asked.

"Please."

His executive officer tapped buttons and aimed his voice above the duo's heads.

"This is the executive officer, Liam Walker. Mister Cahill would be honored to have you as his guest on the bridge during our egress from Toulon. I've just unlocked the door, and we look forward to you joining us."

The latch clicked open and shut, and footsteps echoed up the stairs. Without thinking, Cahill stepped to the handrail and spied the creature who tugged his emotions in every direction.

In this moment, she irritated him, and he glared at her, trying to make sense of her invasion into his world.

As she met his gaze, the effort backfired.

"Which part of my uniform impresses you the most?" she asked.

"Excuse me?"

"You're staring at me. Something must impress you about my uniform."

"Um, the dark green part, I guess."

"It's all dark green. Are you most attracted to my chest, my buttocks, or my groin?"

The jolt woke him up.

"No need to be testy, major. I was merely offering a hand to help you up."

He extended his arm, and she hesitated below him.

"Do you help all guests to the bridge, or just the ladies? I don't want any special treatment other than you refraining from undressing me with your eyes."

"Given that you're the first lady to have ever boarded this ship, that's an unfair question."

She remained a statue, and he returned to his console.

"Suit yourself," he said.

The space felt cramped as she moved between him and Walker. With folded arms, she aimed a strong voice at him.

"I've taught enough horny young Israeli soldiers lessons, and I won't hesitate to use appropriate techniques to make sure your crew pays me the same courtesy. I'm a field-grade officer of the Israeli Military Intelligence Directorate, not a Barbie Doll."

She'd been on board less than thirty minutes, but he knew a sailor needed less than thirty seconds to offend a lady.

"I apologize if any of my men have been inappropriate with you. I will have Mister Walker investigate how my men have treated you thus far, and I will deal personally with any sailor who has wronged you."

She stepped close to him and lowered her voice.

"Your crew has behaved as well as sailors can be expected. My problem is with you. Keep your eyes off my feminine parts."

Petrified, he kept them glued forward at the basin's rising waterline and forced a curt reply.

"Yes, ma'am. Of course."

"You're no longer military, and if you were, you'd still outrank me," she said. "So don't call me 'ma'am'. It implies that I'm old, and that's worse than objectifying me."

He wanted to disappear and hoped for a rescue as his executive officer reached for his blinking screen.

"Pierre's hailing us," Walker said.

"Speak to him in private," Cahill said. "Let him know Major Dahan is with us on the bridge.

Walker exchanged words with their boss.

"He says it's okay to share the news with her."

"Very well. Put him through."

The Frenchman's voice filled the dome.

"Dmitry has just contacted me with a one-way communications buoy on a thirty-minute delay. He's barely cleared Port Said, and he's already been harassed by an Israeli submarine. He managed to disable one, but then he stumbled upon another. This verifies Major Dahan's prediction that the Israeli Navy is poised to defend potential interference from the Egyptians."

"What's his outlook on breaking through?"

"Not good. The Israelis have regrouped from his early moves."

"I suppose that means I need to transport him through or around the problem."

"Indeed," Renard said. "Make haste. I'll have you out of that dock in an hour."

After the line went dead, Dahan spun around and headed for the staircase. Cahill called for her in hopes of salvaging a normal conversation.

"Where are you going?" he asked.

"To check on my team's surveillance equipment."

"You're going to miss the exciting part where we get underway and accelerate to the open sea."

She stopped at the top of the stairs, turned her head, and offered him a profile of her sleek jawline.

"I'll be back when the time is right. And I'll be the judge of what I consider exciting."

After she left, Walker shook his head.

"She's got you by your bloody wanker."

"Do you have to remind me?"

"Maybe I do. This can't be a good thing."

"Well, don't you think she's a beaut?"

"I'm a married man."

"That's not what I asked."

"Fine. I can't deny that she's attractive," Walker said.

Cahill pondered a paranoid thought.

"Do you think Israeli intelligence somehow knew I'd find her attractive?"

"Now that's a dangerous concept. That would mean she's here to manipulate you and not just to help us."

"Perhaps. Or maybe just to assure her bosses that I do what Pierre signed us up to do."

"Maybe."

"Either way, it's a frightening thought. But it's almost unthinkable. How could anyone be so sure she'd turn me to mush?"

Walker snorted.

"Don't know, mate," he said. "Who could imagine the most gutsy, paranoid, and tenacious nation on the planet, one that's supposedly chosen by God to endure forever, daring to seduce the mighty Terrance Cahill?"

"No need for mockery."

"Every bit of humor holds a nugget of truth. We need to watch her, Terry."

Cahill swallowed.

"No, damn it. I need to watch her. If there's any subterfuge here, I'm the victim."

"Right."

"And unfortunately, you'll need to watch me."

"How so?"

"Because if this is a devious ploy against me, it's working."

CHAPTER 3

Jake Slate stood from his folding seat on the *Specter's* elevated conning platform and sensed an inappropriate dullness within his submarine's control room. His team seemed dead, like the waters outside the Port of Gaza.

"It's like a ghost town in here," he said.

Seated at his Subtics station, Antoine Remy, Jake's sonar leader, nodded his toad-shaped head.

"It's like a ghost town out there, too," Remy said. "I would hear a pin drop if there were someone to drop it. All the Israeli ships are enforcing the blockade much closer to shore than expected."

At the *Specter's* control station, the silver-haired Henri Lanier looked at Jake.

"Given the zeal the Israeli patrol boats have shown in enforcing the six-mile limit, we're seeing Palestinian fishermen exercising caution and staying four miles to shore or closer. Nobody likes being shot, and the Israelis are making gunfire a habit."

"It's not a blockade," Jake said. "It's a stranglehold."

"Condemned by the United Nations in multiple ways and in no uncertain terms," Henri said.

"Yeah, well, if you believe everything the U.N. says about Israel, you'd think it was the worst nation in the world."

"There are indeed wrongs to be righted," Henri said.

"Right. But there's a lot of stuff working out just fine that the prime minister shouldn't be messing with. Otherwise we wouldn't be here."

"It's difficult to know whom to trust."

Jake stepped forward and pressed his palms into the polished railing around the conn. A young man wearing the green uniform of an Israeli Army Captain stepped aside.

"In this fleet, we trust Pierre Renard," Jake said. "And if the presence of Captain Mizrahi standing beside me didn't make it obvious, Pierre's siding with the Aman military intelligence faction."

The French mechanic stood from his station, approached Jake, and lowered his voice. The Israeli officer took the hint and started a slow exploratory lap around the control room.

"I've known Pierre longer than you have," Henri said. "And I'd wager my life on his integrity."

"But?" Jake asked.

"But, he lives in a murky gray area where wrong and right are blurred. Impeccable integrity or not, he can pick the wrong side by mistake."

"Or be nudged the wrong way by money."

"You understand my concern," Henri said.

"Yeah, I do. And this mission popped up even faster than the last one. This machine of his–this growing mercenary fleet–may be spinning out of control."

"But you and I both agreed to do this. As did Antoine, Terry, and even Dmitry."

"Dmitry's still auditioning for the job and had no choice but to agree," Jake said. "The rest of us are conditioned to believe anything Pierre says."

The Frenchman shrugged.

"I can see both sides of the Israeli argument. Decisive and resolute force has served them well in the past, regardless of collateral damage and international condemnation."

Jake had thought through the mission many times and had talked it over with his key crew personnel and spiritual advisors. As a fledgling Christian, he considered his pending actions just.

"I'm committed. But you're not getting cold feet, are you?"

"Perhaps," Henri said. "I admit that we've discussed this to my satisfaction already, but I'm now rethinking it."

"So, what's bothering you?"

"It may be that I just realized this is our first attempt to intervene in a civil affair."

"You mean a civil cold war, for lack of a better description?" Jake asked.

"Precisely, if not in name then de facto. Nobody else outside of Israel wants to get involved since the divisions among factions are too complex. Even Palestine is split between Fatah and Hamas."

"Yeah. Egypt is playing it cool, too," Jake said. "They aren't much more fond of Hamas than the Israelis."

The French mechanic shook his head.

"We obviously see ourselves as the heroes in this."

"Well, yeah. Heroes, garbage men, or fools. Whatever it is, we're doing something nobody else can or will do. But we know it needs to be done."

"Do me a favor, and please remind me of this from time to time. I seem to be struggling with discernment on this mission."

The sonar guru's toad-head offered its profile, catching Jake's attention.

"I hear a patrol craft," Remy said.

"What kind?" Jake asked.

"Fast."

"They're all fast. What does that mean?"

"I mean really fast. It's a *Shaldag*-class patrol vessel, based upon propulsion noise."

"That thing can go almost as fast as a torpedo. Can you give me blade rate on the propeller and a speed estimate?"

"I would, except that there's no propeller, at least not outside the ship," Remy said. "The propulsion is a water jet. And... it just slowed. I can't hear its jet anymore, but I can hear a fifty-hertz electric plant."

Jake sat in his chair and watched the icon representing the new patrol craft shift across his tactical display. His mission required making the strength of the Israeli Navy, the submarines, reveal themselves. Patrol craft were deaf to his underwater movements and amounted to distractions.

Until the closest one became interesting.

"Gunfire," Remy said.

"Where? Who?" Jake asked.

"From the _Shaldag_. It's shooting at something, probably the distant civilian ship I was tracking towards the Port of Gaza."

Jake recalled the patrol craft's armaments as a twenty-five-millimeter Typhoon Weapon System and a twenty-millimeter gun. He considered them undersized for naval combat, but he knew his opinion would soften if he found himself on their receiving end.

"Is it hitting anything?"

"I can't tell," Remy said. "I just hear popping in small bursts. It's warning fire, if I had to guess."

"Well, shit," Jake said. "I guess it's time to rescue our first impromptu blockade challenger."

"They're far from the blockade," Remy said. "I'd say they're barely inside Israeli waters."

"Regardless, the Israelis perceived them as a challenge, and we're going to rescue them," Jake said.

"Our orders are reconnaissance," Henri said.

Jake appreciated the periodic challenges from the wise Frenchman and was willing to change his mind based upon the elder's insights.

But not this time.

"It's too damned quiet around here. If Antoine hasn't heard anything by now, I need to make something show itself. It's time to reconnoiter these waters by stirring things up. Let's harass this blockade."

"Understood," Henri said.

"Firing point procedures, tube one. The target is the _Shaldag_. I'll cripple it with a slow-kill weapon."

An impatient glance at the Israeli garnered a somber response.

"I don't expect to use my veto unless you violate the agreed-upon weapon parameters," the Aman officer said. "Otherwise, don't expect me to say a word."

"Just verifying," Jake said.

He turned his head and watched Remy fidget with his screen and glance at the young technician beside him who assigned the targeting solution to the torpedo.

"I'm getting you a targeting solution."

"You had a high bearing rate and knew its speed," Jake said. "It should be a slam dunk."

"It is," Remy said. "I've got a range now. Six miles. The weapon is ready."

"The ship is ready," Henri said. "Are you planning to evade after shooting?"

Jake grunted.

"Evade from a deaf *Shaldag*? No. But from the submarine I hope is out there trying to protect it, yes. I'll turn left one hundred and twenty degrees after shooting."

"Understood."

"But before we shoot, I want to aim ten degrees to the right of the target."

The toad-head turned, stopped at a profile, and then mouthed the sonar guru's understanding.

"I assume you want to shoot wide and steer the weapon back from a waypoint," Remy said.

"Yes."

"Would you like me to program the waypoint in case the wire breaks?"

"Yes," Jake said. "Good recommendation. Eight miles out."

"That's farther than the target," Remy said.

"I know," Jake said. "I want the weapon to pass the target and come back. Eight miles."

Remy watched over the young technician seated beside him as he made the guidance updates.

"The waypoint is set to eight miles out," he said.

"Very well," Jake said. "Shoot tube one."

The pneumatic impulsion system beyond sight in the forward compartment thrust a weapon into the sea while sucking air into its piping. The rapid pressure change popped Jake's ears.

"Tube one indicates normal launch," Remy said. "I have wire control. I hear its propeller."

"How long is the expected run before the seeker awakes?"

"Thirteen minutes," Remy said.

"Left ten-degrees rudder, steer course two-eight-zero," Jake said.

As the deck angled and settled, Henri crossed the control room and stood beside Jake.

"I think I know what you're doing, but can you verify it?"

"Ye of little faith," Jake said.

"No need for quoting Christ," Henri said. "And I didn't come here to pray with you, in case you were worried about it. I don't sense pending death since our slow-kill weapons haven't killed anyone yet."

Jake checked his memory and frowned.

"We sank a North Korean submarine with a slow-kill."

"I rather choose to believe that the North Korean submarine commander opted for suicide. We gave him more than adequate time to save his crew."

"It's a gray area, but I'll agree with you for the sake of argument," Jake said. "What would you like me to verify?"

"The waypoint is unnecessary for a deaf patrol craft. In fact, it extends the time to impact by almost five minutes. I would call it folly except that you're taking a hidden variable into account, and I suspect that variable is a submarine we have yet to detect."

"Go on."

"I think you're intentionally keeping our weapon in the water longer than necessary as a fishing expedition. You want to see if you can entice action from a hidden submarine by running our torpedo around the seas fifty percent more than needed."

"Good guess," Jake said. "That's part of it. I'm also fishing farther north, closer to the blockade, as the point for our seeker to awake. Maybe that can catch us a submarine's response."

Henri frowned.

"I don't like intentionally calling attention to ourselves."

"Neither do I, but I don't want to come up empty on Israeli submarines before Terry and Dmitry get here. I need to learn something about their presence, and I'm taking the risk."

The Frenchman swallowed and assumed a shade of pale.

"On second thought, maybe we should pray."

"You go ahead. I don't see the need."

"You're still Christian, are you not?"

"Muddling through. But you can't pray all the time, or else you wouldn't leave time for anything else."

"True, but I'll do so anyway–silently at my station."

The mechanic returned to the ship's control panel.

Minutes later, the sonar expert broke a silence.

"Our weapon has reached its waypoint and is turning back for the target."

"Very well," Jake said. "Is the target still dead in the water?"

"Yes," Remy said. "It must be inspecting a fishing vessel."

"That's what I was hoping for," Jake said. "Sometimes, you need to have a little luck."

He moved to the central plotting table and watched the icon of the torpedo pursue that of the patrol craft.

"Get tube two ready for the *Shaldag*," he said.

"Tube two is ready," Remy said.

"I may soon ask you to track the *Shaldag* and steer two weapons towards it," Jake said. "So be ready."

"We're ready," Remy said. "Our weapon's seeker just went active. No sign of a reaction from the target."

"This could get interesting," Jake said.

"Detonation in thirty seconds," Remy said.

Jake hoped for a hit, but hoped for something more–his victim's perfect evasion.

"The target's accelerating," Remy said.

"That's what I'm looking for," Jake said. "Get me a course and speed."

"Coming to flank, smartly. Bearing drift is to the right."

"Steer our weapon sixty degrees to the left."

"That's pointing back at us," Remy said.

"It's far enough away. Impart the steer. Also, assume flank speed for the target and give me a course as you resolve the bearing rate."

Remy nodded, and Jake waited while his tactician transformed sounds into information.

"I have a bearing rate and a solution I'm sending to the Subtics system."

"Status on tube two?" Jake asked.

"The solution is ready," Remy said. "The weapon is ready."

"Shoot tube two."

As the soft whine and pressure change hit Jake's ears, he considered the geometry of the battle. His adrenaline kicked in when he grasped a possibility.

Henri joined him at the chart.

"What do you see?"

"A perfect evasion," Jake said. "That patrol craft put our torpedo on the edge of its baffles while trying to slide sideways out of the acoustic seeker's kill zone."

"I see. That's the same geometry we use when we run from torpedoes. Given that ship's speed, it will outlast our first weapon's fuel reserves."

"Not if our second weapon slows it down enough," Jake said. "It's running right into it."

"Nicely done. Even for you, that trap was impressive."

Jake smirked.

"Maybe, but even an old French mechanic saw it coming."

"I don't know whether to take that as a compliment or an insult," Henri said.

"Compliment. Hold on."

Jake swung his hips around the table and positioned himself behind Remy's chair. The sonar ace lowered one of his ear muffs.

"Let the young kids track the target and our torpedoes," Jake said. "You know what I need you to do, right?"

"Listen for a hostile submarine in all directions," Remy said. "Yes."

"I already am. You could slow to four knots to help me out."

"I should have known. You got it."

Jake returned to the table and ordered Henri to slow the submarine and reduce flow noise on its hydrophones. As the mechanic stepped away to obey, the *Specter's* commander retraced his steps and crouched next to the technician seated beside his sonar expert.

"See if you can guide our second weapon in passively."

The youngster nodded.

"Good," Jake said. "Keep the seeker silent. There's no need to announce the second torpedo if we can avoid it, and the target's making plenty of noise for passive homing."

Having tripped the final spring of his trap, Jake retreated to his chair and waited.

The junior sailor announced the detonation of the second torpedo underneath the fleeing Israeli patrol craft. Although unaccustomed to listening to submunitions breaking from the warhead compartment and attaching to a submarine's hull, the new crewman claimed he heard most of the twenty-four limpets detach from the slow-kill weapon and find their mark.

The sonar guru confirmed it.

"Ripple explosion," Remy said. "That's a successful hit."

"You're supposed to be listening for a submarine."

"There's nothing out there within detection range."

Jake trusted his expert.

"Fine. Is the *Shaldag* slowing yet?"

"Not yet. We didn't damage the propulsion train."

"Not surprising. Two dozen small holes don't always have much effect on surface ships."

"There it is now," Remy said. "That's what I wanted to hear. Propulsion is stopped, and I hear a lot of flooding."

"The slowing must be a conscious decision to allow the crew to work the shoring against the flooding," Jake said. "They'll probably keep the ship afloat, if we let them."

"Why would you let them?" Henri asked.

"Economics," Jake said. "Each torpedo costs money. Let's see how the fight to save the ship goes. In the meantime, prepare tube three for the *Shaldag*, same parameters as tube two."

"Will the first weapon hit, now that the vessel has slowed?"

Jake glanced at the tactical chart.

"Yes," he said. "In two minutes, unless I shut it down."

He looked to the Israeli officer, who impressed him with his cool acceptance of shooting weapons at his countrymen.

"Still no veto," the Aman officer said. "You're still following our defined parameters."

"Just checking."

"I can't think of a more humane way to stop our navy than what you're doing."

Two minutes later, the first weapon doubled the holes in the target's hull. Another two minutes later, Remy reported the patrol craft's battle for survival.

"The *Shaldag's* still afloat. I hear a lot of banging and shoring work. It's also accelerating now, slowly. I think it means to head for port."

"Seriously?" Jake asked. "We put forty holes in it."

"It's still afloat," Remy said. "Wait. I hear splashes. I think the crew's launching life rafts."

"That's great news," Jake said. "But I want to be certain. As long as I'm out here, let's remove this ship from our future concerns. Shoot tube three."

The soft whine and pressure change hit his ears as the *Specter* spat its third torpedo to sink the *Shaldag*. He sat back in his chair and welcomed the French mechanic by his side.

"Coming to second-guess me on something?"

"I was going to remind you of the economics," Henri said. "Three torpedoes were extensive for one patrol craft."

"I think Pierre will understand."

"Then what of the primary mission of reconnaissance? Antoine heard no sign of an Israeli submarine."

Jake smirked.

"True enough, but how do you think a deaf ship learned about our first torpedo just in time to run from it, much less the perfect course to run?"

"It could have been good luck. It could simply have been re-positioning to challenge the next fisherman."

"Maybe, but I think Pierre will agree with me. There was a submarine to the north beyond our detection range but close enough to hear our weapon, and I just gathered evidence that the Israelis are dead serious about the intensified blockade of the Gaza."

"I'll leave such matters to the tactical experts."

"You're selling yourself short," Jake said. "You've picked up enough knowledge over years in combat with me to formulate your own opinion."

"Perhaps."

"So, what's your gut assessment?" Jake asked.

The Frenchman offered a quick nod and cautious smile.

"Mission accomplished."

CHAPTER 4

Commander Adam Levy ordered the Israeli submarine, *Crocodile*, to hold its shallow depth. As the deck rocked in the swells, he sought communications with his fleet's leadership in Haifa.

"Link me with headquarters on a secure channel."

His senior enlisted veteran mechanical technician acknowledged the order, and Levy heard gentle static as the channel changed.

"You're linked, sir," the veteran said.

Levy clicked a handset and spoke into it.

"Squadron, this is *Crocodile*, over."

His squadron commodore's amplified response filled the control room.

"This is squadron. Go ahead, *Crocodile*, over."

"Squadron, this is *Crocodile*, I witnessed the attack on patrol craft *Shaldag Three*. I'm ready to report and upload a data link."

"Send me your data link, and I'll have it reviewed. Give me your verbal report now."

"An unidentified platform, likely a submarine, launched three torpedoes at *Shaldag Three*. I detected the first torpedo and came shallow to give *Shaldag Three* an optimum evasion course, but I couldn't detect the second or third torpedoes until I heard the detonations."

"*Shaldag Three* is sinking, but the crew has time to abandon ship. No casualties have been reported."

News of his countrymen's survival left Levy unmoved. Sailors on substandard vessels–which in his judgment meant every surface combatant–were tangential considerations as compared to him winning his battles and accomplishing his missions.

But the vessel's loss and its visible rescue effort would weaken the blockade, and he expected the Palestinian fishing fleet to exploit the weakness. Judging that the Gaza peasants couldn't fend for themselves within the permitted fishing zones, he expected them to spread across the water like a virus.

"I'd like to confirm that I stay submerged and can retain my stealth at my discretion without having to assist in the rescue operation."

"Stay hidden, *Crocodile*. *Shaldag Three's* crew will get all the help it needs, and I've got another *Shaldag* vessel interdicting the blockade runner."

"How many runners are there?"

"Just the one. A lone actor, very unprofessional. It's probably a group of young idyllic humanitarians who haven't given a second thought to the consequences of their actions."

"Good," Levy said. "At least there won't be any weapons entering this forsaken Gaza Strip on this blockade run."

"They won't even get through. I'm more interested in what you learned with the attack on *Shaldag Three*. Can you think of anything else to report about the vessel that attacked it?"

Levy reflected on the observations swirling in his mind.

"The hostile torpedoes weren't standard issue," he said. "They had limpet-type payloads, and I heard multiple small warheads clamp to the hull before exploding, roughly twenty per torpedo. This implicates the same mercenary fleet that attacked the Russians and the Greeks."

"Agreed. I'll have a team review our tactics against these mercenaries since I expect we'll be tangling with them soon. However, this changes nothing about your present orders. Continue your patrol, and make sure the blockade holds. Squadron, out."

Levy looked at his veteran.

"Lower all masts and antennas. Make your depth thirty meters."

"All masts and antennas are lowered, sir. Coming to thirty meters."

The deck dipped forward and then leveled.

"Steady on depth of thirty meters," the veteran said.

As the world became the familiar tranquility of the undersea realm, Levy walked to a central plotting table and stood beside his executive officer, a portly man with thick glasses.

"Any sign of that mercenary submarine?"

"No, sir. We never heard it. It's either drifting quietly, or it's already cleared the area."

Since Levy's crew lacked useful data on his new enemy, the display showed a void where he hoped to see an icon of the hostile submarine.

"Nothing," Levy said.

"Do you want to chase it, sir?" the executive officer asked. "We can make educated guesses about where it evaded."

"I want to, but I won't. It would take a long effort to find it, if it's even still around, and we have more important business."

He tapped an icon, and raw sonar data showed lines to multiple fishing ships expanding towards open water.

"You see," he said. "The Palestinians are moving farther from their shore. They've observed *Shaldag Three* in distress, and they suddenly believe they have the right to fish wherever they want."

"What can we do about it?" the executive officer asked. "It would be overkill to use torpedoes or anti-ship missiles on a bunch of small fishing ships."

"Overkill indeed," Levy said. "Your flair for the obvious underwhelms me. What's more important is that using any of our weapons would reveal our presence, and I'd prefer to preserve the secret that we're dedicating submarines to our blockade."

The stocky man stared at him.

"Then what's on your mind, sir?"

"I'll find a way to keep this blockade enforced."

"I don't see how, without weapons."

"Pick the closest fishing ship, and set an intercept course."

The cowering look in the man's eye revealed his lack of understanding and his obedience.

Levy wanted that look. His men were his pawns, and that suited him for running his ship.

"I've set us on course zero-one-five, speed eight knots, to intercept the closest fishing vessel, sir."

"Very well."

Levy moved behind his seated sonar supervisor, crouched over his shoulder, and verified the visual representation of the targeted vessel's sound on a display.

"What size fishing vessel is it?" Levy asked.

Sitting with a straight back, his new sonar supervisor was skilled and knew it.

Levy made a mental note to break down the man into his control without destroying his technical confidence. He'd later attack him on his division's equipment maintenance or paperwork, to keep him unbalanced. There was always a weakness in his underlings that his position of commanding a naval vessel could exploit.

But for the moment, the man oozed self-esteem, and his voice was strong.

"Best I can tell, it's small, sir, like most of them. It probably holds a dozen men."

"Best you can tell?" Levy asked.

"Yes, sir. There are very few ships in this fleet that stand out as having any respectable size. Ninety-nine percent of them are thimbles used to feed a hundred people at most."

"Very well," Levy said. "You exaggerate, but I consider your point good news. It will minimize the risk of the task."

Levy saw inquisitive eyes in the control room awaiting his explanation of his meaning, and he glared at each man, ensuring silence from those who dared meet his stare.

But the supervisor challenged him.

"What task is that, sir?"

"Why, ramming the fishing ship, of course. Can you think of a more efficient way for me to enforce a no-fishing zone with our surface combatants spread too thin to do it themselves?"

The portly executive office spoke with a squeaky voice.

"Sir, it's my duty to inform you that intentionally ramming a fishing ship could pose a threat to our ship's safety."

Levy scoffed.

"Duly noted. Annotate that in the deck log, if it makes you feel better. But I'll take three inches of steel against a fraction of an inch of wood or fiberglass."

As his hefty second-in-command waddled towards the section's quartermaster to annotate his precautionary but ineffective protest, Levy returned to the back of the room and sat in his captain's chair.

"Does anyone else object to what I'm about to do?"

Though grammar framed his words as a question, his tone made them a statement. Even the impertinent supervisor offered a silent and dumbfounded look.

"You?" Levy asked.

The man shook his head and twisted his chest back towards his sonar screen.

"Good."

He looked to his mechanical technician.

"You, keep me on an intercept course with this fishing vessel. I don't care if it maneuvers or if another ship in violation of the fishing limits gets closer to me. I've decided that this one will serve as the example."

"I'll keep us on course, sir," the veteran said.

"Very well," Levy said.

"I'm tracking the targeted vessel in our system as contact thirty-eight, sir," the supervisor said.

"Very well. Contact thirty-eight is my target. How long to intercept?"

"Twenty-four minutes, sir."

"At what target angle?"

"The target angle is presently three-two-six, sir."

"That's not what I meant. I can see that on my tactical display. I mean when I slice my conning tower through its keel. What will my target angle be then?"

The supervisor tapped his screen and advanced icons forward

in time.

"Two-nine-one, sir."

"Good. That's close enough to a broadside to assure no damage to my sail. Scraped paint, at worst."

A few minutes of silence passed during which Levy ignored routine reports of other Gaza vessels seeking better waters. The supervisor then surprised him.

"You'll need your periscope, sir."

"Excuse me?"

"Your periscope. There's not a sonar system accurate enough or an operator skilled enough to guarantee that you'll be able to ram a target that small. If you want to do this, you'll need visual data."

The man's insolence infuriated Levy, and he stood to bark out an order relieving him of his duty.

But then, as he wagged his finger, he realized the truth.

He gritted his teeth and forced himself to appear appreciative of the comment but strong while still giving orders.

"Of course, I'll use the periscope, and I'm assigning you the role of counting down the time to impact. You'll announce when you predict exactly thirty seconds, twenty seconds, and then ten seconds prior to impact so that I can lower the periscope at the precise time."

A junior sonar technician who habitually avoided direct speech with Levy stirred and murmured to the supervisor, who nodded his understanding.

"Contact thirty-eight is slowing, sir," the supervisor said. "It's drifting, probably getting ready to lower its nets."

"Very well. Get me an updated intercept course."

The supervisor ran his finger across icons.

"Course one-three-two at our present speed, sir."

Levy gave the order to adjust the *Crocodile's* direction, sat in his chair, and waited.

The mounting stench of tension in the control room validated his hopes that his intentions disturbed his crew. Their uneasiness–their fidgeting hands, their tight postures, their curt interchanges–verified the brutality of his pending attack.

He shot periodic glances at a display beside his seat, and the stationary icon of his target presented a trivial prey. The hunt lacked challenge and seemed unsporting, but he rationalized that the impertinent fishing fleet needed a clear message.

Getting his veteran mechanic's attention, he ordered the ship shallow for the final minutes.

"Bring us to periscope depth."

The deck angled upward and then levelled and rocked.

With three minutes to impact, Levy needed visual guidance.

"Raising the periscope," he said.

He tapped an icon, and hydraulic valves clicked above him. A dark monitor awoke with a clear view of the sky. After tapping his screen to aim the optics on the bearing of the fishing vessel, he saw his target's profile.

The ship spanned less than fifty feet.

"Are you tracking this?" Levy asked.

"Yes, sir," the supervisor said. "The propeller is stopped, but I have the fifty-hertz electrical generator and frequent transient noises from the crew's deck operations."

"What's your best bearing?"

"One-three-two, sir. You're pointing our bow right at it."

"Good," Levy said. "Good."

In the screen, the ship grew, and Levy saw a wisp of smoke rising from a crewman's cigarette.

"Thirty seconds to intercept," the supervisor said.

"Very well," Levy said. "Count out every ten seconds."

"Twenty seconds to intercept."

Levy saw a shocked fisherman's face.

"Excellent," he said. "One of them sees my periscope. Let's see if the idiot has enough sense to jump overboard."

"Ten seconds, sir," the supervisor said.

"Very well. Lowering the periscope."

Levy tapped his screen to retract the optics within the safety of his submarine's conning tower.

The crunching impressed him with its puniness as the *Croco-*

dile's conning tower shattered the vessel's hull. Though violent, the splintering passed in seconds.

The silence seemed stark after the collision.

"Raising the periscope," Levy said.

He swiveled his view backwards to see the carnage, but he saw empty water.

"Do you hear anything?" he asked.

"I do, sir," the supervisor said. "Just enough noise to know that it's sinking."

"Good," Levy said. "Executive officer, draft a message to squadron informing the commodore how I'm enforcing the blockade and why I expect the fishing fleet to reconsider respecting our enforced borders. Send it as soon as possible."

"I'll draft and send the message, sir. Do you want to schedule a trip to the surface after sunset to inspect our ship for damage?"

Levy smirked.

"No. Just keep a watch on the other fishing vessels to make sure they're behaving per my will. If any of them are still lingering beyond the boundary in half an hour, plot an intercept course to the closest one and have me summoned to lead the next ramming operation. I'll be in the wardroom. You have the bridge."

CHAPTER 5

Volkov admired his adversary.

"He's like a mother bear protecting his wounded cub."

"Who is?" Anatoly asked.

"The commander of the *Splendor*."

Aman's estimates of Israeli submarine patrol responsibilities and scraps of sound captured during hours of Volkov's cat-and-mouse maneuvering had identified the healthy submarine that stood against him as the Israeli Navy Ship *Splendor*.

Similar intelligence coupled with American satellite photography identified the wounded animal that had suffered ten holes by Volkov's dolphins and his slow-kill weapon as the INS *Leviathan*.

As the *Leviathan* limped at eight surfaced knots towards the naval base at Haifa, the *Splendor* guarded its retreat. That had suited Volkov for the first six hours, but his patience waned.

"What can you do about it?" Anatoly asked. "He sprints ahead, turns, and faces us with all his sensors and, best we can tell, at least one drone. It's a perfect protection of his comrade's retreat."

"These Israeli submarine commanders are cool bastards. I'm not going to rattle this one into making a mistake."

"Well, at least we injured one and kept another busy for most of the day. That's two submarines that weren't causing anyone else trouble today, and one of them will spend a good deal of time in port getting repairs."

Considering himself in an extended job interview to retain command of the *Wraith*, Volkov scoffed.

"I don't know that Pierre will be so kind in his assessment."

"Regardless," Anatoly said, "you can't push a bad situation."

"You're right. I have to back out of this."

Convinced the Israelis had grown wary of his ship's recorded dolphin calls, Volkov had restricted the distance he'd send his mammalian assets, limiting their value. He looked to the trainer seated beside his sonar expert.

"Vasily, call your dolphins back. It's time to withdraw."

"With pleasure," the trainer said. "They're due for rest and feeding anyway."

The trainer called up a screen of stored sounds and invoked the chirps and whistles the cetacean duo would recognize as a command to return to the *Wraith*. The watery garbled rendition of the submarine's emissions played through a loudspeaker in the compartment, and moments later, Andrei's response arrived.

"They acknowledge," the trainer said.

Volkov glanced at an overhead view of icons to verify the geometry allowed the animals to return to his vessel. He then caught his gray-bearded veteran's attention.

"Slow us to four knots to retrieve the dolphins."

Before the gray beard answered, the sounds of a responding dolphin resonated throughout the room.

"Was that a repeat of the last message?" Volkov asked.

"Yes," the trainer said. "A repeat of the acknowledgement of our return-to-ships order."

"That's odd, isn't it? I've never heard them do that."

"Odd, yes. No cause for alarm, though."

The trainer's tightening face contradicted his words.

"What might make them do that?" Volkov asked.

"Technically, it's just Andrei who's responding. Maybe he thought we transmitted the order twice. Mikhail wouldn't talk unless Andrei was in trouble."

"And vice versa, I assume? Andrei has a call he'd give in case Mikhail was in trouble."

"Yes, yes, of course."

"Good," Volkov said. "Then since we've heard neither of them send a distress call, there's no cause for alarm."

Andrei retransmitted the acknowledgment, and a shadow formed over the trainer's face.

"I don't like this, Dmitry. I don't know what's happening."

"Be calm," Volkov said.

While retreating to his foldout chair, Volkov realized he considered his dolphins more rational than most humans. Stimulus in–predictable result out. No adlibbing, no deviations. Andrei's repeated acknowledgments implied his hearing of repeated orders.

"Anatoly, please verify that our return-to-ship order was sent only once."

"I'll have a man listen to our system's recording of the last ten minutes to be certain. I know it went out only once at the proper power level, but it's possible that a glitch in the system sent out echoes by accident at lower power levels."

While his sonar expert's words swam around his head, Volkov realized the *Wraith's* sonar system had sent the order only once. Confirming his suspicions of foul play, he heard the dolphin's fourth acknowledgement.

Someone else was sending commands.

"Dmitry!" the trainer said. "I don't understand. What can I do?"

"Send the order again."

Second order sent. Fifth acknowledgment received.

"Anatoly, come here, please," Volkov said.

The sonar expert placed his headset on his console and walked to the commanding officer's seat. Volkov leaned toward him and gestured him downward to whisper.

"I don't know how they're doing it, but the Israelis are giving our dolphins orders. They must have recorded one of our outgoing orders."

The technician's eyes became wide.

"That would explain their strange behavior."

"Set up a sonar search plan to listen for our return-to-ship order. Either the *Splendor* is playing it from its sonar system, it's playing it from a drone, or another asset has been deployed against us."

As Andrei sent another response, Anatoly stood and nodded.

"I'll get right on it," he said.

"Before you do, be sure to get a range check on the dolphins," Volkov said. "I think you'll find that they're swimming towards the Israelis, or at best in circles. But wait until I leave the room with Vasily. I'm going to escort him to the torpedo room to calm him."

"He's about to break down."

"He can't put it in words, but he's quite aware that his dolphins are in grave danger."

"Even if I hear the Israelis duping our dolphins, what can be done? If they can draw the dolphins close to the *Splendor*, they could kill them with a single blast of sonar energy."

"I know. That's what I intend to prevent."

"At the risk of our ship? You can't just overpower the Israeli calls with acoustic energy from our ship. You'd give away our position. They'd then shoot a torpedo, and we'd all be dead."

Volkov grunted.

"I wouldn't risk the ship for that, but I will risk a drone."

In the torpedo room, Volkov watched the trainer pace along the center corridor.

"Andrei is sick," the trainer said. "He's sick. That's it. He's sick. He's sick."

"He's not sick," Volkov said.

"He can't make it back to the ship if he's sick. He's my baby. I've lost my baby."

"He's fine, Vasily."

"He's sick, Dmitry."

Grabbing the man's shoulders, Volkov thought he held the thin frame of a child.

"Steady, my friend. I know what's happening. I can fix it."

"You can fix what?"

"Promise me that you'll trust me."

"Why do I have to trust you? What's wrong? What's wrong with my babies? You're scaring me, Dmitry."

"I believe the Israelis managed to record our return-to-ship signal and are rebroadcasting it to confuse your babies."

The trainer gave a look of horror.

"They'll be killed!"

"No, they won't. I have a plan."

"You just said they're being called to an Israeli submarine. What do you think will happen? They'll be baked alive when that submarine kills them with the sonar system! Or they could just detonate a torpedo near them. Jake did that and almost killed them when he was fighting against us. There's so much that can be done to hurt them."

"You're overreacting," Volkov said.

"How can you say that?"

"If the Israelis knew the signal they intercepted was a return-to-ship signal, why would they keep broadcasting it?"

"I... I don't know."

"Because they don't know what it means. They're broadcasting it to confuse our dolphins. But they have no idea what response to expect."

"But if they swim towards the Israelis and Andrei keeps responding, they'll figure out that they're getting closer. They'll figure it out and kill them!"

Volkov looked over the trainer's shoulder at his lead torpedo technician and nodded. The man approached.

"Keep it quiet because we know the Israelis are listening. Backhaul tube three and reload it with a drone. And I mean quietly–if you want to live. We can't be heard."

The man obeyed and rallied a team.

"What's going on?" the trainer asked.

"I'm going to use that drone to overpower the Israeli signal and get our dolphins back."

"You will? You're sure it's not too late?"

Volkov lied.

"I'm sure."

After returning to the control room, Volkov glared at his sonar technician.

"Is my drone ready yet?"

"You told the team to be quiet. They're moving slowly."

"Damn."

"Shall I tell them to hurry?"

"No. I'm sure they're moving as fast as they can."

Volkov had lost count of Andrei's responses, and another one filled the room as the latest iteration of his hypnotic mammalian mantra.

"They're getting father away, aren't they?"

"The power level of Andrei's responses is falling, but it could be a matter of angles as much as distance."

"I know that," Volkov said. "But my gut tells me we're losing them."

"Shall I perform another range check?"

"They've ignored your last two attempts?"

"My last three."

"Then they either can't hear us, or they've found a closer sound source they consider their mothership."

"I still don't hear any sign of a fake source," Anatoly said. "If there really is one as we believe, it's far away, or it's broadcasting at very low power."

"Just enough power to illicit Andrei's response."

As Volkov pondered his own words, he lowered his head.

"Dear God. The Israelis are hearing Andrei, too. They know exactly where he is based upon the direction to his sound and the time delay between their transmission and his response."

"But they wouldn't risk walking the dolphins to their ship, would they? Not after what they did to the *Leviathan*. That would be too risky."

The insight offered hope.

"No, you're right. They're still retreating while protecting the *Leviathan*, but they're dragging our dolphins away with them. Back to Haifa, to be captured."

The sonar expert pressed a muff to his ear and lowered his head. Volkov pursed his lips while awaiting his report.

"The drone is ready."

"Finally," Volkov said.

He aimed his chin at the technician beside his sonar guru.

"Is he ready to handle the damned thing?"

"Yes. It's his first time, but an expert from Jake's crew trained him. He'll do fine."

"He has to. Launch drone one from tube three."

"Drone one is swimming out of tube three," Anatoly said. "Drone one is clear of our hull and deployed. We have wire connectivity and confirmation of propulsion."

"Set drone speed at its maximum of ten knots, straight for the dolphins."

"The drone is at maximum speed, heading for the dolphins."

For five minutes, Volkov watched the display above his seated guru's head as the crosshair of his *Wraith* slipped away from the imaginary line between the dolphins and his drone.

Satisfied any reactionary Israeli torpedo targeting the drone would pass behind him, he sought his cetaceans.

"That's good enough," he said. "Send the return-to-ship command through the drone at its maximum transmit power."

With the distant hydrophones facing away, Volkov heard no sign of the transmission, but he heard the dolphin's response, and his sonar guru's face lit up.

"I hear the acknowledgement on our ship's arrays, and it's stronger on the drone."

"As it should be. Get a range check."

The technician beside Anatoly tapped buttons, and three round-trip exchanges of sound followed.

"I've got the range check," the young technician said, "but I don't like the answer. They've gone two miles in the wrong direction."

"Let's keep this up, and see if we can turn them around."

Darkness crept up the guru's face, and Volkov allowed him to process the sounds.

"Torpedo in the water! Detected by the drone."

"Give me a bearing," Volkov said.

The direction to the hostile weapon fit between those of the dolphins and the drone.

Volkov exhaled.

"It's not a dangerous shot," he said. "It's reactionary in hopes that our drone was our ship. We'll maintain course and speed."

"The dolphins just announced a new submerged contact," Anatoly said. "It's probably the torpedo."

"Acknowledge the report and send a reactionary torpedo down the bearing of the Israeli weapon."

The Israeli Aman officer lifted his gaze to Volkov, reminding him of his mission's limits.

"Set half the bomblets for detonation," Volkov said. "I don't want to risk overwhelming the crew's damage control abilities."

Anatoly's fingers flew across icons.

"Tube two is ready, fifty-percent bomblet yield."

"Shoot tube two."

Volkov's ears popped.

"I have control of the weapon from tube two," Anatoly said.

"If you hear the *Splendor*, let me know and recommend a steer for our weapon, but I doubt that cool commander will make a mistake."

"Of course, Dmitry."

"Now, keep trying to get our dolphins back home with commands to return."

"I will, but I'm concerned they won't consider a drone a large enough target to be a mothership."

"That's a challenge," Volkov said. "Can you keep the drone far enough away to keep them guessing about its size?"

The guru shrugged.

"Maybe. In these waters, their echolocation isn't what we've seen elsewhere. If we get lucky, they'll hear the return-to-ship signal and follow it without knowing it's coming from the drone."

For ten minutes, Volkov fought a tug-of-war for his dolphins against the distant Israeli submarine. The cetaceans seemed caught in the middle, and as their trainer lumbered into the control room and forced his way into the seat beside Anatoly, Volkov feared his mammalian assets lost.

Then he caught a break.

"I hear the fake call!" Anatoly said. "On the drone, bearing three-four-nine from the drone."

"You've still got wire control of our weapon?" Volkov asked.

"Yes. I recommend a steer to the left of twenty degrees."

"Agreed. Twenty degrees. Do it."

The trainer looked up with forlorn eyes.

"At least you'll make them pay if they take my babies?"

"I'm getting your babies back."

"But if you don't? You're only human."

"Then, yes. I will make them pay. Not with their lives, since I'm using a slow-kill weapon. But they'll pay with the shame of defeat."

The sonar expert stirred.

"I've intercepted another fake command to our dolphins. Bearing three-four-seven from the drone."

"Send the raw bearing to the tactical display," Volkov said.

He looked to the lines connecting his drone to the source of sound he suspected as the *Splendor*.

"Assume the source of the fake calls is the *Splendor* and assume its speed is five knots. Plot it."

The technician the trainer had forced to move to an empty Subtics console seat tapped his screen, and an icon of the Israeli submarine appeared on the chart before Volkov. A velocity vector of five knots became wedged between the two sniffed sounds of the vessel's attempts to dupe the dolphins.

"Steer our weapon another five degrees to the left," Volkov said. "This is our chance."

"I've imparted a steer five degrees to the left," Anatoly said. "If we're right, the weapon can acquire the target in four minutes and will have eighteen percent fuel remaining to chase it down."

"Turn on the weapon's seeker five minutes from now. I don't want to give the Israelis any extra time to evade."

While waiting for his torpedo to end the battle, Volkov urged his team to continue salvaging his cetaceans.

"Get another range check from the drone," he said.

Three exchanges of acoustic signals later, his sonar expert confirmed the dolphins' stagnancy in purgatory.

"Still caught between the *Splendor* and our drone," Anatoly said. "At least they're not losing ground, but this will be difficult if the *Splendor* keeps fighting us."

"They're terrified," the trainer said. "They can't possibly understand what's going on. Turn on the weapon's seeker and scare away that submarine!"

"It's too soon, Vasily," Volkov said.

"Please, Dmitry! My babies!"

"I will get them, and I will rid this campaign of the *Splendor*. Be patient."

The trainer stood and ran from the room.

After minutes of watching the tactical scene unfold while wrestling with his guilt for the trainer's suffering, Volkov whispered to himself.

"Damn him."

"Say that again please, Dmitry?" Anatoly asked.

"Nothing. It's just... never mind."

Unwilling to admit compassion for the trainer with whom he shared a blossoming friendship, Volkov welcomed the distraction of a tactical milestone.

"Per your timing, it's time to energize our weapon's seeker," Anatoly said.

"Energize the weapon's seeker."

"The weapon acquired a target on its second ping! It's accelerating and changing its ping cycle to prosecute the target."

"Excellent," Volkov said.

"I hear the *Splendor*!" Anatoly said. "High-speed screws. Cavitation. Reduction gear noises. It's trying to evade."

"It won't. It's a perfect shot."

"Right, Dmitry. You turned on the seeker less than a mile away. Brilliant! Impact is in ninety seconds. And wait... Countermeasures!"

Volkov glanced over the guru's shoulder at a green icon indicating continued wire connection with the torpedo.

"Drive our weapon through."

"The countermeasure field has blinded us to the *Splendor*," Anatoly said. "We've lost the *Splendor*."

"Understood. That's expected."

"Our weapon is approaching the field. Passing through it now. And... I've regained the *Splendor*. I have blade rate now. It's making turns for twenty-seven knots on one seven-bladed screw."

Volkov caught the glare of the silent Aman officer who offered a dour look.

"Your countrymen will be fine, I assure you," Volkov said.

"I would protest if I thought otherwise. But don't expect me to share your crew's jubilation."

"Hull popping," Anatoly said. "The *Splendor* is heading shallow. Our weapon is diving below it... the magnetic influence field is broken... and detonation!"

"Count the attachments," Volkov said. "Everyone!"

He watched the sonar team stare at their screens and listen while blocking out distractions. Anatoly stood, walked behind the backs of his technicians, and gathered their input."

"Nineteen of twenty-four attached. Nine or ten should detonate based upon our fifty-percent yield setting."

"Count the detonations."

The sonar technicians repeated their listening efforts.

"I heard the first," Anatoly said. "Several just went off together. The *Splendor* is surfacing."

"Get me a final count."

Half a minute later, the sonar guru made his report.

"Eight. Perhaps nine. It's hard to tell given their timing."

"Good enough," Volkov said. "The Israeli commander became greedy and tried to take our dolphins. That was his mistake, and we were fortunate to capitalize upon it."

"The dolphins," Anatoly said. "We still need to get them back."

"Keep using the drone."

Five minutes later, Volkov frowned.

"They're rejecting the concept of the drone as their mother-ship, aren't they?" he asked.

"I can't get them to move," Anatoly said. "They must be in shock or something. Now that the *Splendor's* no longer a factor, should we just blast out the return-to-ship command at maximum power from our bow sonar?"

"No. We'd announce ourselves to the world. For all we know, the entire Israeli anti-submarine helicopter fleet is coming for us now, and there's no guarantee the dolphins would respond."

"We can't abandon them."

"No," Volkov said. "We can't."

He walked to his gray-bearded veteran, leaned beside him, and whispered.

"Can you patch the sound-powered phone system through the Subtics system for broadcast through the drone?"

"That's impossible directly, but I could move a receiver close enough to a Subtics microphone to give you a workaround. Anatoly should be able to adjust the amplification to any power level you'd want coming out of the drone."

"Good enough."

He explained his plan to his veteran and stood to leave. As he departed, he looked to his executive officer.

"Sergei, you have the deck. I'll be setting a plan in motion."

In the crew's berthing area, Volkov walked to the trainer's rack and rapped on the locker under the bed.

He heard a sobbing voice.

"Go away," the trainer said.

"Oh, you wouldn't send away an old man trying to help a friend, would you?"

"Yes, we are friends. But I want to be alone. As my friend you have to respect that. I just want to be alone."

"What if I told you I think we can still save your babies?"

The curtain flew aside, revealing a reddened face glistening with tears.

"Don't tease me."

"I'm not. I have an idea. Will you at least try it?"

"I'll try anything for them."

"I'm going to grab the sound-powered phone over there and bring it to you. I've arranged for your voice to be transmitted through the drone. I believe that if they hear you, they'll follow the drone back to the ship."

The trainer's eyes became wide.

"Really? What about the Israeli submarine?"

Volkov responded with a hint of pride.

"It's no longer a problem."

"It could work. I'll try it."

The *Wraith's* commander paced across the berthing area and returned to his friend with the receiver.

"What should I say?"

"Tell them to come home. Speak slowly and calmly. Tell them how important they are to you. They'll follow your voice. At least I sincerely hope they will."

The trainer spoke into the phone.

"Andrei? Mikhail?"

"Good. Keep going."

"Come home, my babies. Vasily misses you."

"Keep that up. That's fine."

After five minutes of the trainer's repeated hails, the sonar guru appeared at the door to berthing.

"I wanted to bring you the news personally," Anatoly said. "The dolphins are following the drone. We're bringing it back to the ship, and they're coming towards us."

"See?" Volkov asked. "I told you it would work. We'll have them back in our torpedo tube in no time, and then back into their tank for food and rest. You'll have your babies."

The trainer lowered the phone and looked at him.

"You do care, Dmitry, don't you? About me. About my babies. About everyone on your team."

"Yes, my friend. Indeed, I do."

CHAPTER 6

After a day at sea, Cahill watched moonlight glimmer atop the waves.

"We're still two days away from our operational theater, even averaging more than thirty knots," he said.

"Two days exactly, give or take a few hours, depending how you define our theater," Walker said.

"It still feels like a long time."

"Losing patience?"

Cahill found the question odd but gained personal insight pondering it.

"It may not be about patience," he said. "It's probably got more to do with feeling naked above the waves for days on end. I'm better suited to be hidden underneath."

"Don't be that way. This is a rare opportunity. We're lucky we can run all out on the surface."

"What do mean? We're lucky because our port bow is withstanding the load, or because nobody's trying to kill us?"

"Both. But it's nice to unleash the engines and run like a destroyer across the open waters. You may find it foreign with all your time on submarines, but this is the best part of being a surface warfare officer."

Cahill faced his executive officer and smiled.

"Getting romantic on me?"

"Nice choice of wording, mate. I expected you to be more romantic with our Israeli guest, but I haven't seen you string two sentences together with her."

Cahill felt like a prisoner on his own ship, fearful of encountering the woman who consumed his thoughts. The *Goliath* became tiny as he tried to avoid her.

"What could I possibly say to her? What could I possibly hope to accomplish other than losing my credibility by letting a Sheila distract me?"

"Come on, mate. Half the crew is pulling for you to have a go at her, and the other half doesn't think you have the stones."

"Seriously? You're joking."

"I didn't run a formal survey, but it's me job to be in touch with the rumors."

"So be it," Cahill said. "I can't do anything about what the men say, and I'm not going to let their talking dictate me life."

"Nor should you. But what do you want to do?"

Cahill frowned and headed towards the stairway.

"Well, good night, Liam. You've got the bridge tonight."

"Indeed, I do. But you're avoiding the question."

"Why are you so interested in me personal affairs?"

"I see the way you look at her."

"So what? I must appear pathetic when she's near me. I'm trying to avoid her so that I don't."

"I wouldn't worry about looking pathetic, mate."

"And why's that?"

"Because I see the way she looks back at you. She's trying to hide it, but she's got an eye on you, too."

After walking to his stateroom, Cahill slid under his crisp sheets and fell asleep.

He dreamt.

Exasperated, he lowered his head while his steps echoed through a steel serrated brow connecting the submarine to the pier.

"Executive officer!"

He turned his head and saw his commanding officer behind him, standing on the back of the Australian vessel, *Collins*.

"Yes, sir?"

"That was disgusting."

His crew had lost ten out of twelve mock engagements with a Malaysian submarine during a four-day international training exercise. Part of him wondered if the two victories had been gifts from his northern neighbor's superior tactical team.

"I know, sir."

"The fleet suffers from a horrible manpower shortage, but I won't tolerate that as an excuse for incompetence."

"Nor should you, sir."

"Good. Then I assume you'll have the crew rounded up for remedial training early tomorrow."

Having returned to port on a Friday evening, Cahill had planned on personal time over the weekend, as had the entire crew. He swallowed his desire to be with his fiancée and prepared to dash her hopes and those of his sailors.

Though harsh, his commanding officer was right. His tactical team would die if faced with real combat.

"Of course, sir. I'll see to it."

Fast-forwarding in his dream, he met his would-be wife at the Stirling base's officers club. Her athletic lines shaped a black evening gown that failed to hide the musculature of the former gymnast's body.

She frowned and sat without speaking.

"Thanks for coming," he said.

"Do you know how long it took me to get those reservations you just made me cancel?"

He had no idea.

"A long time."

"Three months. It's the most popular restaurant in Perth."

"I'm sorry," he said. "I needed to be on the telephone this evening and call the crew back to work tomorrow. I couldn't possibly have made the trip."

"But you expected me to make the trip out here instead?"

"I wanted to see you. I hoped you wanted to see me."

"I did," she said. "But this is all I get? One night in this waterfront hangout for sailors. Then you're back at it tomorrow?"

"Sometimes duty calls."

Her face glowed an ugly red, the remembered pain morphing his subconscious mind's imagery.

"Well, life is calling me, Terry, and I can't wait for you to go back and forth to sea on your deployments. This is no way for me to advance a career. This is no way for us to start a family."

"What are you saying?"

She ripped her finger off and flung it like a javelin into his chest. With each pump of his dying heart, blood spurted over the engagement ring.

Time slipped to a nearer nightmare, and he stood in the port bow section of the *Goliath*. The ringing of a torpedo's acoustic seeker hammered the barren walls of the lonely ship.

The echoes pounded his head.

He was alone.

Darkness surrounded him.

Louder... louder... impossibly loud in his bones.

Detonation.

Deluge. Burning lungs. Drowning.

Death.

Cahill awoke with the rapping at his stateroom door, and he choked out a response.

"Enter."

"Terry," a sailor said. "Liam wants you on the bridge."

"How urgent?"

"He says to take your time, but he needs you in the next fifteen minutes. He has an update from Mister Renard."

Allowing himself an abridged toiletry routine, Cahill made himself presentable before exposing himself to the skeletal night crew.

As he stepped through the berthing area and into the tactical control room, his heart fluttered when he saw Dahan walking behind the men seated at consoles.

Trying to mimic normal, he clenched his jaw to avoid verbalized stupidity.

"Captain," she said.

"Major," he said. "I see we're both awake at an odd hour."

"Yes."

He struggled for words.

"Are your accommodations to your liking?"

"The tunnel between the hulls causes an unnecessary delay between my team's berthing and the control center."

"I can't shorten the length for you. It's made of steel and has dimensional constraints I can't change."

"You can move my team into starboard berthing. You have enough spare racks."

"But you'd lose your privacy. You'd be... exposed... to conceivably every man aboard."

Her glare negated his statement.

"I see that you don't care," he said.

She cocked her head.

"And apparently any concern I have about the matter is irrelevant. Very well, I'll have your team moved to the starboard side in the morning."

She cleared her throat and folded her arms. Over her shoulder, he saw his evening watch sonar supervisor bury his chin into his chest to hide a giggle.

"I see," Cahill said. "May I assume that you've already identified four racks of your choosing for your team and will move yourselves at your leisure?"

"Yes."

"Well then," he said. "It's settled. Good night, major."

"You're not very observant."

"What now, major?"

"Did you notice that my team's evening watch is missing?"

Having avoided eye contact with his own men for fear of ridicule, he'd missed the absence of the empty seat he'd reserved in the control room for the section's Aman soldier. To protect a shred of his dignity, he lied.

"There are other places on the ship where your team can listen to radio traffic."

"Two," she said. "The port control center, which doesn't interest me since it's separated from your team, and the bridge."

"Okay. So he's with Liam."

The hard shadow her brow cast over her eyes suggested he'd epitomized buffoonery.

"Yes," she said. "And with your permission, I will join you on the bridge."

"So, you had your night watchman wake you when he saw Liam wake me?"

"That's part of my standing orders to my team."

"I could make this easier and have you informed any time I'm summoned. No need to go the trouble of spying on me."

"If you wish," she said. "But it's no trouble at all."

On the bridge, Cahill cowered against the port end of the room's circular boundary, wishing for a corner in which to hide. Trying to avoid Dahan, he stared into the starry night outside the plexiglass. Despite its energized nautical running lights, the *Goliath* remained a blackened silhouette bouncing atop the waves.

The makeshift port bow section withstood its stresses better than Cahill's nerves.

"Captain Cahill?" Dahan asked.

He turned to face her, Walker, and an Aman soldier who appeared muscular for an intelligence technician. The soldier's voice was deep and strong.

"I intercepted orders mobilizing our airborne reconnaissance and early warning craft, manned and unmanned," he said.

The Aman man speaking in the first person about Israeli assets concerned Cahill.

"You need to refer to Israeli craft as 'Israeli' and not 'our'. Our assets consist of the three ships in Renard's fleet."

Dahan shot a glance at the soldier.

"I apologize," he said. "It's a habit."

"It's also part of the charade," Dahan said.

"Which charade?"

Hearing the Frenchman's familiar voice over the loudspeaker, Cahill stepped closer to the room's center to see his boss on a screen.

"The charade that Aman remains loyal to the prime minister," Renard said. "Such pretense may serve us well."

Cahill realized the deployment of Aman personnel aboard

Renard's ships had happened beyond the knowledge of the military forces upon which they spied, allowing them an influx of trusted sensitive data.

He felt himself a fool for having failed to see that advantage. After he grasped it with Renard's prompting, the tactical value of Dahan and her team doubled per his estimate, and he shamed himself for letting her sexual allure blind him to ways she could help him succeed and survive.

"Yes," he said. "That charade. It's understandable, but to avoid confusion aboard this ship, we must refer to Renard's fleet's assets in the first person and Israeli assets in the third person."

"We will," Dahan said. "The Israeli airborne assets are now a threat to detecting our ship while it runs at high speed. We'll need to slow to avoid being identified as a combatant."

Cahill reflected upon the detection ranges of the adversary's assets.

"The Phalcon system on your Gulfstreams has an advertised tracking range of only two hundred nautical miles," he said. "Granted, detection range for a ship this large may be a bit farther, but we're barely east of Malta."

"The detection range is three hundred and fifty nautical miles for this ship and its large radar cross section," Dahan said. "A Gulfstream could fly from the Israeli coast to detection range in less than two hours."

"They won't fly directly towards us, unless they're fanning out several aircraft across the Mediterranean to search for us. And I need to stay on the surface to get to Dmitry."

She offered the gruff gaze.

"Then a tactical decision must be made," she said.

Cahill welcomed his executive officer's interjection.

"I can resolve this," Walker said. "That's why I called you up here. Dmitry doesn't need us."

"I assume that's good news?" Cahill asked.

"You bet," Walker said. "He's an ace as I see it. He took out two Israeli submarines and can maneuver at will to the operational theater without our help."

"No shit, mate? Dmitry's putting Jake at risk of being our second-best submarine commander."

"It's not all good news," Renard said.

Cahill focused on the video screen.

"I assumed not," he said. "Otherwise we wouldn't all be awake now."

"Indeed. Jake and Dmitry have enjoyed rapid and successful engagements, but an unintended consequence is the Israeli's certitude about whom they face as an adversary. We've left no room for doubt."

Pondering the implications of becoming known, Cahill glared at the screen in hopes his boss would offer a clue. The Frenchman's fatigued, sullen sockets framed steel blue eyes that betrayed no hint. He tried to lure a clue.

"Three slow-kill torpedoes and two dolphin bombs pretty much equate to your calling card, mate," Cahill said.

"Agreed," Renard said. "They're adjusting their defenses to account for our technology and our tactics, which are unfortunately becoming too easily recognized for my tastes."

The Frenchman's tone revealed the hint of caution Cahill sought. For a man who planned every move to control his world, Renard appeared to be shifting to a backup option.

"So they know a lot about us, but what's it all add up to?" Cahill asked.

"They know that the *Specter* attacked *Shaldag Three* and that the *Wraith* attacked the *Leviathan* and the *Splendor*," Renard said. "And they know they can't defeat us in open waters, if I surmise their behavior correctly."

Dahan exchanged quick words in Hebrew with her soldier, and then she aimed her voice at the screen.

"That's correct," she said. "The Israeli Navy is warning all unit commanders about Renard's fleet and its latest actions, and the information is accurate. In response, the submarine fleet ordered the *Revival* to cease an intelligence-gathering mission and to join the *Crocodile* in the Gaza Strip blockade. Jake's interference there caught the prime minister's attention."

Cahill questioned her definitiveness.

"How are you sure the *Revival* is in one place and the *Crocodile* in the other?"

Her hips glided as she shifted her weight and cocked her head, leaving Cahill to wonder if every statement he uttered offended her.

"We know from historical briefings that the *Revival's* crew is experienced in offshore intelligence missions while the *Crocodile's* crew has trained for open sea combat."

"So it was the *Crocodile* that Jake discovered at the blockade?"

"Yes," she said.

"Okay," Cahill said. "Two Israeli submarines are stranded on the other side of the Suez Canal. Two are disabled thanks to Dmitry. One is laid up in dry dock, and that leaves only the *Crocodile* and the *Revival* to support the blockade. Isn't this the best outcome we were hoping for at this point?"

"It was," Renard said. "But I had planned on the Israelis being aggressive and pursuing Jake and Dmitry, and their defensive reaction to protect the blockade is the worst of the outcomes I analyzed. It places obstacles in the way of the humanitarian aid convoy we intend to escort to Gaza."

"So that's the bad news," Cahill said. "But you did analyze it and consider other options, right?"

A glint of pride glimmered in the Frenchman's eye as the corners of his mouth angled upward.

"Indeed, I did, and I'm sure you'll embrace the change in plans."

"I'm listening."

"I'm going to have Jake and Dmitry both loiter outside the blockade awaiting your arrival."

"Ah, another mission where me transport ship doesn't do any transporting—only fighting, not that I'm complaining."

"Well, you may complain about this," Renard said. "You're going to have to submerge, but not for the reasons Major Dahan suggested. You won't be hiding any time soon from the airborne early warning assets. In fact, I want you to stay surfaced until you can verify that an airborne asset has identified you."

Cahill folded his arms.

"If I had to guess, you're setting another one of your traps."

"I am, my friend," Renard said. "And what better bait than the *Goliath*?"

CHAPTER 7

Jake tapped a nervous finger on the *Specter's* central plotting table and looked to his French mechanic.

"This doesn't seem fair," he said.

"That's because it isn't," Henri said. "But this is warfare, and ambushes are an acceptable means to victory."

Across the table, the Israeli Aman officer shrugged.

"I can't lend any judgment," he said.

"But you do confirm that I'm facing only one submarine?"

"You could have surmised that for yourself, but yes. The most logical place for the *Revival* to be gathering intelligence is off the coasts of Lebanon and Syria, which means it's too far away to interfere with you before you reach the *Crocodile*. You didn't need me to tell you this."

"Still, I appreciate the confirmation," Jake said.

He lifted a stylus from its magnetic mount and stuck its tip into the oval of uncertainty about the *Revival's* location.

"That's as good a guess as any," the Aman officer said. "I have little knowledge of the *Revival's* operating area. I only know the latest intelligence coming from the submarine fleet refers to Hezbollah, and that places it near Lebanon."

"It would be a challenge for the *Revival* to reach Terry before he can attack the blockade, especially since it lacks air-independent propulsion," Jake said. "It would have to snorkel a lot. The Israelis would be wiser to send the *Crocodile* without delay for a head-to-head battle with Terry."

"I agree," the Aman officer said.

"Then I'll focus on just the *Crocodile*."

Jake double-tapped the stylus in the ellipse of uncertainty around the *Crocodile* and then selected a hostile submarine icon from a dropdown menu. With the system adjusting his free-handed attempt, he drew a straight line from the Israeli submarine and snapped it to the expected future track of the *Goliath*.

Submerged after offering Israeli early warning aircraft a blatant opportunity to detect it, the *Goliath* made eight knots towards Israel. Jake dialed up an eight-knot speed for the *Crocodile*, and the line between the Israeli submarine and the *Goliath* shifted to bring both vessels to the same place at the same time.

"This only works if the *Crocodile's* crew knows where the *Goliath* is heading," the Aman officer said.

"Leave that to Terry," Jake said. "He'll pop up every hour or so to track Israeli assets on his radar, and if he finds something within range of his cannons, he'll show off his itchy trigger finger. The *Crocodile's* crew will have plenty of knowledge of where he's going."

"They won't suspect the trap?"

"They'll assume that Terry's zig-zagging at his maximum submerged speed of thirteen knots, which makes eight knots in his baseline direction believable. I expect he'll throw a little variance into his path so that it's not an exact straight line, but the *Crocodile's* crew will know where to intercept him."

"And if you stick at your present speed of four knots in a straight line, you'll set up an ambush roughly here."

The Aman officer pointed at the chart.

"Good guess," Jake said. "I'll head in that direction at four knots and deploy two drones a few hours before we get within reach of the *Crocodile*. I'll probably do some zigging of my own, but four knots average over ground. Slow, methodical, easy. The *Crocodile* is being handed to me on a silver platter."

"Yet you appear anything but confident," the officer said.

Jake snorted.

"That's because I've never had any battle set up so easily in my favor. So that means something has to go wrong."

"*Merde!*" Henri said.

The French mechanic turned and walked to his station.

"What'd I say?" Jake asked.

"You just jinxed us," Henri said.

"I didn't know you were superstitious."

"I'm not. I just know when I need to start praying, and when you jinxed us, I felt the urgent need to pray."

Jake glanced at the chart.

"Before you tune in with Jesus, can you get us on course one-three-five?"

"Coming to course one-three-five."

"Very well," Jake said. "We've still got eight hours until we're near the *Crocodile*. I'm going to take a nap. Have someone make sure I'm awake in five hours. Get your replacement at the ship's control panel up here to relieve you, Henri. You have the bridge while I'm gone."

In his stateroom, Jake added an entry in the ongoing journal he kept for his wife. He wrote it on waterproof paper under an unproven belief that the writing would last for her as a final salvageable gift if his mission ended on the bottom of the sea.

After affirming his love and adoration for her with annotations of his mindset about the mission, he slid under his sheets and slept for the first time in a day and a half.

The thumping at his stateroom door felt early, and he glanced at his watch. He'd slept for two hours.

"Enter," he said.

A young sailor opened the door and spoke English with a heavy French accent.

"Henri requests your presence on the bridge. He has news from Pierre Renard."

After shaking his head to swish mouthwash between his cheeks, Jake stopped at a scuttlebutt, spat, and washed the green ooze down the drain.

He continued to the control room and joined the French mechanic beside the central chart.

"I received an update from Pierre over the low-bandwidth feed," Henri said. "He wanted to call your attention to two Israeli *Sa'ar 5* corvettes moving together in formation with two *Sa'ar 4* missile boats and three patrol craft that have formed a task force. The task force also is on course to intercept the *Crocodile* before it can reach the *Goliath*."

"Interesting," Jake said. "They only have three *Sa'ar 5* corvettes in their entire fleet. This is a serious response for their limited surface combatant firepower."

"Quite interesting. Pierre thinks it's positive evidence that the *Crocodile* is seeking the *Goliath* with anti-ship missile support from the corvettes."

Jake did quick addition.

"That's thirty-two Harpoon anti-ship missiles if my math is right. So I'm thinking the Israelis are going to try the squeeze play to put Terry in a bind between running from a torpedo and diving under missiles."

"I'm sure Pierre has warned him," Henri said.

"But he hasn't changed our plans, which means Terry's still the bait for the trap I'm going to spring. And now I'm springing our trap while facing two extra bow-mounted sonar systems, two extra towed sonar systems, and four helicopter decks."

The Aman officer folded his arms.

"And remember the unmanned vehicles," he said. "The corvettes can carry unmanned helicopters and Seagull robotic undersea hunters."

Jake recalled having daydreamed during the briefings the Aman officer had given him about the vast array of domestic techno-gadgets. The tiny nation behaved like a leading developer of everything automated and deadly, but Jake thought only a fraction of the ideas would reach mass production.

"Would the helicopters carry weapons?" he asked.

"No, they'd be just scouts. Miniatures, really. But the Seagulls would be armed with small torpedoes."

"How small?"

"About the same size as an air-dropped weapon."

"That's big enough to sink us," Jake said.

"Yes, it is. Each Seagull carries two of them, and each corvette can carry two Seagulls, which hunt as a pair and can make thirty-four knots."

Jake realized he needed to respect the automated hunters.

"How good's the Seagulls' sonar?" he asked.

"They're high-frequency, as you'd expect on a small craft," the Aman officer said. "Terrible at long distance, excellent if close. The Seagulls are optimized for minesweeping. Anti-submarine warfare is their secondary function, but they are dangerous. If a Seagull gets within a few miles, we'd be in a dire situation."

"Got it," Jake said. "I'll try to avoid them."

"At least there's a benefit from this," Henri said. "We now can use the surface ships as a guide for the location of the *Crocodile*."

"Somewhat," Jake said. "We have at least five and half hours until we tangle with this new Israeli task force. Henri, let's hash this out a bit."

The Frenchman leaned into Jake's ear and spoke in his native tongue. Jake shifted his brain into the thought and speech patterns of the Romance language.

"Something seems wrong," Henri said.

"Like they're trying to gift us the bulk of their fleet all at once?" Jake asked.

"Exactly. The Israelis are too smart to sacrifice so many ships to an ambush."

"But that's the point of an ambush. They're not supposed to know it's coming. They're supposed to be only thinking about Terry."

"But they know we're out here somewhere after sinking the patrol vessel in the blockade."

Jake scoffed.

"We could be on the other side of the Mediterranean by now as far as they know."

"Do you believe that they'd be so naïve?"

Jake sighed and slouched.

"No. And that's what's bothering me. I thought this was going to be an easy ambush on just the *Crocodile*, but now I've got a creepy feeling about it being too easy."

"But what to do about it? You can't just retreat."

"No, I can't. We'll stick to the plan of taking out the *Crocodile*. The submarine remains the meat of our attack. All the surface ships are just gravy."

As Jake feared he might overanalyze the scenario, the Frenchman compelled him deeper into the matter.

"What do you make of the old *Sa'ar 4* missile boats?"

"Relics with only one purpose," Jake said. "To shoot Harpoons at the *Goliath*. They'll probably be mothballed by the end of the week."

"I thought they were already mothballed. I hardly remember them from our reviews of the Israeli fleet."

"I'm honestly impressed that they're at sea making more than thirty knots. I guess the Israelis thought it was worth putting Harpoons on them and getting them within strike range of the *Goliath*. They'll be loud, but remember that they're just distractions. We're taking out the submarine."

Appearing content with Jake's position, the Frenchman switched to English.

"Shall I have the tactical A-team stationed in three hours, to include a team briefing of your intent with the task force?"

"Make it three and a half," Jake said. "Let's give our aces a final chance for some food and rest before battle."

To clear his mind, Jake went to his stateroom and reclined in his rack. After a minute of racing thoughts tormenting him about possible outcomes of the pending battle, he found the solitude unsettling. As he sought companionship, a quick walk brought him to the entryway of the crew's mess.

He pushed his head into the space and saw his French veterans huddled around a dining table.

"You guys plotting a mutiny?" he asked.

His top mechanic lifted his white-haired head.

"I've been working on that for years," Henri said. "So far, progress has been slow."

"I'll take that as a compliment," Jake said.

"I guess it is," Henri said. "Claude has been my biggest supporter, but even he seems safely back in Antoine's camp of remaining loyal to you."

The wiry frame of his engineering officer, Claude LaFontaine, twisted and exposed a cigarette hanging from the corner of a curled mouth. Jake also noticed a book in the man's hands.

"Henri exaggerates," LaFontaine said. "I haven't even thought about mutinying against you since our latest campaign in Taiwan. We're all with you, and we know we'll succeed in the next battle."

"I appreciate it. What are you guys doing?"

"Bible study," Henri said. "Would you care to join us?"

"It depends what you're studying. If you're studying some sort of glorious historic battle, I'm not interested."

"Not at all. We're in First Corinthians."

Jake had read every canonical book, and though he'd internalized a fraction of the contents, he considered the repetitive guidance of the Pauline epistles hard to digest.

"I don't think I want to read about a bunch of do-gooders before I take a bunch of cheap shots at Israeli sailors."

The Frenchmen chuckled in unison.

"Corinth was a mess," Henri said. "It was a harbor town with pagans, Jews, and the worst sort of scum—sailors. They were horrible sinners and struggled to figure out how to adopt their new beliefs. Since Paul said there was hope for them, there's hope for everyone."

"That's good to know," Jake said. "But I'll pass. I need to think through some more possible scenarios against the Israelis."

He wandered farther aft and entered the MESMA plant and heard hissing steam. The compartment's billowing heat warmed him, and he sat at a workbench to gather himself.

A passing technician garnered Jake's nod and then departed down a ladder to the room's lower section, leaving the *Specter's* commander alone with his thoughts.

Though the words he shared with his crew preached a focus on the *Crocodile*, the urge to succeed drove Jake to strike the entire task force. With one smart salvo of his torpedoes, including the reloads he expected he'd have the time to employ, he could cripple the remainder of the Israeli fleet.

Then the humanitarian support of the blockade run would be a foregone conclusion, and the ensuing political embarrassment would force the militant prime minister to reshape his strategy of expansion–or have it reshaped by his emergency successor.

A fledgling Christian, Jake sought divine guidance.

"I need your help, God," he said. "Please let me know what to do. I'm trying hard not to pretend I'm you anymore. So help me figure out if I'm supposed to hit the *Crocodile* and run or take down the entire task force."

He glanced around the room and saw temperature sensors on steam piping but no divine signs.

"I guess you'll guide me when you need to."

He returned to his stateroom where he took a quick shower and put on fresh clothes. After a few minutes of relaxing, he headed to the control room and found his A-team.

Beside his mechanic, he stood at the central charting table.

"Would you like to deploy the drones?" Henri asked.

"Soon," Jake said. "Where are my drone operators?"

Seated at adjacent Subtics systems consoles, two young Frenchmen turned and raised their hands. Though untested in combat, they'd undergone training with Remy.

"You guys ready?" Jake asked.

Two confident faces affirmed their eagerness.

"Okay, then," he said. "Let's deploy them at the same time to make all our noise at once. And let's do it now before we're close enough to the *Crocodile* to be heard."

"Tubes five and six are ready with drones," Henri said.

"Simultaneously launch drone one from tube five and drone two from tube six."

After hearing confirmation of the launch relayed from the torpedo room, Jake watched his sonar guru gather input from his protégés.

"Drones one and two are deployed and clear of our hull," Remy said. "We have wire connectivity and confirmation of propulsion on both drones."

"Set the speed for both drones to ten knots," Jake said. "Fan them out forty-five degrees off our track for five miles. After five miles, turn them parallel to our track."

To give his sonar arrays workable listening geometries, he accelerated the *Specter* to six knots and began zigzag legs across the path leading to his prey. Then, for thirty minutes, he took periodic views of the tactical chart as the crosshair of his submarine slipped behind the icons of his twin drones.

The triad of the submarine and its extended listening machines appeared on an imaginary line Jake drew connecting the distant *Goliath* to the approaching Israeli task force. He considered his lurking *Specter* ready to swallow the hidden but predictable *Crocodile* and its surface escorts.

"Too easy," he said.

Exercising the patience submarine commanders valued, Jake retreated to his foldout chair on the conning platform, slouched in it, and let his crew search for its victim.

After two hours, the familiar curl in his sonar ace's upper torso caused Jake to sit straight. Remy pressed his muffs against his ears as he discerned phantom sounds from reality.

"Fifty-hertz electric plant," Remy said. "I have it on the towed array, bearing zero-eight-three. Sending to the system."

The line of bearing to the sound sliced the ellipse of uncertainty of the *Crocodile's* location. Jake stepped down to the central chart, snapped a stylus from its mount, and then tapped a location on the sound's line.

"Correlate the fifty-hertz tone with the *Crocodile*. I've set the *Crocodile's* location in the system. I'm setting its speed to eight knots, heading directly for the *Goliath*."

Jake glared at a young technician.

"Anything on drone one?" he asked.

The young operator shook his head.

"That's fine," Jake said. "Let's risk an active transmission. Aim drone one at my estimated position of the *Crocodile* and prepare for a half-power, one-hundred-millisecond burst."

The technician tapped keys and expressed his readiness.

"Transmit," Jake said.

A wall of sound crept up a display over the technician's head, and a small blip appeared within half a mile of Jake's guess of the Israeli submarine's position.

Extending his head over his protégé's shoulder, the sonar ace studied the display to confirm his understanding.

"Active return," Remy said. "It's a submerged contact. It's got to be the *Crocodile*."

"That's it, then," Jake said. "Can anyone think of a reason I should wait?"

He scanned the room and saw shaking heads, including a nonchalant shrug from his Aman officer.

"Very well," Jake said. "Shoot tube one."

CHAPTER 8

Commander Levy sprang from his seat as the *Crocodile's* tactical system klaxon blasted its alarm.

"Active torpedo seeker," his sonar supervisor said. "Bearing two-six-one."

What had seemed impossible prior to the *Goliath* exposing itself was happening. He'd set a trap, and the mercenary submarine was taking the bait.

"Signal the task force at maximum sonar transmit power, and assign tube one to a reactionary shot down the bearing of the incoming torpedo."

The supervisor stood, crouched, and hovered over two technicians as they tapped keys. Levy heard the bow-mounted sonar system belching its repeated low-frequency tones as a warning to the ships above him.

"The signal is being sent, sir," the supervisor said. "And tube one is ready."

"Shoot tube one."

Levy heard the pneumatic whine as the pressure change popped his ears.

"Executive officer, send the incoming torpedo's bearing to the task force on the underwater phone until you get an acknowledgement."

The portly man waddled across the compartment, twisted dials, and spoke into a microphone.

"Bearing to hostile torpedo is two-six-one," he said. "Bearing to hostile torpedo is two-six-one. Bearing to–"

A watery-electronic response interrupted the repeated report.

"Acknowledge bearing two-six-one for incoming torpedo.

Counterstrike is now underway."

Levy looked at his senior veteran mechanical technician.

"All stop. Use our momentum to surface the ship smartly."

The veteran acknowledged the order, and the deck lifted Levy's stomach into his chest. He grabbed a railing for balance.

"Get the radio lined up on the task force channel," he said. "Maximum power."

As the submarine surfaced and levelled, the room rocked.

"Raise the radio mast," Levy said. "Give me voice and a high-bandwidth data link with the task force."

"You're linked, sir," the veteran said.

Levy grabbed a handset.

"Task force commander, this is *Crocodile*, over."

"*Crocodile*, this is task force commander, over."

Since he'd planned on spending most of his time submerged, Levy had allowed for a surface warfare officer to command the naval group. But the concept was his, the trap was his, and the true command was his. He gave the orders.

"Give me a status report," he said.

"The *Arrow* and *Lance* are doubling back to locate themselves four hundred and two hundred yards ahead of you respectively in sacrificial positions. Also, the full counterstrike has begun on a base bearing of two-six-one."

Levy glanced at the room's central chart to verify updates to his countrymen's tactical data. The icons and information he desired appeared. Four anti-submarine warfare helicopters fanned out to bar the mercenary submarine's escape while the two corvettes and two Seagull pairs navigated towards the spaces between the aircraft.

The formation reminded him of an animal trap with interlacing razor teeth. A gap allowed for his *Crocodile* to seek the enemy vessel from the center of the group.

"Very well," he said. "Update the task force's tactical data for the exclusion zone around my hunting waters."

"We're updating it now around the bearing you recorded for the hostile torpedo. One moment."

"I don't have all day," Levy said.

"It's coming now."

Lines on the tactical chart showed the *Crocodile's* water.

"It appears acceptable," Levy said. "Make sure none of the task force's assets wander into my water, or I'll punish them with a torpedo. I won't tolerate the remotest chance that you confuse me with the mercenary."

"There will be no such mistake, I assure you. We are professionals–not idiots."

"I'll be the judge of that when this is over," Levy said. "But since I have no choice but to trust you, make sure you attack any submerged target you find outside my exclusion zone. That order applies to the Seagulls, too. Today is not a day for hesitation."

He returned the handset to its cradle and pointed at his executive officer.

"Raise the periscope and watch the missile boats to make sure they maneuver in front of us," he said.

As his hefty second-in-command struggled to balance his mass over the rocking deck, Levy stepped to the central table to review his brainchild, the counterstrike against the mercenary submarine's ambush.

The ships and aircraft followed his designs, and he considered the mercenary doomed.

Lusting to begin his hunt, he looked to his sonar supervisor, the man he'd lacked time to break into an obedient minion.

"Supervisor, where's the hostile torpedo?"

Levy judged the man's self-esteem as remaining strong, and after stomaching this lingering threat to his dominion, he appreciated the expert's confidence in waters that held the most complex undersea battle of his career.

"It was practically a shot in our face, sir. There's no bearing rate to track it. The only good news is that the *Lance* is now between us and the torpedo. The *Arrow* is still maneuvering."

"The *Arrow* is maneuvering at what speed?"

"Thirty-two knots, sir. It's making the effort."

"Good. I won't tolerate the cowardice."

"The *Arrow's* now slowing into position."

Levy walked to the stocky officer seated at the periscope control console.

"Step aside."

The executive officer leaned from his chair and then stumbled to the adjacent seat, giving Levy a field of view through the periscope's optics.

"Good," Levy said. "Both ships are doing their duty."

"The hostile torpedo has shortened its ping cycle to terminal homing," the supervisor said.

Levy thought about asking which surface combatant would be his sacrificial anode, but he didn't care. Skeletal propulsion and conning crews staffed each ship, and they all expected the laughable limpet warhead that characterized the Frenchman's fleet's self-imposed limits.

"Excellent. Executive officer, lower the periscope. Now we can submerge again."

As the portly officer obeyed, Levy commanded his mechanical veteran at the ship's control panel.

"Make your depth thirty meters, slowly."

The deck assumed a gentle angle, and the rocking receded.

"I request a change in course to drive some geometry on the hostile torpedo, sir," the supervisor said.

Levy turned his head.

"Why?"

"There's a good minute or two before it detonates. I'd like to track it to be sure."

The *Crocodile's* commander agreed with the tactic but rejected the recommendation as a show of strength.

"The hostile torpedo's fate is now a foregone conclusion. The missile boats have served their purpose. My hunt begins now."

He turned back to his mechanical veteran.

"Make eight knots, and steer course two-six-one. Take me right back down the bearing of that damned torpedo. The sonar team will continue its search for a *Scorpène*-class submarine, and I will rid these waters of this accursed menace."

As the supervisor announced the success of the first phase of the counterstrike–the sacrifice, Levy's confidence rose.

"The hostile weapon has detonated," the supervisor said. "I have just enough bearing separation to place it under the *Arrow*. It's not a heavyweight. Limpets are attaching to the *Arrow*. And now, the limpets are detonating."

"Belay your reports on the *Arrow*," Levy said. "That ship's now finding the best retirement it could hope for with a burial at sea."

"Its crew, sir–"

"Is of no concern to us. Shame on them if they can't find their way to lifeboats. Now that the *Lance* is the surviving missile boat destined to an ignoble retirement, it will pick up the *Arrow's* crew. Focus on finding the *Specter*."

"Why do you think it's the *Specter* and not the *Wraith*, sir?"

Levy had received intelligence that the *Wraith* had transited the Suez Canal, making it the likely aggressor against the idiots who'd let it cripple their two submarines north of Port Said, Egypt. That left the *Specter* as the culprit that had defied his blockade, and the geometry of undersea, undetected transit favored his target being the *Specter*.

"That's a commanding officer's privileged information," he said. "I am hunting the *Specter*."

"Okay, sir. Let's assume the mercenary submarine is the *Specter* since–"

"It is the *Specter*. There is no assumption."

After a brief silence, the sonar supervisor continued.

"Yes, sir. I would bet the *Specter's* commanding officer is smart enough to have repositioned himself so that he's no longer on a bearing of two-six-one. I'm sure he kept moving along the line of sight after he shot at us. So he's gone far to the left or to the right."

"Of course, he has," Levy said. "But that will only matter in resolving ambiguity if I pick him up on the towed array, and if I pick him up before someone else in the task force does."

The long line of hydrophones he towed behind the *Crocodile* sensed low-frequency sounds and distant noises, providing him his first warning of danger. But exposed to the water without any mechanical backstop, his towed array was helpless to tell its left from its right.

"Given our limits in maneuvering, we could save some time in resolving ambiguity if we knew what side it's on now."

"There's no rationale beyond a coin toss for that."

"Maybe not, sir, but let's take a guess. I think the *Specter's* heading south to go help the *Goliath*."

Levy saw a flaw and attacked.

"I'm sure that's what they want us to think, these mercenaries. But we know the *Goliath's* primary purpose is to serve as bait, which, of course, backfired through my insights when I outsmarted them with my counterstrike plan. For all we know their entire fleet could be heading to Cyprus to escort a blockade run or even be withdrawing."

"I just wanted to get ahead of the *Specter*, sir."

"That's my job, and I will make no assumption about its behavior beyond what the data tells me."

"Yes, sir."

"Well, what does the data tell me?"

"Acoustically, nothing yet," the supervisor said. "I see that we're getting useful low-bandwidth updates from the task force's tactical data feed though."

Levy lowered his gaze to the central table.

Icons representing helicopters that had taken off from the four largest ships stopped and hovered twenty miles from the torpedo-detection point. He expected their dipping sonar systems to shriek their dangerous frequencies and drive the *Specter* back into the pursuing task force.

The corvettes marched forward at half speed, closing the formation's jaws while blaring their sonar systems and listening for a return, and the Seagulls patrolled the outer edges of the formation.

With a mistrust of the robots, Levy hoped a manned asset

would find and prosecute the *Specter*. Though he personally wanted to find the mercenary submarine, he conceded that he needed a large net to capture it.

Though suffering from misplaced loyalties, the *Specter's* commander had talent. He could mount an escape in any direction, and Levy wanted him to double back into a submarine-versus-submarine encounter.

But a kill of the *Specter* would be his victory, and he would claim credit regardless who pulled the trigger.

"Where's my torpedo?" he asked.

"Fifteen miles out with eight percent fuel remaining," the supervisor said. "Do you want a steer?"

"No. There's nowhere smart I could steer it. Cut the wire and reload the tube."

Ten minutes passed, and as doubt threatened him, Levy leaned over the chart to assure himself his trap would succeed.

The counterstrike was brilliant, he convinced himself. Flawless. The net was wide and tight, and fate lacked the cruelty to allow the *Specter* to escape. He commanded his patience to endure, and he waited.

Two minutes later, his adrenaline spiked as he reaped the rewards of his genius.

A new icon appeared on the display, two miles from the southern pair of Seagulls.

He smirked.

"After all this elaborate planning and putting the best ships of the surface fleet forward, a damned robot finds the *Specter*."

He waited for an update to the mercenary submarine as the Seagulls tracked its course and speed.

"Good," he said. "Only twelve miles away. I will chase it. Assign tube two to the *Specter*."

The executive officer voiced his weak protest.

"Sir, it's my duty to inform you that leaving our exclusion zone is a danger to our ship."

"Noted. Annotate your protest in the deck log again to protect your career. I don't care. I know where our ships are, and I know how to avoid them."

"But why seek the *Specter* when the Seagulls will prosecute it? You're incurring risk for no reward."

"Don't be a fool, you buffoon," Levy said. "A Seagull has never been tested against a commander as skilled as that of the *Specter*, and I'm making a calculated assessment that my intervention as an insurance policy is necessary."

"May I at least inform the task force with a communications buoy, sir? For our safety."

Levy flipped his wrist backwards.

"Bah. Very well. Prepare a buoy and launch it when you're ready. But hurry so we're not close enough to the *Specter* that it can hear the launch."

He looked to his chart to check his target's tracking, and then he dragged a stylus over the display to confirm his intent before calling out to his veteran.

"Increase speed to eighteen knots, come left to course two-one-five."

"We're at eighteen knots, sir," the supervisor said. "Coming to course two-one-five. We're incurring a heavy load on the battery at this speed. Remaining time on the battery is seventy-eight minutes."

As the deck rolled through the turn, the supervisor requested his commander's attention. Sensing the man might utter words best kept private, Levy walked to his side and crouched.

"I couldn't help but notice the *Specter's* heading towards the south, sir. It looks like it was heading that way to help the *Goliath* after all."

"How dare you gloat," Levy said.

"That's not what I'm doing, sir. I mean we need to consider the *Goliath*. It's still out there, and we haven't seen any sign of it since we launched our counterstrike at the *Specter*."

Digesting the insight, Levy stood, walked to his executive officer, and whispered.

"Before you send the communications buoy, place an order to the task force to request constant air observations over the

Goliath and constant updates back to us. If that ship so much as snorkels, I need to know where it is and what it's doing."

"But the *Goliath* shouldn't be a factor, sir. Not given the distance where it was last found."

"It's almost laughable how you try to defy me to protect your career, but in this case, I actually agree with you. No, the *Goliath* shouldn't be a factor. But given the history and luck of these mercenaries, I refuse to leave that accursed ship's undetected intervention to chance."

CHAPTER 9

Jake considered surfacing and surrendering.

"What the hell's going on, Antoine?"

"You said it," Remy said. "Hell is going on."

Leaning over the tactical chart, Jake stared at interlacing lines of sounds to hostile ships, aircraft, and robots. The noise cast an inescapable net with webbing attached to Israeli assets his sonar guru struggled to locate. It felt like a locust swarm.

"Get me a solution to the closest threat."

"The raw bearings are on the chart," Remy said. "You can draw a solution as well as I could estimate one."

"Damn it. At least tell me which threat is the closest based upon sound power levels."

The guru offered Jake his facial profile while yelling over his shoulder. He appeared flustered for the first time Jake could recall.

"At what power level is each sonar transmitting? At which depths are the dipping sonars? How fast is water moving over the surface ships' sonars? Answer these questions, and I'll tell you which is closest."

"Shit. Can you tell me which ones are the greatest threats of detecting us?"

"I can give you power levels hitting our hull, but I can't tell you about the return paths or sensitivity of every hostile hydrophone. If you want my guess, a good half of them have more than a fifty percent chance of detecting us."

Jake sensed fear in the control room but lacked the confidence to override it. Feeling vulnerable, he wished for divine intervention.

Then help came from above.

Hostile icons jumped on his screen as Renard's data feed tightened to the threatening war machines while the merchant shipping went dark. With the constrained focus on the assets that could kill him, the updates arrived faster.

"Thank you, Pierre," Jake said. "Antoine, Pierre's giving us updates every thirty seconds. Get your team to correlate what you're hearing to his feed."

One by one, the haphazard lines of sound from the crosshair of the *Specter* disappeared as the sonar ace's technicians matched them to a truth Jake assumed Renard garnered from an American satellite or a NATO aircraft.

"Henri, cut the wires to tubes five and six. Reload both tubes with Sidewinders."

As the Frenchman relayed the orders to the torpedo room, Jake reflected upon his loaded weapons. Having never used the encapsulated anti-air Sidewinder missiles, he doubted their efficacy. But Volkov's success three months earlier against multiple helicopters offered Jake hope in their design.

A simple casing held one anti-air missile in its torpedo tube and protected it against moisture after launch. Once at the water's surface, the canister would open and aim the missile's heat seeker to the sky. Bladders under the tail would inflate to tilt the weapon in a crude preset direction. But with a two-thirds chance of hitting its target, the missiles left Jake with a need for insurance.

"Get a Stinger missile team up here, too."

The French mechanic looked at him with raised eyebrows.

"You expect that we may surface?"

"I don't know what to expect. Just get them up here."

As Henri obeyed, Jake walked around the table to gain his sonar guru's attention.

"Assign tubes one through four to the four closest contacts, based upon Pierre's feed."

"Tubes one through four to the four closest contacts," Remy said. "We'll take care of it."

Jake stepped back to the plotting table and enjoyed a moment of comforting insight into the machines maneuvering above him. But his moment evaporated when he realized a pair of Seagull hunters had turned towards him.

He looked across the table at the Aman officer.

"The Seagulls are a risk at three miles, right?"

"Yes," the officer said. "But it varies with many factors. Two to six miles, depending–"

"Then the pair to the south is a threat already."

The officer nodded.

"Tell me everything you know about them," Jake said. "Speed, hunting tactics, launch parameters."

"Maximum speed is thirty-four knots. They usually hunt in pairs where the ships take turns slowing for short periods to listen while the other is transmitting. This gives them an average speed over ground of twenty-five to twenty-eight knots."

"What else? Would their behavior change if they detect us?"

"I expect the same sort of aggressive behavior you'd see from a surface combatant that lacks a helicopter and must fight with its organic torpedoes, except there's no human element of fear of your counterstrike."

While weighing his escape options, Jake wanted to avoid the unafraid robots, but they represented one of several evils. He could risk running under a helicopter, he could turn back towards the task force that included an alerted submarine, or he could try to slip under the southern pairs of Seagulls.

Each option stank of death.

Hoping for a clue of discernment, Jake welcomed the French mechanic's presence by his side.

"Pierre just sent a text note in his data feed," Henri said. "He's commanded Terry to come shallow and render assistance.'"

"I'm glad I didn't have to ask," Jake said. "I would've felt like a coward asking Terry to expose himself."

"If the roles were reversed, I'm sure you'd help him."

"Yeah, you're right. Okay. This tells me which way to run. We're heading south to make it easier for Terry to help us."

"That's logical. But it means we need to pass near the southern group of Seagulls. Maybe right under them, depending how they maneuver. They're fast."

"Everything hunting us is fast."

"Then I leave it to your skills."

For lack of a rational basis to hope for his survival, Jake trusted his instincts.

"Henri, come left to course one-five-zero. Increase speed to fifteen knots, slowly."

The mechanic acknowledged and walked to his station to administer the order.

As the deck rolled through the turn, Jake pressed his palms into the table for balance. He looked down at the icons that shifted about the display at the fastest speed Renard could provide him information through the submerged antenna trailing the *Specter*.

An update to the Seagulls kicked his adrenal glands into overdrive.

"The Seagulls just turned towards us."

"I don't hear them," Remy said. "If they turned towards us, that puts their bow nulls facing us. That's their quietest aspect."

"I know that. Shit. That's enough. Do you have weapons ready against them yet?"

"Yes, tubes one and two."

"Very well," Jake said. "Shoot tubes one and two."

The impulsion system beyond sight popped Jake's ears.

"Tube one indicates normal launch," Remy said. "I have wire control. I hear its propeller. Now I hear tube two and have wire control."

"Hand off weapons control. I want you to focus on listening."

The guru tapped keys and uttered quick keywords to his team. As he settled back in his seat, his torso became taut and began to curl forward.

While Jake waited for him to sort seaborne sounds from auditory hallucinations, he turned his head to the ship's control station.

"Henri, reload tube one with a Sidewinder, tube two with

a slow-kill weapon. Make noise and get it done fast. Get two teams down there if they're not already."

"I already have two teams in the torpedo room," Henri said. "I'll have them load tube one with a Sidewinder, tube two with a slow-kill weapon."

From the corner of his eye, Jake saw his sonar ace stir.

"Torpedo in the water," Remy said. "From a Seagull, bearing two-zero-four. The seeker is active."

"Bearing rate?"

"I don't have one yet."

"Bearing drift?"

"Drifting to the right. On the left, drawing right. It looks like a good intercept shot."

Icons on the chart shifted to show the robotic hunters three miles away. Realizing the impossibility of outrunning weapons launched in a nearby damning geometry, Jake shifted his thoughts into the third dimension.

"Henri, all ahead flank, and make your depth three hundred and fifty meters, smartly. Get us down fast!"

Grabbing a handle on the charting table for stability, Jake braced himself against the thirty-degree descent. He twisted his sneakers on the diving deck to face the stern and give his toes a chance to bend in his favor.

"Prepare to launch one pair of gaseous countermeasures on my mark."

"I'm ready," Henri said.

Watching the depth gauge pass through two hundred meters, Jake gave his order.

"Launch countermeasures."

"Countermeasures are launched," Henri said.

"Prepare to launch a second pair on my mark."

At two hundred and fifty meters, Jake ordered the second pair of bubble-makers into the water, and then the deck's tilt receded with the *Specter's* steadying at its deepest depth.

"I've lost the torpedo to our countermeasures," Remy said.

"Then it's lost us, too," Jake said. "Henri, prepare to launch a noise-making countermeasure."

"One moment… it's ready."

"Launch the countermeasure."

"I hear our noise maker," Remy said. "It's transmitting our recorded frequencies."

"That may not fool the torpedo," the Aman officer said. "I can only speculate that its seeker would use passive listening to regain us after our gaseous countermeasures blinded its active seeker. I can give you no guarantee."

"The only guarantee is that we need to fool it or we're dead," Jake said. "Henri, left full rudder, steady on course zero-six-zero. Make your depth fifty meters smartly. Get us up fast."

Jake twisted his feet and braced his arm against a seat as the *Specter* tried to toss him towards a corner.

"What are you doing, driving down and up like this?" the Aman officer asked. "How can this work? How can you save us?"

The Israeli's distress revealed he'd reached the extent of his undersea warfare knowledge. Jake had little patience for his ignorance, but he needed to quell the fear.

"The torpedo was too close to outrun. So I blinded it and dived below its seeker's acquisition cone. Now that it's diving blindly, the first thing it should hear on the other side of our gaseous countermeasures is our noise maker. That should keep it aiming downward while we rise above its seeker's acquisition cone and slip away."

"Can it work?"

"We'll know soon enough."

"We lost the wires to our weapons during our erratic maneuvers," Remy said. "But they looked like good shots at the Seagulls. We'll track them acoustically."

"Very well," Jake said. "Let me know when the hostile torpedo pushes through our gaseous fields."

"That's in twenty-five seconds, best estimate."

Time working in his favor, Jake waited half a minute.

"I hear the hostile torpedo's seeker," Remy said. "It passed through our second gaseous countermeasures. Bearing two-one-zero."

"Bearing drift?"

"One moment," Remy said. "Slight right. Yes. On the right drawing right."

"We're clear," Jake said. "Henri, slow to eight knots."

The hull's trembling ebbed, and the deck leveled. Across the table, the Israeli Aman officer's shoulders slumped.

"That really worked?"

"The torpedo's moving away from us, isn't it?" Jake asked.

"If you say so. That was... amazing."

"We're hardly free yet. Those Seagulls have three torpedoes left and are still chasing us. Antoine, how long until our weapons hit?"

"Less than two minutes," Remy said. "The Seagulls are driving right into them, making no effort to evade."

"The manufacturer claims that the Seagulls can evade torpedoes," the Aman officer said. "But I don't see how someone could write software elegant enough to do what you just did."

Though running with severed wires, the *Specter's* torpedoes appeared on the display thanks to the sonar team tracking their propellers and seekers. Matching them to Renard's updates on the Seagulls, Jake expected his weapons to reach their targets.

"Our weapons will detonate under the Seagulls," he said. "My concern is what happens if both weapons hit the same Seagull. Or what happens when limpet bombs designed to spread across multiple compartments of a frigate try to land on a tiny robot. Most of them will miss."

"How many need to hit to stop them?" the officer asked.

"I was hoping you could tell me."

"I could only speculate."

"Then I can only speculate on the number of warheads needed to cripple them, and I hope to find out. But you asked a good question. Antoine, reassign tube three to the closest Seagull, tube four to the farthest Seagull."

"That's really one target in our system, given how close together they are," Remy said.

"Fine. Just reassign the weapons."

"Done. Tubes three and four are assigned to the Seagulls. Do you want me to shoot?"

"Hold your fire. Let's see what our deployed weapons do."

"Thirty seconds to impact of our first weapon–roughly–I can't tell exactly without the wire," Remy said. "Both weapons are pinging for terminal homing."

Jake glared at the chart while the icons merged.

"Our first weapon is detonating," Remy said.

"Any idea if the second weapon is on the other Seagull?"

"It's a coin toss," Remy said. "Limpets are attaching to the first Seagull."

The technician seated beside the guru became animated and rattled off a report to Remy.

"He thinks the second weapon just detonated under the second Seagull. We may have gotten a lucky coin toss."

"Count the detonations," Jake said.

The guru leaned over a technician while listening to his headset and watching multiple screens. After quick banter with his two closest accomplices, he turned his toad-head to Jake.

"Eight detonations on the first Seagull. Four on the second. The first Seagull is already slowing, probably with water weight and extra friction caused by riding lower in the water."

"The first Seagull is sinking?"

"Yes."

"But it can still shoot a torpedo until it's underwater. Have one of your guys listen to it. I want you listening to the other one."

Renard's data showed the hunters four miles away and driving behind the *Specter*, but Jake knew they posed a continued threat to his submarine.

Worse, with the battle against the robots revealing his location, the rest of the task force angled towards him. The speedy helicopters presented the greatest new danger, provided he survived the Seagulls.

"The first Seagull is under water," Remy said. "The second is still making turns for thirty-four knots."

"It's adjusting its protocols to hunt alone," the Aman officer said. "It knows it lost its partner and will reduce its sprint cycle and increase its drift cycle."

"But its sprint would still be full speed, right, slowed for any damage we may have inflicted?" Jake asked.

"I believe so, but I only know what the manufacturer shared in confidence while selling the product to the Navy. I don't have access to any data which was shared beyond that. And I don't understand why you're asking"

Jake pointed to the line of sound between the crosshair of the *Specter* and the remaining Seagull.

"Because the bearing to the Seagull is lagging where it should be if it's moving at thirty-four knots. So it turned towards us, turned away from us, or slowed. But I'm hoping it slowed due to taking on water from our weapon."

"It's taking on water," Remy said. "I hear sloshing."

"You hear..."

The guru angled his head and offered a cold stare defying the questioning his abilities. Jake had lost count of the times Remy had heard noises he'd considered beyond audible discernment.

"Of course, you hear sloshing. That's great news. Reassign tube three to the closest corvette, tube four to the farthest corvette."

"Tube three is assigned to the closest corvette, tube four to the farthest corvette," Remy said. "And the second Seagull is now under water."

Jake felt the mortal fear of the robotic threat flush from his flesh. In a moment of calmness, he braced himself for the next phase of battle.

Helicopters, corvettes, a second pair of Seagulls, and the *Crocodile.*

"Do you want to shoot at the corvettes?" Remy asked.

"Yes. God willing, we've got some time to drive slow and regain the advantage while keeping wire control of the weapons against the corvettes."

"I hope so, too," Henri said. "But look at the chart. The helicopters are getting close. We may need to shift our focus."

"Let's get the torpedoes out there and let them make their runs. Then we'll focus on the helicopters."

"Understood," Henri said. "Shall I prepare a communications buoy for Pierre informing him of our status?"

"Yeah, good idea. Give him a feed from Subtics and let him know I'm going to try to double back towards Terry. Launch it when it's ready."

The mechanic acknowledged and departed.

"Antoine," Jake said.

The toad-head faced him.

"Shoot tubes three and four."

CHAPTER 10

Cahill wedged himself between the shoulder of his sonar supervisor and that of a seated technician.

"How bad is it?" he asked.

"Bad," the supervisor said. "I've never seen pressure on Jake like this."

"Worse than the Black Sea?"

"Yeah, because there's no deterrent this time. The Israelis know he's using slow-kill weapons, and I'd bet me arse Jake doesn't even have a heavyweight loaded."

"I know he doesn't, mate," Cahill said. "But he can reload fast enough, and the Israeli's know it, and so does Pierre. Negotiating is always a possibility when Pierre Renard is our boss."

"That's a crutch we can't always lean on."

"And I plan to avoid putting Pierre in that position."

"You mean to rescue your friend?" Dahan asked.

Her voice stunned him, as always. He found it strong, sexy, and distracting.

"Yes," he said. "Jake is me mate, and I plan to rescue him."

"You can achieve your mission objectives without him."

Her words infuriated him, and he clenched his jaw.

"Join me on the bridge," he said. "We'll discuss it there."

He escorted her to the other side of a watertight door and stopped at the bottom of the stairs. Though cramped and within muffled earshot of Walker above, the space provided the best privacy he could find.

"Do you have no soul?"

"Are you questioning my comment about not needing Jake to finish your mission?"

"Yes!"

"I pointed out a fact. Was I incorrect?"

Her coldness continued to stymie him.

"Yes. No. I mean, it's the way you say things."

"I see no need to waste words."

"But you know I'm close to the *Specter's* crew, yet you suggest I abandon them like pawns on a chessboard."

"If you can't see your colleagues as expendable during battle, your emotions will poison your judgment."

Though unsympathetic, she made sense to him.

"I'm not arguing that. But you can at least be discrete when you talk about them."

He braced for her escalation to a shouting match, but she lowered her voice.

"I wasn't discrete because I needed your attention. I can see how important the *Specter's* crew is to you, and I know that strong team cohesion is a valuable military asset. But you were planning to put this ship at risk without considering the larger picture."

"You're bloody well right I was thinking about Jake and his crew first, but I am also considering the fleet's objectives."

"Even if you are considering the objectives, I'm concerned. If you're that invested in your colleagues' safety, you risk going insane if you lose them."

"Then let's make sure I don't lose them."

As her frame relaxed in resignation of the argument, he turned from her and yelled up the stairway.

"Liam, maintain propulsion on the MESMA systems and surface the ship."

The stairs angled upward, complicating the climb, and Cahill used the handrails to yank himself forward. Nearing the summit, he continued his orders to his executive officer.

"Set all rounds in both cannons for splintering until I say otherwise, and get the weapons bays ready for battle. We'll control the firing from the bridge."

He heard Walker relay the order to the relevant crewmen as he reached the bridge's leveling deck and saw the sun glimmering through translucent fluid above the broaching dome. As Dahan entered the space behind him, the *Goliath's* speed created an artificial wind that whipped liquid sheets over the plexiglass.

"Energize all radar systems and elevate all weapon systems," Cahill said.

The executive officer tapped keys.

"Pierre's video is coming through," Walker said.

The Frenchman's face appeared on a screen next to a display showing the tactical scenario. As Cahill watched, the icons on the adjacent screen hopped to their updated locations.

"Bloody hell. It's even worse than I feared."

"I assume you're seeing the real-time information on Jake's situation," Renard said. "It's dreadful, but he's managing as well as could be expected. He appears to have sunk a pair of Seagull hunters without suffering any damage, but he needs help with the aircraft."

"It's the helicopters," Cahill said. "It's always the helicopters. Shall I start shooting? Say, ten rounds at each aircraft?"

"Agreed," Renard said. "I will have them guided on target."

Cahill knew better than to ask in front of Dahan how Renard would control his rounds, and her silence conveyed her acceptance of the secret. His experience suggested American satellite technology, local NATO airborne military assets, or both.

He tapped keys as he talked.

"I have control of both cannons. I'm aiming ten rounds at each of the four Israeli helicopters. Commencing fire."

He saw Walker lift binoculars to his face and point them off the *Goliath's* quarter as the first duo of hypersonic rounds cracked overhead. From the corner of his eye, he saw Dahan's startle response. For the first time in his presence, she'd revealed a hint of frailty.

"I apologize, major. I should've warned you of the sound. You get used to it."

"No need to apologize. It's just, with the railguns so far aft, I didn't expect the explosions to be so loud up here."

"It's the sonic boom, major. It's loud anywhere near one of the moving rounds."

Every five seconds, the *Goliath's* computers ordered the railguns to send a pair of projectiles over the horizon.

"Why hasn't Jake tried a Sidewinder?" Cahill asked. "It's not like him to wait for me to bail him out."

"Good question," Renard said. "Perhaps his tubes were all loaded with torpedoes."

"Why would he do that?"

As the Frenchman's answer came, Cahill realized his mindset had changed from commanding a submarine to commanding a ship with railguns.

"It's my fault," Renard said. "I hampered him with the rules of engagement. I denied him the use of his heavyweights, and he may have loaded all his tubes with slow-kills to allow multiple shots at the ships and robots."

"He's smart enough to reserve at least one tube for a Side-winder," Cahill said.

His boss' eyes grew wide as he looked away from the screen.

"Wait. He's launching a Sidewinder now."

Cahill wanted to see the images the Frenchman saw, but he exercised restraint in front of Dahan. Then shadows cut across Renard's face as he frowned.

"*Merde.* A miss."

"That's okay, Pierre," Cahill said. "Sometimes the Sidewinder misses. The targeting is crude."

"No. A well-defended miss. The helicopters are using defensive flares."

"Your Sidewinder attacks in the Arabian Sea are known," Dahan said. "The fleet is adjusting."

"I need to hurry to Jake," Cahill said. "He just gave away his location to a nearby helicopter."

"The Sidewinders come with timers," Renard said. "I pray he used a delay to clear the location before it launched."

"He may have," Cahill said. "But I'm still coming for him. Shifting propulsion to the gas turbines. Coming left to course zero-two-zero."

Liquid sheets walking over the dome began spitting spray, and the deck's undulations increased.

"Let's see what I can do with your rounds," Renard said.

After a minute of hypersonic flight, the arcing icons of railgun projectiles reached the helicopters. On the adjacent screen, the Frenchman's face became ashen.

"*Merde*. They're jamming our guidance and using chaff."

"Your tactics for shooting down aircraft are known, too," Dahan said. "I expect the helicopters have transmitters in the same frequencies you use to guide your rounds. The chaff is blocking your airborne tracking systems. They're probably defending themselves both ways."

"You don't seem too disappointed," Cahill said.

"You're trying to kill my countrymen."

"Fair enough," Cahill said.

"Damn," Renard said. "All the rounds are missing."

"Are you at least forcing them into evasive maneuvers?" Cahill asked.

"Yes. We're keeping Jake safe for the moment. They can't hunt while they dodge bullets."

"Let's see how brave they are if I make this harder on them," Cahill said. "Pierre, order Jake to transmit his location and give him mine. Have him drive straight towards me at high speed. I'll get the helicopters off his back by raining down metal above him."

"Yes, I see," Renard said. "That could work. I'll send him word of your location and get an update from him."

As the Frenchman rattled off commands in his native language to a man seated off screen, an alarm whined in the *Goliath's* bridge.

Cahill looked down and noticed two supersonic aircraft coming from the east.

"I thought the Israeli Air Force was against the prime minister and was staying on the sidelines," he said.

"The helicopters you're shooting at are staffed by the Air

Force," Dahan said. "I suspect you've created a new enemy."

"What's coming at me?"

"To drop bombs on us, my assessment is that those are F-15 Strike Eagles," she said.

"She's right," Walker said. "They're painting us with APG-70 radar. They're Strike Eagles."

"Very well, Liam. Take charge of the starboard cannon and start shooting the Strike Eagles."

The Frenchman's voice carried the day's first shred of enthusiasm.

"Splash one helicopter!" he said. "I had all your rounds diverted to the one closest to Jake, and it's finally down. It looked like a controlled water landing."

"That buys us some breathing room," Cahill said. "But the next one is only five minutes away per your data link."

"You can use four of those minutes to defend yourself," Renard said.

"Liam, use both cannons against the Strike Eagles."

The sonic booms became gentler as the rounds streaked towards the eastern horizon.

"What could those Strike Eagles hope to accomplish?" Cahill asked. "We already have them on our phased array radar. They can't jam that very easily."

"I think it's just a distraction," Walker said. "Every round we aim at them is a round a helicopter doesn't need to dodge."

An alarm whined again, and another pair of supersonic jets appeared.

"Another distraction?" Cahill asked.

"You said it yourself," Dahan said. "The Air Force is neutral in this conflict. I suspect all the strike aircraft are distractions designed to protect the helicopters."

"You'd bet your own hide on that?" Cahill asked.

"I'm standing next to you, aren't I? If they bomb you, they bomb me."

"I now have the APG-70 radar systems painting us from the new Strike Eagle contacts," Walker said.

Cahill felt the satisfaction of having seen through a ruse.

"Don't the strike aircraft seem too obvious about advertising their interest in us?" he asked. "A bit aggressive with their radar use, but a bit timid in their flight speed?"

"Agreed," Walker said. "I think this confirms they're just trying to distract us."

"Right, then. Turn the port cannon back towards the helicopters. Make them work to chase Jake. Keep the starboard cannon on the strike aircraft to call their bluffs."

The Frenchman's image became animated.

"Jake launched a communications buoy," he said. "He acknowledges the order to sprint to you. I'll send you his coordinates for your verification, but I recommend you come right to zero-two-two."

Cahill made the adjustment in the *Goliath's* course and saw the icon of Jake's position appear on his display.

"Forty-five miles away," he said. "We'd take station on each other in forty-four minutes if Jake held his maximum speed, but he can't hold his speed that long."

"No, he can't," Renard said. "Let me have the numbers run."

Again he turned and issued orders in his native tongue to a French naval officer who sat beyond his camera's field of view.

"Eighteen knots," Renard said. "You'll intercept each other in fifty-two minutes. He has enough charge per his report to sustain that speed."

"Okay," Cahill said. "But I hope to scare away those helicopters long before then. They should turn back when I have them on the phased array. Do you know what altitude they're operating at?"

"Quite low," Renard said. "They'll rise up to two hundred meters when they reposition, though."

"I can use that against them," Cahill said.

He did a quick mental horizon calculation and then tapped a stylus onto a display to analyze the possible movements.

"Then they'll be vulnerable to me phased array at thirty-four miles when they reposition. And at that range me rounds get there in half a minute."

"Then you could begin to provide Jake a stronger safety net after eleven miles of closure," Renard said. "Less than thirteen minutes."

Cahill reviewed the larger scene.

"The strike aircraft are keeping their distance," he said. "They're not suicidal, and we've called their bluff. Liam, use both cannons against the helicopters."

For slow minutes, time dripped like molasses.

Then good news arrived when one of Dahan's Aman soldiers shared a report over the loudspeaker.

"I'm able to hear the orders to the helicopters," he said. "It's encrypted, but it's a common military channel we can decrypt with our listening equipment."

Cahill cast his voice towards a microphone.

"Is there any useful data?"

"Yes," the soldier said. "They understand the threat of our phased array radar. They have orders to turn back when we're able to track them with it."

"Good," Cahill said. "Liam, have our own translator draft a manuscript of the communications and have the tactical team review it as he scribes it."

He caught Dahan sighing through her nose with disapproval.

"It's not that I don't want to trust your team, major," he said. "It's that I can't afford the luxury of blind trust."

"I didn't say anything," she said.

"But I could tell me order to verify your man's report bothered you."

"Wouldn't it bother you if the roles were reversed?"

"Yes. Probably. So let's move past it. If the information is correct, I believe it changes the tide of this battle. Time now favors us, but let's see if we can hasten things."

"What more could you do?" she asked.

Cahill checked his new idea against the display to verify its plausibility.

"The helicopter crews are starting to fear us," he said. "And given how long they've been in the air, their fuel is becoming a limit. They're too far away to reach the nearest coast."

"I don't see your point," Dahan said. "They can land on any of four ships in that task force."

An Aman soldier within the tactical control room overheard and corrected her assumption over the loudspeaker.

"Make that three ships, Major Dahan. I just overheard a report that the *Arrow* has been declared a loss. They have no crew aboard to perform damage control, and it's sinking."

"That's still three ships that can support flight operations," she said. "They thought out this task force well."

"Then we'll just have to bring that down to zero," Cahill said. "Liam, turn the starboard cannon to the nearest corvette."

"Shall I target the propulsion gear as usual?"

"Yes. See if you can cripple it."

"They know the techniques the Russians and Greeks used to counter such an attack," Dahan said. "They'll use evasive maneuvers and the point defense systems while they maintain flank speed towards Jake."

The Aman soldier's voice over the loudspeaker preempted Cahill's rebuttal.

"They're turning back!" he said. "The entire task force, except for the submarine. They've been ordered back. I just intercepted the message."

"The evidence I'm now seeing agrees," Renard said. "Apparently, the Israeli Navy is using common sense to determine what causes are worth risking one's life. Chasing down a fleeing mercenary submarine fortunately isn't one of them."

Cahill's enjoyment of the victory was brief.

"At least not today, mate," he said. "But a retreat still leaves us with a challenge in our primary mission. If we can't defeat this task force now, those assets will just head home to beef up the blockade. This just delays our final conflict."

"Indeed it does," Renard said. "But have no fear. I have a backup plan that addresses this."

"Don't you always have a backup plan?"

"Yes. And for now, continue to Jake and pick him up. He's dangerously low on battery, and I don't want him snorkeling with the *Crocodile's* whereabouts unknown."

"Leave it to me," Cahill said. "I'll grab him."

"Then bring him southeast. Once you're both safely disengaged, I'll share our next steps with you."

CHAPTER 11

Volkov digested Renard's data feed trickling across the *Wraith's* central plotting table.

"This is undesirable but not entirely unexpected."

His sonar ace spoke over his shoulder.

"Is everyone okay on Jake and Terry's ships?" Anatoly asked.

"Yes. Our ambush yielded one mothballed missile boat, and Jake's narrow escape from a counterstrike with Terry's help yielded one helicopter. But the *Crocodile* still remains at large."

"You make it sound like it could've been worse."

"That task force that materialized around the *Crocodile* appears to have been a well-planned reaction to Jake's ambush. You could call it a reactive ambush, if such a thing may be defined."

The supervisor shrugged.

"Whatever you call it, it puts more pressure on us," he said. "We're a great crew, but other than our skill, we have no advantage over the *Revival*. In fact, we have a disadvantage since it's defending water while we're the aggressor."

Volkov reviewed his tactical chart. An ellipse of uncertainty of the Israeli submarine's location covered a sizeable chunk of water off the Gaza Strip's coast.

"Yes, we are at a disadvantage," he said. "And we will remain so until we alter our circumstances."

"Your tone suggests you have an idea?"

"I've been considering an option."

"Are you going to share?"

"Yes," Volkov said. "But not with you. Not unless I can convince someone else first."

In the torpedo room, Volkov noticed an oddity in a spare

weapon rack.

Atop the arced metal recess which had once held a reload torpedo, sprawled blankets and a comforter. A bright foam plug jutted from the sleeping man's ear as drool rolled from the corner of his mouth to a pillow.

The senior torpedo technician approached.

"I was going to tell you, but he begged me not to. He's not hurting anything. He just wanted to be close to his dolphins."

"How long has he been... relocated here?"

"Ever since we brought the dolphins back, after we almost lost them."

Floating in the centerline tank, each cetacean aimed a lazy eye into the ceiling as half of each animal's brain stood guard over the sleeping half.

"And he wanted to be near them, even when he sleeps?"

"Right, sir. He's even convinced the guys down here to grab food for him, though he hardly eats."

"I'm surprised he hasn't asked for a chamber pot."

The man looked away and rubbed the back of his neck.

"Well, he did, but the guys and I have our limits."

The chronometer on the torpedo control station indicated the late afternoon.

"It's an odd time for him to sleep," Volkov said.

"He stood over his dolphins talking to them for a day straight," the technician said. "The guys said he did it constantly. He hardly slept. He finally passed out for good about an hour ago."

"Damn. I need him."

"I thought we were giving up on the dolphins due to the Israeli tricks."

"Perhaps," Volkov said. "But perhaps not. I need Vasily's perspective to be certain."

"I'm afraid he'll be useless until you give him at least a couple more hours."

Volkov took another look at the motionless dolphins.

"Agreed," he said. "I have some time I can give them for their recovery. I may as well let them all rest."

After walking to his stateroom and allowing himself a short nap, Volkov refreshed himself with a shower and changed into a fresh version of the fleet's uniform. The white starched shirt smelled soothing, and his beige chinos felt crisp.

He passed through the control room to verify the *Wraith* remained undetected, and then he returned to the torpedo room where the dolphins and their master continued their slumber.

He walked beside the weapon rack that cradled his crew's oddest man. He cleared his throat, but the sleeper slept.

Then he whispered the trainer's name.

"Vasily."

He raised his voice.

"Vasily."

The sleeper stirred.

"What is it, Mikhail?" he asked.

Volkov collected himself while stifling a chuckle.

"It's not Mikhail, you fool. It's Dmitry."

"Dmitry? Yes? What?"

"Slowly, my friend," Volkov said. "You were suffering from exhaustion and in a very deep sleep."

The waking man jerked his torso upward.

"My babies?"

"They're fine."

As the trainer looked over Volkov's shoulder at the tank, his face softened.

"Oh, there they are. So peaceful."

"Indeed, they are," Volkov said.

The trainer's eyes became pained.

"But they failed, didn't they? My babies are useless."

"The Israelis certainly developed a potent countermeasure. That was unfortunate."

"I should've seen this coming. I didn't protect my babies."

"I, too, should have seen it coming. As should have Jake, Terry, Pierre, and every other man who's been benefiting from their efforts. You can't blame yourself."

"It's easy for you to say that, but that's not how I feel. If you had children of your own, I think you'd understand better."

As the legitimacy of the trainer's paternity claim swam in his head, Volkov willed his mind back towards his tactical needs.

"I think it's possible that we can make your babies useful again, against anything the Israelis can conjure."

"No, Dmitry. It's impossible. They'll use too many strange sounds to confuse them. Not just from submarines, but from surface ships, aircraft, or even sonobuoys. It's not safe for them outside."

Volkov mustered the courage to ask his partner in a fledgling friendship to risk his children.

"I have an idea to make them useful again."

"I don't know how that could be possible."

"It's possible. You remember how they followed your voice through the drone to get back to the ship?"

"How could I forget?"

"They could follow a drone and stay close to it while you speak to them."

"I don't like this."

"You don't want your babies to become relics, do you?""

"No, but I don't want them to become corpses."

"That won't happen. I believe they'll ignore all signals except the one coming from the same drone as your voice."

The trainer shrugged and looked to his cetaceans.

"I imagine they would. They were so good when I brought them home."

"They were remarkable."

"But so many things could go wrong."

Volkov attempted a soothing, paternal tone while trying to protect the dignity of his listener.

"Yes, you're right, of course. According to Pierre, the Israelis are already dropping sonobuoys, and I wouldn't be surprised if most of them are blaring out faked dolphin calls."

"You see? There are so many distractions for them."

"True, but sonobuoys are harmless, and every one of them

eventually runs out of battery power."

"Harmless? They could confuse my babies and lure them away from me forever."

"Yes," Volkov said. "Yes, they could. And then your babies would be lost to us but free to roam the seas."

He let his gentle words linger and watched the trainer's face soften as he absorbed them.

"Your point is that their accidental freedom would be an acceptable outcome?"

"Yes, if it comes down to it."

"I don't like it. Let me take them home and train them. I can teach them to avoid fake signals."

"I don't doubt that, but how long would it take? Years?"

"I don't know, Dmitry. Why are you pushing so hard?"

"I want to avoid an exchange with even odds against the *Revival* while it's shooting heavyweight torpedoes. The risk to its crew against our slow-kill weapons is much less than the death we face. In fact, with even odds, they could force a one-for-one exchange and celebrate it over drinks while we begin rotting in our watery tomb. I must have the odds in our favor."

"Can't we just turn back?"

Volkov scolded the trainer.

"Would you have me leave Jake to fight the *Revival* and the *Crocodile*, in addition to all the surface ships and helicopters?"

"Of course, not. But how can you be sure the *Revival* is even part of the blockade?"

"Pierre's data feed says there aren't any anti-submarine warfare helicopters in the blockade. That's either an oversight on the part of the Israelis, or it's a conscious decision to avoid the risk of fratricide with their own submarine."

"So, maybe it's an oversight."

"What are the chances of an Israeli military oversight?"

"Fine, I see your point. But how can you hope to keep my babies from the *Revival*? If they get too close, they could be killed."

"I've been developing tactics that will prevent that."

After convincing the trainer to release his dolphins and

verifying his submarine operated far from Israeli interference, Volkov leaned over the charting table and checked his assets' positions for his test.

Icons showed two drones three miles abeam of the *Wraith* and vector lines showed each manmade object moving forward at four knots. The status of Andrei and Mikhail remained a matter of estimation and instinct as he'd had the machines maneuvered around the cetaceans.

Wearing a headset microphone, the trainer sat between the sonar expert and one of two technicians who controlled the drones.

"Remember the new procedures, everyone," Volkov said. "All communications to the dolphins are now being channeled through drone one."

The drone operator nodded.

"Hail them for a response. Minimum transmit power."

With the sounds in the *Wraith's* sonar hydrophones amplified and relayed over loudspeakers, the recorded chirps and whistles piped through the drone filled the room.

Then came the welcomed response.

"They responded," the operator said. "Range, two and a half nautical miles–five thousand yards exactly–from the drone, based upon the roundtrip speed of sound."

"Andrei figured it out," the trainer said. "He's smart enough to respond the drone."

"Let's see he how he interprets direction," Volkov said. "Send them to twelve o'clock relative to our position."

"I've sent them a command to swim at twelve o'clock relative to our position... well, relative to a reference position... of twelve o'clock, and they've acknowledged."

"Very well," Volkov said. "Give it sixty seconds."

Counting time, the drone operator stared at his screen.

"That's sixty seconds," he said.

"Get a range check."

"Five thousand, two hundred yards from the drone."

"They don't see the drone as reference," the trainer said.

"They're moving towards the ship. They see the ship as reference."

"That's fine," Volkov said. "We'll adjust our commands and our tactics."

"You can't use the drone to take them too far away, or they may lose sight of the ship."

"I'll be careful, Vasily. Trust me. I'll also trust you to keep a watchful guard on this."

The trainer flicked a hurried wrist in the air

"Yes, yes, of course. Let's get through this training, please."

"Indeed. Send them to six o'clock."

"I've sent them a command to swim at six o'clock relative to our position, and they've acknowledged," the operator said.

"Count off two minutes."

"May I speak to them?" the trainer asked.

"I had your volume set low on the drone," Volkov said. "And your voice will be overridden by any command signal. So, you may speak to them whenever you wish. However, I caution you to speak sparingly since they may instinctively follow your voice in opposition to a command."

The trainer pressed an icon on his console.

"Hello, my babies. I'm so proud of you."

"That's fine," Volkov said. "Try not to overdo it."

"Two minutes, sir," the operator said.

"Get a range check."

"Four thousand, eight hundred yards from the drone."

"Very well," Volkov said. "That verifies that they're considering the *Wraith* as a reference. Send them to nine o'clock."

As the drones and dolphins drove forward, Volkov slowed the submarine to a drift.

"Let's see how they withstand a distraction," he said. "Aim drone two at the dolphins and play the return-to-ship message from drone two at maximum volume."

The second technician-operator tapped his console.

Two minutes later, Volkov ordered a range check.

"They're still swimming at nine o'clock," the trainer said.

"Very well. That's what we want. But let's make this more challenging. Increase drone two's speed to ten knots and set it on an intercept course with the dolphins."

As the second drone approached the cetaceans with its confounding cacophony, Volkov tested the animals further.

"Let's see what they see," Volkov said. "Query them for submerged contacts."

"I'm ready to query them for the bearing to a contact," the operator said.

"Transmit the query."

"They have a contact at three o'clock," the operator said.

"Get a bearing and range."

The information suggested the mammals were reporting the presence of the order-issuing drone.

"Excellent," Volkov said. "They're accepting orders from the drone but are still following their conditioned reporting protocols. Continue with the next contact."

"They report a contact at nine o'clock. I'll get the bearing and range."

Chirps and whistles defined the second drone as the next contact in the cetaceans' view.

"Good," Volkov said. "They've identified our drones. Query them for the next contact."

"I'm querying... and they have nothing."

"Perfect," Volkov said.

"Wait," the operator said. "The bearing to the dolphins was a degree to the right farther than I expected."

"Get a range check."

After another triple cycle, twice-verified query of the dolphins' location, the evidence showed them heading towards the distracting second drone.

"Vasily, talk them back," Volkov said.

"Come home, my babies. Vasily misses you."

"They need a new order to coincide with Vasily's voice," Volkov said. "Send them away from the distracting drone. Send them to four o'clock."

"I've sent the order," the operator said. "But they haven't acknowledged."

"Come to Vasily. Daddy wants you to be safe."

"Increase the transmission of the order and of Vasily's voice from drone one to half power and retransmit."

"I'm transmitting... and I have a response!"

"Keep talking, Vasily, until we verify their direction."

Two minutes later, a range check proved the dolphins were responding to their master's voice and verified their ability to overcome a distraction—one distraction.

Volkov turned his ship, his drones, and his mammals towards the blockade and towards a battle where countless distractions awaited.

Eight hours later, he approached the center of the ellipse of uncertainty around the *Revival's* expected position within the Gaza Strip blockade. Looking at his chart, he scoffed at the vector history showing the ease with which he'd slipped between the repositioned corvettes from the task force that had attacked Jake.

Equipped with information from Renard, Volkov had enjoyed an unfettered map through the dispersed surface combatants that patrolled an extended distance from the coastline in a defensive formation against the long-range railguns of the *Goliath*.

Convinced he'd circumvented the anti-submarine-capable combatants, he triple-checked the geometry governing the *Crocodile*. Starting where Jake had encountered the Israeli submarine, time and distance precluded its possible interference of his hunt for the *Revival*.

But the *Crocodile* was coming, and he needed to act fast.

A submarine commander's patience under pressure paid off as he guided his assets around threats.

"Drone one and the dolphins are passing sonobuoy twenty-two," the operator said. "The bearing rate to the sonobuoy reached a maximum of two degrees per minute and is now dropping off."

"Very well," Volkov said. "Maintain the search pattern."

"There's another source broadcasting the fake return-to-ship signal bearing three-one-one from the drone."

Volkov trusted the dolphins' discernment of submerged contacts to include submarines and drones. But the smaller, vertically-oriented sonobuoys skirted their threshold of interest. Assuming the local waters free of surfaced sonar systems and anti-submarine helicopters, he concluded the offending sound source was another sonobuoy.

"Designate that source as sonobuoy twenty-three," he said. "Maintain the search pattern."

The operator drove the first drone in a straight line by the next sonobuoy and took a range check to verify the dolphins swam where expected.

Then the cetaceans offered an unsolicited report.

"They say they have a submerged contact at eleven o'clock," the operator said.

Volkov's back stiffened.

"Anything on either drone?"

Two heads shook.

"Query the dolphins for the range."

"It's medium range," the operator said.

"But it's not transmitting, since we don't hear anything on the drones," Volkov said. "That's the *Revival*. Bring the dolphins and drone one back to the ship. Send drone two straight at the *Revival*, and prepare tube three for the *Revival*."

As the buzz of activity rose, climaxed, and then fell during an exciting minute, Volkov received the reports of his orders having been followed.

The dolphins were returning, and the *Revival* was his.

Confident in his pending success, he pulled the trigger.

"Shoot tube three."

CHAPTER 12

Commander Levy balanced against the *Crocodile's* rocking deck.

Having raised his radio antenna, he watched the icons on his tactical plot adjust to the updated data.

A vector line showed the damaged *Revival* slinking away towards Haifa. His blood pressure surging, he reached for a microphone.

"*Revival*, this is *Crocodile*. Where are you going?"

No response.

"*Revival*, this is *Crocodile*. Answer me, damn you. I am the leader of this task force. Where are you going?"

"*Crocodile*, this is *Revival*. The leader of this task force is Captain Cohen aboard the *Spear*."

"That's just a formality. Since when would you dare consider him superior to me?"

"Since you failed to sink the *Specter*."

Levy heard a new voice.

"This is Captain Cohen, task force commander. Stand down, Commander Levy. I've taken command of the blockade task force and am giving the orders now. Check your data feed if you have any doubt."

The concept of being supplanted had seemed impossible, but Levy scanned the new orders in a phone notification backlog he'd ignored.

"I acknowledge, sir," he said.

"I would've taken command of the assets earlier, but you used back channels to pull that stunt of getting ships to support your attack on the *Specter*. Such games end now. This task force is now designed to protect the blockade from all interference, and it begins with you following my orders. Am I clear?"

Knowing he could submerge and claim a communications loss at his whim, Levy feigned compliance.

"Yes, sir."

"Good."

"But there's no need to send the *Revival* back to port when it can remain here as a weapons launcher, even if pinned to the surface with damage."

"That is my decision. The *Revival* is returning to Haifa."

"Can you explain why, sir?"

After a brief pause, Levy received his answer.

"Very well," Cohen said. "The *Revival* took damage from the *Wraith* and surfaced before we could defend it with electronic jamming. Then the *Goliath* entered cannon range and landed rounds in the torpedo room. You should know that a surfaced submarine is too sluggish to maneuver around high-velocity rounds, and without jamming support, it was inevitable."

"Damn it," Levy said. "So it's me, three corvettes, and a handful of missile boats against two submarines and the *Goliath*?"

"We're not trying to win a slugfest. We're protecting our boarding parties so they can enforce the blockade."

Levy took a closer look at the noncombatant vessels on his display and made a quick count of thirty ships tagged as part of a blockade run.

"This is three times the size of any prior attempt," he said. "Where did this liberal band of vandals find so many ships?"

"It's obviously coordinated with the well-funded attack by the mercenary fleet. They all appear to have loaded their supplies in Turkish Cyprus. Why our intelligence community didn't see this coming is a failure to be explained."

"What's the plan, then, sir?"

"Protect the boarding teams. You keep the *Wraith* away from them while the corvettes do the same against the *Goliath*."

Levy unfurled a long mental list of flaws he analyzed in the plan, but he withheld his protest since he had the permission he wanted to attack a mercenary submarine.

"I understand, sir. But this still leaves the *Specter* unaccounted for between you and the *Goliath*."

"We'll use anti-submarine zig-zag approaches with helicopter support. The *Goliath* can't shoot helicopters, Seagulls, and speedboats at the same time. We have numbers against the *Goliath*, and helicopters will keep the *Specter* in check."

"I'll take care of the *Wraith*, sir."

"Very well. Head deep now and get to it."

Levy took the *Crocodile* to one hundred meters and ordered his team to correlate the overload of sounds hitting his ship's hydrophones with the task force's radar data.

His self-confident sonar supervisor marched over the hunched backs of his seated technicians making sense of the busiest waters Levy had experienced. With a deep baritone, the man looked at his commanding officer while sending his verbal report throughout the control room.

"I'm tracking the blockade runners as hostiles in the system, sir. There's thirty-two of them, and we need to keep them separate from the fifty or so neutral merchants and fishers."

"Very well," Levy said. "But keep separate tabs on the *Goliath*. Keep track of it."

"Of course, sir. I'm commencing the sonar search plan for the *Wraith* now. I'm assuming a threat vector to the east, listening for *Scorpène*-class propulsion sounds, launch transients, and Black Shark torpedo noises."

Levy found the supervisor's confidence threatening, but he needed his competence against the mercenaries. The dichotomy unsettled him.

The distractions of speedboats trying to board a swarm of blockade running vessels unsettled him, too, but he needed to understand the maritime mess.

"Executive officer," he said.

The portly man looked up from across the table.

"Yes, sir."

"Make sure the low-bandwidth feeds from the task force land on the tactical plot correctly," Levy said. "Make sure they align with our organic acoustic data. Make sure you can predict when each speedboat will intercept its targeted blockade runner."

"I'm working on it, sir. There's a Shayetet 13 commando team within five minutes of intercepting the northernmost runner."

"But there are many more boarding operations," Levy said. "You must track them all. Get some more junior officers and technicians here to help you. This will be intense work."

During five minutes, the room swelled with bodies.

Then after several hours of driving northwest, the stench of armpits wafted over Levy's nose as he turned the *Crocodile* east. As the deck tilted during the turn, he hovered over the tactical plot.

Five commando teams had boarded and stopped five blockade runners, but more than two dozen ships crossed within two hours of the Gaza Strip coast.

As he wondered if any outcome of such a coordinated breach of Israeli security could end with an international political victory, he reminded himself to focus on his personal success. He expected to survive the conflict as the only submarine commander to avoid damage from the mercenaries. The distinction would bring him advancement.

Then, as his sonar supervisor announced an opportunity, he sensed his chance for greater glory.

"Torpedo in the water," the supervisor said. "I hear the high-speed screws. On the left, drawing left. No threat to us."

"Can you classify it a Black Shark?" Levy asked.

"I have no acoustic evidence supporting that. I can't tell you until I hear an active seeker."

"Damn it. Use situational awareness and classify it as a Black Shark. Assign a speed of forty-eight knots."

After a moment studying the plot, Levy surmised the weapon's destination. He lifted a stylus and tapped the icon of a speedboat that approached a blockade-running cargo ship.

"I've determined the weapon's target," he said. "Plot it on an intercept course to the speedboat I've highlighted. Then track it backwards with the bearing rate to its origin–the *Wraith*."

"I'm taking care of it, sir," the supervisor said. "That gives us a line through the *Wraith's* launch point, but it doesn't give us that point. And it's an old launch origin. The *Wraith* has repositioned since shooting."

Levy raised his voice.

"I'll determine what the *Wraith* has or hasn't done."

In the silence following his proclamation, he decided to seek the mercenary submarine. With the *Crocodile* already following a direction Levy deemed acceptable for hunting the *Wraith*, a glance at his chart confirmed his need to alter the direction of his solitary deployed drone.

"Have your operator accelerate the drone to nine knots and steer it to bearing one-two-five."

"The drone is on course one-two-five, accelerating to nine knots, sir," the supervisor said.

"Very well. Prepare one of your technicians to manage a second drone, which I will launch as soon as possible."

Realizing aggressive actions could pin his adversary against the coast, Levy gained his veteran mechanic's attention.

"Prepare tube six for launch," he said.

"Tube six is ready, sir," the veteran said.

"Launch drone two from tube six."

"Drone two is swimming out of tube six," the supervisor said. "Drone two is clear of our hull and deployed. We have wire connectivity and confirmation of propulsion."

"Give drone two a speed of nine knots and steer it on bearing zero-three-five."

"Drone two is at nine knots, bearing zero-three-five, sir."

For ten minutes, Levy watched his central chart as the icons of his drones fanned out in a trident formation with the crosshair of his submarine. The data feed from the task force above him showed the *Wraith's* torpedo converging on a commando speedboat.

"I hear the torpedo's bomblets attaching, sir," the supervisor said. "It's on the bearing of the speedboat you identified. Bomblets are detonating now."

"I'm sure you'll hear the speedboat slowing," Levy said. "It was a good shot, and our commandos aren't running anti-submarine zigzag legs."

"The speedboat is slowing, sir. I've lost its propellers."

"I can't protect those fools from poor tactics," Levy said. "But I will demonstrate smart tactics myself. I'll roust the *Wraith* before it stops another one of our countrymen. Transmit active search from both drones, half power, forward-hemispheres."

The drones' active energies sought the mercenary submarine's hull but found nothing.

As Levy considered another drone-based active transmission, his sonar ace preempted his decision.

"I hear another torpedo, sir. On the right, drawing right. It's no threat to us, heading towards the south."

"Classify it as a Black Shark and set its target... here."

Levy tapped a stylus on a southerly speedboat heading to intercept a sprinting cargo ship. The line tracing the weapon back to its launch origins assured him he hunted the *Wraith* in the proper quadrant of water.

As he returned his thoughts towards sending another active search into the water, the supervisor's words chilled him.

"Dolphin calls, sir."

"You're sure it's not one of our decoy sonobuoys?"

"We're far from any decoy sonobuoys, sir. It's a real dolphin, or it's a mercenary's recording of one."

"Damn," Levy said. "Begin a broadcast of the decoy sounds from the drones. Let's see if this forces a mistake."

After technicians tapped keys, the solitary signal his otherwise unsuccessful comrades captured during their interchanges north of Egypt rang throughout the water.

Levy lacked clarity on the nature of the decoy command and if it told the *Wraith's* dolphins to lay explosives, swim in circles, or stop and rest. But given the minimal impact the mammals showed since his fleet had begun rebroadcasting the signal, he trusted it would stall the cetaceans.

Then the forced mistake happened.

"I hear a human voice, bearing zero-seven-three," the supervisor said. "It's Russian or some Eastern European language, if I had to guess."

"A human voice, like underwater communications?"

"It didn't sound like military communications, sir. It sounded more like a man talking to a child."

"That's someone calling to the dolphins," Levy said. "Prepare tube one for that bearing. Set the range to five miles. Set the seeker to awake in two miles."

"I'm preparing tube one for that solution, but it doesn't make sense versus the *Wraith's* torpedo trajectory, sir."

"I'll decide what makes sense."

"The voice might be coming from a drone, sir. You could be giving up our position by shooting."

Levy yelled.

"Shut up and prepare my weapon!"

The unfazed supervisor looked over a technician's shoulder, looked back at Levy, and nodded.

"The weapon's ready, sir."

"Shoot tube one."

As his torpedo began its journey, Levy hoped to hear more clues about his intended victim.

"What more human voices can you hear?" he asked.

"None, sir. The voice went silent after about thirty seconds."

"Hostile torpedoes? Dolphin sounds? The *Wraith* itself?"

"Nothing, sir. But it might help to get that voice's message translated and figure out what was being said."

Levy felt vulnerable for letting the good idea escape him. So his instincts told him to weaken it.

"Of course, I considered this," he said. "But I don't have a translator onboard that speaks the language, and there's nothing to be learned from the translation that warrants exposing a radio mast. I'll have it translated when I deem the time appropriate."

The supervisor's silent acceptance satisfied him, and he turned back to his tactical display. Uninterested in the unchanging icons, he called up a side window to view raw sonar input.

Teasing his eyes, the *Crocodile's* acoustic integrators churned out a faint hint of a new sound. A trace tickled the screen.

"Look at bearing zero-eight-four," he said.

"I see it, sir," the supervisor said. "I just put a man on it to listen."

"It can't be the *Wraith*," Levy said. "The bearing is too far from where I shot."

The supervisor took a hurried report from his technician, steered the selection of his hydrophone input to the direction of the new sound, and pressed his muffs into his hairline.

When the man looked at him, Levy saw defiance and scorn.

"It's a torpedo, sir. On the left, drawing right slowly. It's a shot in our face."

"Why the hell did you take so long to hear it?"

"Because we were listening down the bearing of the torpedo you shot, sir, per protocol, and the incoming torpedo is coming from a different bearing. I recommend you evade to the left."

Feeling victimized, cheated by some trick, Levy lacked the time to defend himself from the supervisor. He needed to save himself.

"All ahead flank, cavitate. Deploy active countermeasures. Left full rudder, steer course three-three-zero. Launch tube two down the bearing of the incoming torpedo with reactionary firing protocols."

As the rumbling deck angled through the turn, Levy experienced a moment of good luck.

For scant valuable seconds, he held the *Wraith's* torpedo on his hull sensors and his towed array sonar. The geometric separation of his hydrophones allowed him to triangulate a distance to the incoming weapon.

He had time.

A minute into his evasion, he dropped gaseous countermeasures and steadied at the *Crocodile's* top speed. The system showed eight minutes before impact, and any delays his countermeasures could achieve would improve his lot.

But the torpedo shot through his countermeasure fields, indicating intelligent wire control. The *Wraith's* crew heard his sprinting escape, and they would condemn Levy to the harshest laws of physics their torpedo could enforce.

What had seemed like time to orchestrate an escape had become inevitable failure.

Expecting to survive based upon the mercenary's merciful limpet tactics, Levy felt more shame than fear. As he prepared to accept the revolting disgust of defeat, he cast a final desperate look over his tactical chart.

Hope sprang in the form of a blockade runner. He grabbed a stylus and connected the *Crocodile's* crosshair to the irreverent ship.

"Come right to course three-four-eight," he said.

As the ship turned, Levy felt the supervisor step beside him.

"I see what you're doing, sir. It's brilliant."

Having churned through rapid and paradoxical doses of vulnerability, hubris, and luck, Levy kept silent and nodded.

"You're going to turn the *Wraith's* torpedo against a blockade runner," the supervisor said. "They intended to shoot us, but instead they'll hit a ship they're trying to protect."

His throat tight, Levy forced a response.

"Yes."

"If the *Wraith* set that torpedo with a ceiling like it should have, you'll have to surface us, which will make us vulnerable to the *Goliath*."

With renewed hope and the transformation of the supervisor from his judge to an ally, Levy felt calm again and allowed himself a deep breath before responding.

"I'm not worried about the *Goliath*," he said. "We'd face long-range cannon fire with the blockade runner as a shield."

"That ship will protect us from the *Wraith's* torpedo and the *Goliath's* railguns, sir," the supervisor said. "It escaped the reach of our limited boarding parties, but it's perfectly placed for us. You've turned a defeat into a victory."

Still processing the emotional overload, Levy scoffed.

"There's still some deft seamanship to be demonstrated."

"After you sawed that tiny fishing boat in half, sir, I don't think you'll struggle at all with this."

Five minutes later, Levy surfaced on the far side of the cargo vessel, matching its speed and course. With assistance from the task force, he monitored the *Goliath*, which kept its guns working against helicopters and speedboats.

The supervisor tracked the *Wraith's* weapon under the sacrificial vessel's keel and then announced its uneventful climax.

"The incoming torpedo has shut down."

"Commanded by wire?" Levy asked.

"Probably, sir. It's too close to the merchant vessel to hear, but I suspect the *Wraith* sent a message up the weapon's wire to cut off propulsion and flood it for sinking."

Though he failed to fool the mercenary into damaging his side's blockade runner, Levy had escaped. He sighed in relief and collected his bearings.

The battle would continue, and he needed electric power.

He came shallow and settled at snorkel depth to charge his batteries and to communicate with his countrymen. While receiving tactical updates, he remembered to transmit the underwater message intercepted from the *Wraith* for translation.

As he recovered from his near defeat and began to focus on his next steps in the battle, his veteran mechanic got his attention.

"I have the written text of the translation, sir."

"What was being said?" Levy asked. "Read it out to me."

The elder sailor cleared his throat and grinned.

"Come home, my babies. Vasily misses you."

CHAPTER 13

Cahill noticed his shaking leg, and he shifted his weight to quell it.

Then the other one trembled.

"Bloody hell," he said.

The comment passed unnoticed as tactical considerations consumed the bridge's other occupants.

Seated in a rarely used, rear-facing console behind him, Dahan chattered in Hebrew into a headset that connected her with the Aman officers in the *Goliath's* tactical control room.

She then switched to English, raised her voice, and offered another periodic update of the intercepted military traffic.

"The fifth Shayetet 13 commando boarding party has declared their vessel under Israeli control," she said. "That leaves three boarding teams in process of boarding three vessels."

"Very well," Cahill said. "I count only four more speedboats at large. The commandos can't board even half our vessels."

"Overwhelming the defenses with our numbers is part of the plan," Dahan said. "Why do you seem surprised?"

"I'm not surprised. I'm just verifying. Okay, I'm a little surprised. I'm not used to battles unfolding per plan, especially not backup plans where Pierre spends extra money to double the size of our blockade-running armada."

As she faced away, he sensed her unspoken annoyance, and he shifted his focus to the less humiliating subject of warfare.

Beside him, Walker led the surface and air battle.

Conditioned to fight one-on-one submarine encounters or attacks on a handful of surface combatants, Cahill considered himself his executive officer's student in tracking the swarm of ships and aircraft comprising the blockade and its challengers.

While trying to thwart the boarding operations, Walker had toggled the *Goliath's* railgun rounds between speedboats and troop helicopters that attempted to hover over the blockade runners. With the quasi-neutral Israeli Air Force gaining interest in the mercenary fleet, electronic control aircraft patrolled the shoreline, providing jamming protection over the commandos.

Cahill's executive officer had missed with every round, but the harassment had forced evasive maneuvers and had slowed the Shayetet 13 teams' efforts. As the commandos boarded ships but ran out of bodies, Walker shifted his attention closer to the *Goliath*.

"The last speedboats are getting too close to our flotilla for me to target," he said. "I'm pulling our fire back to the helicopters to protect Jake."

Already within range of all adversarial Harpoon anti-ship missiles, Cahill would have gained nothing by trying to slow the weak guns of the Israeli surface combatants. So he let Walker commit his shots to defending the hidden *Specter*.

"Very well," he said.

With the *Goliath* pointing northward, the cycling sonic cracks continued piercing the night off his starboard bow.

He then reconsidered threats to his ship.

"Major Dahan, are you sure we've seen the last of the Air Force's Strike Eagles?"

"The pilots don't want to dodge phased-array-guided hypersonic railgun rounds. It's not worth the risk to try to drop bombs on a ship that can submerge."

"That makes sense. Wait, though. Are you getting this as intelligence from intercepted orders?"

"No, I'm getting this from analytical observation of their tactics in this campaign. My team was only able to procure decryption keys for the most important naval channels."

"I understand. You just sounded so confident in your assessment that I... never mind. But, still, the Strike Eagles could load anti-ship missiles as ordnance and attack from distance."

"They won't," she said. "The surface fleet has plenty of anti-ship missiles for any imaginable tactic against us, and most Air Force generals want to see the prime minister fail."

"Very well," Cahill said. "We'll keep targeting the helicopters. I don't think Liam's going to hit any, though."

Keeping his face aimed at his screen, Walker looked back at Cahill from the corner of his eyes and smirked.

"Ye of little faith," he said.

"The helicopters are beyond our phased array, and I expect the Air Force is providing jamming protection to their brethren."

"If I shoot close enough for the pilots to hear the sonic booms, I'll test their courage. Only an idiot would hover over Jake as an easy target."

"Good point."

Fate rewarded him for letting Walker follow his instincts.

Equipped with satellite radar and infrared from Renard, his executive officer sent dangerous rounds towards small but slow airborne submarine hunters. As the helicopter pilots honored their self-preservation, they broke from their searches for the *Specter* to dodge bullets.

Dancing data on Cahill's display showed defensive aerial acrobatics, which stymied the aircrafts' effort to find Jake and allowed the *Specter* to protect the *Goliath* from the *Crocodile*.

Maritime momentum moved in the mercenary fleet's favor, and Cahill watched the icons of his flotilla fight for landfall. As the blockade runners overran the Israeli defenses, he sensed a resounding victory, until his moment to intervene arrived.

"Vampires," Walker said. "One each from missile boats two and three."

Cahill surprised himself with his verbalized first thought.

"Only two?" he asked. "The Greeks proved that the optimum against us is three."

"The fleet knows this," Dahan said. "The third will come."

"The first two are veering away to the north and south," Walker said. "They're using waypoints."

With his plan unfolding per his desires, the Frenchman on the video screen had remained silent until the anti-ship missiles threatened his property and his staff.

"Major Dahan was correct," Renard said. "The third missile was just launched by a corvette. I'm sure it's a three-axis attack timed for simultaneous arrival. You need to submerge."

"Understood," Cahill said. "I know the protocol well."

His response sounded cavalier as he uttered it, and his boss detected the overconfidence.

"Don't be a hero, Terry. The Israeli warships hold enough anti-ship missiles to keep you underwater until our flotilla is ashore. Don't risk the *Goliath*."

"There's three corvettes and half a dozen missile boats out there," Cahill said. "If I don't harass them, they'll stop coming for me and chase down our blockade runners instead."

"The Israeli guns are too small to matter," Renard said.

"Enough rounds in an engine room can stop any ship."

"A few ships, perhaps, but our flotilla has all but succeeded. Adequate humanitarian aid will reach the Gaza Strip to humiliate the prime minister. Gaza will be self-sufficient for at least six months."

Cahill frowned and looked at his boss' face on the screen.

"What about boarding parties from the Israeli surface combatants?" he asked.

"The ships' crews aren't allowed. Eight years ago, a flotilla one-third our size captured and exploited Israeli commandos who were trained for the boarding. This is politically-sensitive work, and the Israelis allow only specially trained commandos to partake in the assaults."

"He's correct," Dahan said. "My team is intercepting message traffic verifying it. They've expended their trained boarding parties. They're out of options."

Cahill struggled to accept an untroubled victory.

"So, they're out of commandos, and their bullets are too small to cripple our flotilla. But what about shooting anti-ship missiles at our cargo ships?"

The Frenchman scoffed.

"That would be political suicide for the prime minister. Even his own supporters would turn against him."

"So that's it then? You'd have me just turn and run?"

"It's not running. The mission is accomplished. I want you to return me my ship undamaged for once."

"Okay," Cahill said. "I guess I owe you that."

A hint of tension in the major's even tone chilled Cahill.

"Not okay," Dahan said. "My team just intercepted a command. The corvettes are going to launch two pairs of Seagulls. We won't be able to evade submerged."

"That's all the Seagulls they have, though, right?"

"Yes, one pair per corvette. The *Specter* destroyed the third pair during its failed ambush of the *Crocodile*."

Cahill studied the geometric impositions on his display.

"Clever," he said. "We'll have to dive below the first wave of vampires in four minutes. That'll slow us. Then the Israelis will keep launching vampire salvos to keep us slow while the Seagulls catch us."

"We've faced similar challenges before," Walker said. "We could porpoise."

"The timing has to be impeccable," Cahill said. "And we've pushed our luck with that technique in the past. I prefer to avoid it. I'm accelerating away from the battle."

After tapping a new course and speed into his screen, he watched stars walk across his bridge dome.

"Running is a good start, but it doesn't solve the problem," Walker said. "We need a plan."

"Right," Cahill said. "And I've got one."

As the *Goliath* sliced through swells, the bounding bridge fell silent, save for the washing of waves. Cahill let his promise hang while he let his plan solidify in his head.

"Well?" Walker asked.

"Torpedoes," Cahill said. "We carry six of them for a reason. The rules of engagement preclude using heavyweight torpedoes against Israeli assets, but I assume our boss can change that policy for defeating robots?"

"I don't like it," Renard said. "Those Seagulls are highly maneuverable and one missed shot would beget a wild torpedo that could easily acquire a manned ship. Killing an Israeli surface combatant crew is unacceptable."

"I'll have wire control."

"You'll be maneuvering erratically and at great risk of breaking your wires."

Cahill wondered if his employer had forgotten the burden of facing mortal danger.

"If you see a better way out, now's the time to mention it."

"I'm thinking."

"It may be your ship, but it's not your arse out here."

"I said I'm thinking, man."

"I'm two minutes from being turned into a fiery mist of goo if I don't submerge, and once I'm under, we won't be able to have this conversation. So I suggest you either come up with something brilliant fast or let me fight the battle."

"Very well, then," Renard said. "Use your torpedoes. But establish conservative fence protocols to shut them down in case they miss the Seagulls."

Tired of rules forcing his fleet to fight at a disadvantage, Cahill had ignored the risk his heavyweights would pose to the Israeli seamen, but he considered Renard's comment valid.

"I will," he said.

Unsure if he expected a congratulatory or condescending remark, he glanced over his shoulder, but Dahan ignored him while listening to her headset.

He turned back to the display and noticed a rare glimpse of the Frenchman's humility in his softened eyes and facial rosiness.

"You're out of time," Renard said. "Best that you submerge now for your safety."

"Right," Cahill said. "But next time we talk, I'll remind you to give me some anti-air missiles. A dozen vertical launch cells in each bow section would have turned this day into a vacation."

"I understand your plight but make no promises."

"Seventy-five seconds," Walker said.

"Very well, Liam. Prepare to crash dive."

Walker tapped keys, and Cahill watched multiple graphics representing the induction mast, the turbines, the phased array radar system, and the railguns merge into a group of systems to be lowered or turned off upon the touch of a single key.

"One minute to missile salvo arrival, Terry."

"Very well. Flooding the forward trim tank and securing the Phalanx close-in weapon system."

Cahill tapped an image that ordered huge centrifugal pumps to inhale the sea and drive water towards the forward-most internal tanks. He hit another key and then watched the cylindrical silhouette recede into the port bow.

"Placing full rise on the stern planes."

The Israeli officer's voice distracted him.

"We intercepted traffic," she said. "The task force commander just ordered the release of the Seagulls."

"Very well, major. I suggest you stand and grab a railing."

He tapped another graphic that drove the sterns downward to counterbalance the heaviness of the bows. The added weight lowered the ship in the seas and increased flow friction on the hulls, sapping three knots.

He pressed a button to send his voice throughout the ship.

"Prepare to crash dive in five seconds. Four. Three. Two. One. Crash Dive!"

He stabbed his finger against a graphic that ordered the preselected group of systems to shift to their undersea states, and then he walked his hand across the screen to command the stern planes to their opposite extreme.

"Hold on, major. This is our roughest maneuver."

He grabbed a railing and took a wide stance as the rising rear drove the proper prow and the stubbed prow into the waves. Speed pushed the rakish bows under tons of water, and the ship glided through liquid and canted to the right with the extra downward force on its longer starboard forecastle.

The sea's darkness rushed to the domed bridge and engulfed it in opaqueness. The rapid and steep angle tugged the *Goliath* below the waves and created a fulcrum that lifted the propellers above the water. Momentum carried the hulls under.

"The ship's submerged," Walker said.

"Right. That always gives me the willies."

"And that bloody stubbed port bow didn't help matters," Walker said

"But it held. Bring us back up to twenty meters. Make us light with a ten-degree down angle."

As the ship rose, Cahill balanced against the new decline, and a glance over his shoulder showed the Israeli officer as a statue. Her knuckles were frozen white over the railing, and even in the bright lighting, her skin appeared as green as her uniform.

The *Goliath's* most violent maneuver had rattled her air of invulnerability, and she looked spooked. Cahill capitalized upon the opportunity to explore her weakness.

"Are you alright, major?"

"Fine."

Her tone contradicted her words. She sounded frail, human, and her vulnerability increased Cahill's desire.

"Propulsion is on the MESMA systems," Walker said. "All plants running normally. We're at sixteen knots, slowing to our maximum sustained submerged speed of thirteen knots."

Cahill spoke to a microphone.

"Sonar supervisor, listen for Harpoons overhead."

"I'm tracking them. They'll pass in twenty seconds."

Cahill knew the weapons would circle back seeking him until they exhausted their fuel. He expected them to pin him below the waves for another ten minutes while the robots sprinted towards him at twice his speed.

"Stay on them. Also, listen for the Seagulls."

Distance kept the paired hunters silent to the *Goliath*, but Renard's low-bandwidth feed showed them inching closer. Cahill analyzed the geometrical limits he'd invoke to attack the robots while protecting the humans that launched them.

Despite touching the world's best technology, his fingertips failed to find an automated answer, and he taxed his mind.

The huge rate of closure between his torpedoes and the speedy corvettes left little leeway for error to the east. A rampant weapon would reach the Israelis without extensive limitations–limitations so restrictive he estimated they prevented him from launching.

"I can't shoot yet," he said.

"Sorry?" Walker asked.

"A wayward weapon would pass over any fence I could set before reaching the robots. At least I think so, if I've done the math right."

His executive officer intensified his glare on his display.

"Let's see what happens if I advance forward in time."

Walker tapped his screen, and Cahill glanced at his visualized predictions.

"You're right," Walker said. "But we'll have a narrow launch window in about ten minutes that should remain open about two to three minutes. Any sooner, and we'd risk hitting those corvettes. Any later, and the Seagulls could shoot at us."

"That's good enough. We'll hit them."

"If our predictions of their paths are accurate."

"We know how they hunt, based upon Jake's escape."

Walker reset the display to the present moment, and Cahill noticed that the combatants had sent another Harpoon salvo his way. A quick analysis showed the new weapons' arrivals timed with his expectation of the prior salvo's fuel exhaustion.

A perfect shot to prevent his single Phalanx point defense system from defending three axes and knocking down all missiles. A perfect shot to keep him submerged while the robots hunted.

His blood pressure rose as he considered his tight window.

Then he enjoyed good fortune as the corvettes turned away.

"You see that, Liam?"

"If you mean the corvettes peeling off, yeah."

"I do. I trust this means they're heading back to deal with their busted blockade."

"Agreed. Dare we shoot now?"

"Perhaps. Major, does your team hear anything?"

She shook her head.

"No."

She still seemed spooked, and Cahill coaxed her to reality.

"Is it possible that the corvette commanders already had permission to turn back at their discretion?"

"Yes," she said.

"Is it also possible that the commanders know it's risky to provoke me, and after launching Seagulls, they know their time is better spent salvaging what they can of the blockade?"

"Yes."

"I hope we're right, major," Cahill said. "Pierre will kill me if I get this wrong, even if nobody gets hurt. If I put Israeli sailors in mortal danger, I'll be looking for a new job."

"Is job insecurity worth the risk to your life?" Walker asked.

Cahill scoffed.

"No. I'll shoot now. Standby."

He verified his torpedoes' targeting, tapped through warnings, and pressed a button to launch one weapon from each bow section.

His launch of torpedoes from the *Goliath* impressed him with its gentleness. With the tubes mounted in inaccessible bow tanks, the pneumatic systems thrust the weapons into the sea without a pressure impact on Cahill's eardrums.

But the tactical information before him showed two flawless shots reaching out beyond the ship's beams and then turning backwards to pursue the Seagulls.

Ten minutes later, his weapons exploded and halved the number of hunters. Guided by Renard's feed, the wire-guided targeting proved trivial.

With the two remaining Seagulls slowed to solitary hunts, Cahill studied his display. His reduced speed disadvantage created a degree of freedom, and he expected to navigate a safe path away.

"I think we did it," he said. "Mission accomplished."

"I agree," Walker said. "So does Pierre, per his data feed."

Cahill's once-shaking legs felt warm and numb, like he was standing in a hot bath. As he shed his instinctive paranoia, he wondered if the strange calmness was his first feeling of victory unhindered by a near-death experience.

To be safe, he prepared two more torpedoes, in case the remaining robotic hunters got lucky.

CHAPTER 14

Ariella Dahan willed herself still to hide the shaking.

She couldn't let Terry Cahill see her weakness.

Clenching her jaw shut, she hated herself for letting her first submerged experience under the *Goliath's* bridge dome happen during battle. Though predictable, the crash dive had surprised and shaken her.

She deemed herself incompetent for having avoided the bridge during prior submerged hours. Having restricted herself to the steel-encased sections of the vessel, she realized she'd masked her fear of being underwater. The sudden enveloping of windows that looked so thin had terrified her.

A voice in her headset startled her.

"Ma'am?"

"What? Say that again."

"Can we stand down from battle stations and return to a normal watch rotation?"

"Yes. Yes, of course."

"If it's okay with you, ma'am, Silverstein and I will switch watch sections. My adrenaline's still pumping, and I want to stay here in the control room. He's okay with it."

"Fine. Go ahead."

Unsure what she'd agreed to, she slid the headset to the console and stood. After clearing her throat, she excused herself.

"Good night, gentlemen."

"Aren't you going to attend the battle reconstruction, major?" Cahill asked.

With the dark heaviness of the sea's infinite abyss surrounding the dome and encircling the edge of her vision, she aimed her eyes down the staircase.

"Of course. Whenever you want."

"We usually do it immediately after a battle."

She paused to gather her bearings as the steps seemed to spin and twist below her.

"I need a break."

Cahill's reply was a muted echo as she skirted down the stairs to the watertight door and fumbled through it. Once on the other side of the steel, she noticed her panting.

A gathering of her men and the *Goliath's* tactical team crowded the control room's central plotting table. In unison, they seemed to dissect her.

Feeling exposed, she froze.

One of her soldiers broke an uncomfortable silence.

"The remaining Seagulls turned back, ma'am. We're in the clear now."

She understood his English but responded in Hebrew.

"Seagulls. Good."

The Aman warrior responded in her native language.

"Are you okay, ma'am?"

"Fine."

"I think you should sit down, ma'am. Perhaps get some water and food. Let me escort you to the mess deck."

She remained motionless until he stepped to her, grabbed her elbow and led her away. Time slipped unnoticed until her buttocks hit the hard seat and the smells of coffee and buttered rolls wafted under her nose.

Sipping the bitter drink calmed her, and she gulped half the porcelain cup's volume.

"What happened?"

"I was hoping you'd tell me, ma'am."

"I was fine, and then all of a sudden…"

As she replayed her memory of the sea swallowing the bridge, the cup trembled in her hands.

"Never mind," he said. "Just drink and eat. I'll get you some water so you can rehydrate."

She nibbled, imbibed, and regained her awareness.

"How bad do I look?" she asked.

"Just a little sick, ma'am."

"Thanks for taking care of me. I guess I needed it."

"No problem, ma'am."

"Go ahead and get back with the team," she said. "I'll join you soon. I just need a little time to freshen up."

"You're sure, ma'am?"

"Yeah, yeah, I'm fine. Go on."

She powered down her snack, stood, and then deposited her dishes in the scullery. Continuing around a corner, she found the empty crew's head and relieved herself in a toilet stall. After washing her hands, she splashed water on her face and wiped it dry with paper towels.

As she walked forward, she reminded herself to stand tall. Taking a place at the center plotting table, she watched the system replay the battle as Cahill led a review. Though she forced herself to appear strong, she was grateful that the *Goliath's* commander let her remain silent. She watched him guide the team through a replay of the blockade run, sharing insights on tactics for future use.

She judged him as plain, with the average military build of a trim and fit man. Nothing in his physical stature suggested grandeur, but his demeanor oozed an easy, earned confidence.

That made him interesting. That made him charismatic. That made him sexy.

Given her emotional day, she felt susceptible to his stimulation. She stuffed away the slight tingle she felt in her stomach when he smiled.

When the tactical recap ended, the *Goliath's* commander read aloud the low-bandwidth update from Pierre Renard.

"Let me see if I can decipher our French boss' shorthand gibberish," Cahill said. "Seventeen ships ashore. Sufficient aid received. Painful to my bank account but worth it. Successful run. Congratulations."

Dahan withheld her insider knowledge that most of the food, fuel, and medicine would land with Hamas and that the ruling party would use the aid as a tool of control. She instead let the men celebrate since she believed the Gaza Strip's general populace would benefit despite its leadership's corruption.

Though feeding upon corruption, the people would enjoy months of surplus. Hope would replace despair. Full stomachs would replace full rifle magazines and mortars at checkpoints and border tunnels. The evening's maritime-driven loosening of the prime minister's damning grip over Gaza–a step towards peace–deserved a moment of cheer.

But Cahill's demeanor kept the men subdued.

"There's more," he said.

"Well, you've shared the good news," Walker said. "Now why do you look like we've still got work to do?"

"Because we've still got work to do. Pierre wants us to attempt a new trick. He wants us to pick up Jake and Dmitry and carry them both in our cargo bed."

A short silence preceded a growing chorus of groans.

"What's wrong, gents?" Cahill asked. "This'll be the first time we try it, but the ship's designed for it."

"It's not the work, Terry," Walker said. "It's the waiting. That's at least two days for rendezvousing and loading their slow and ugly arses. Then the extra weight will slow our trip back. That's a full day we could be in the pub, lifting pints."

"If you like your paycheck, you'll do what Pierre says."

"I like me beer, but I like me paycheck, too. So, I imagine we need to review the two-submarine loading procedure."

"We'll first need confirmation from Major Dahan's team that the *Crocodile* has returned to port. We can't risk that its commander is still coming for us."

As he looked at her, she felt ashamed of her fearful reaction to the crash dive. She wanted to hide from him, and her usual curt and reserved manner served her in hiding her emotions.

"My team will confirm it," she said.

"Very well, then," Cahill said. "Since Jake and Dmitry have to move west to catch up to us, everything can wait until morning. It's the middle of the night, and I'm ready for the rack. Or for a snack. Maybe both–a snack in the rack. I'm not quite sure."

"I'll have the cook set up midnight rations," Walker said.

"You heard him, gents," Cahill said. "Get some rest, food, or both. We're relaxing until I say otherwise."

As the group disbanded, an unwelcomed finality crept over Dahan's heart. With the blockade run accomplished, her relationship with Cahill skipped from its clumsy and ephemeral dawn to its jolting twilight.

Tired, confused, and depressed, she sought solitude and began her journey to the port hull. As she walked away, the thought of the mission's end saddened her.

The thought also frightened her.

She'd sought Cahill's attention since seeing his image in a dossier two months earlier. From the narrative of his career as an Australian Naval College top graduate, a submarine commander in his domestic fleet, and lord of the *Goliath*, he'd struck her as a lion, a king among men.

Acknowledging her attractiveness, she knew she could pick from among the male officers of the Israeli Defense Force, and she'd enjoyed her fair share of attention. But a failed engagement to a cheating fiancé had soured her to the population of available suiters. But before she'd resigned herself to a bachelor-ette's life, her commanding officer had placed a fantasy before her.

Terrance Cahill.

Rule-breaker who defied the Australian admiralty. Captain of the world's most daring vessel. Rescuer of a stranded South Korean submarine. Scourge of the North Korean Navy. Freedom fighter against the Russian annexing of Crimea. Vandal-activist against Greek political corruption.

Her clandestine assignment to lead the intelligence team on the *Goliath* was a gift, and having fought beside him during his role as feeder of the Palestinians, she affirmed her intuition.

She wanted him in her personal life.

And with its tale of romantic solitude, his dossier proved his need for companionship. She wanted to rescue two souls from loneliness.

Her rational mind protested the logistical absurdity of courting a man living across the globe in Australia while she advanced her promising military career in Israel. But her heart made her hope and warned her of regret if she failed to try.

But as she contorted herself through the door into the tunnel between the *Goliath's* hulls, she realized she hadn't tried.

"Stupid Ariella," she said.

Instead of enticing him, she'd overcompensated by being her curt and direct self, the military professional that had enjoyed advancement thanks to her devotion to decisive action. Though her former lovers had taken months to accept her brusqueness, she lacked time with Cahill to reveal her true personality.

Then she questioned if she retained a shred of Ariella, or if Major Dahan had consumed the woman. As her inner demons tormented her, she defended herself aloud as she crawled.

"Can't a man tell? Isn't it obvious?"

Confounding concerns consuming her, she reached the midpoint of the tunnel before recognizing the bondage of her cramped confines. At the deepest point in the tunnel, she considered the crawlspace an elongated coffin that smelled stale with its damp, thick air tasting dusty as she labored to expand her lungs.

Bowing her head to avoid the air-intake cross-connect, she watched her multiple shadows stretch under the thin grating that served as a floor. Her labored breathing echoed off the bilge, where condensation reflected light from the twin rows of LED bulbs that ran beside the crossing air duct.

The same sickness she'd suffered on the bridge assaulted her, and she hastened her movement beside hydraulic lines that fed an oversized block of metal. Dahan craned her neck and watched steel arms move outward through grease-coated holes into an invisible nook that shaped the hydrodynamic rear of the ship and housed the rocker that swung the stern planes.

Scrunching her shoulders, she slipped past the stern planes

controller and forced herself onward. She focused on her breathing, which taunted her with its tinny echo, and perseverance rewarded her with a dogged-open door that gave way to the heat and hissing of the port hull's MESMA plant six.

As her head emerged into freedom, she twisted and grabbed a bar attached above the door. She pulled her shoulders through the portal and then reached for a higher rung. With her waist freed, she walked her heels out and pushed her buttocks free. She drove her haunches backwards, making space for her legs to back into the compartment and transfer her weight to steps mounted below the door.

She felt free as she stood and gathered her bearings.

Within the ethanol-liquid-oxygen propulsion MESMA plant, the hiss of steam rang, and soothing heat wafted over her.

With his jumpsuit's torso flopped over his waist, a technician exposed a sweat-marked tee shirt. He was examining gauges on a control panel when he looked up.

"What brings you to the port hull, major? We don't get many visitors, not even from our own crew."

Recovered from her confined crawl, she told the truth.

"I'm walking the ship to clear my mind."

"Good idea," he said. "My name's Johnson, if you need anything."

"I could use some solitude."

"If you head forward through the next two MESMA plants and keep going, you'll find the best privacy on the ship."

Dahan marched through MESMA plants four and two, reaching the open space that paralleled the starboard side's galley and mess. The quiet compartment had dining tables, housed spare parts, and served as the recreational space for the crew.

Hundreds of spare railgun rounds covered the free spaces between pieces of exercise equipment. Some crates formed short walls around a treadmill, and others concealed the lower half of a Bowflex machine.

She continued to the port hull's berthing area and crept through the space to reach the abandoned tactical control room that served as a redundant brain of the *Goliath*. She sat in a cool chair and faced a dark screen.

Alone in the dim light, she placed her elbows on the console and rested her forehead in her palms. The hull's rhythmic rumbling relaxed her, and fatigue began billowing in her bosom.

She spread her arms over the console, leaned, and rested her cheek on her sleeve. Her mind slowed and took hold of the thought that bothered her.

Her time with Cahill was ending.

If the Israeli Navy stood down while awaiting the prime minister's response to the blockade run, Renard's fleet would revert from hired mercenaries to an insurance policy, and then to a memory. And her boss would deploy a helicopter to take her home, leaving her Australian lion in her past.

She dragged her nose across her sleeve while flipping her face to her other cheek. The forward bulkhead filled her view as she recalled the list of the prime minister's possible reactions to his maritime defeat at Gaza.

He could become a political survivor, giving ground to hold his job and opening talks with those who opposed him. But the more likely scenario was his doubling down on his fierceness and mounting a military offensive somewhere–anywhere– to divert the world's attention from the defeat of his Gaza Strip blockade.

Theories ranged from him retaking Gaza, pushing into the Sinai, rolling into Lebanon, extending his hold on the Golan Heights deeper into Syria, or even purging the West Bank of Palestinian settlements with block-by-block advances. While she waited for the prime minister to reveal his next steps, she realized the chances of a continued naval intervention grew slim.

Her involvement with Terry Cahill would end, and she'd failed to invite the mercenary hero into her personal life.

As a mist glazed over her eyes, she was unsure if the tear rolling down her cheek signified sadness or fatigue.

The giant ship's gentle vibrations drew her into calmness, and sleep released her from her self-inflicted mental torment.

CHAPTER 15

The next day, Jake Slate checked the *Specter's* location on the chart. Since he'd lingered by the Israeli coast to protect his colleagues' departures, he'd let Volkov reach Cahill ahead of him.

With confirmation from the Aman team, the icon of the *Crocodile* had appeared beside a pier in Haifa three hours earlier, assuring safe waters for the two-submarine cargo exercise.

Renard's low-bandwidth feed placed the *Wraith* on station with the *Goliath* seventy nautical miles to the west of Jake's *Specter* with the boarding process underway.

"Terry has to do all the work," he said. "Dmitry's just along for the ride from here on out."

"It's Dmitry's first time–at least willingly," Henri said.

Jake chuckled as he recalled Cahill's ensnaring of Volkov in his crippled Russian submarine six months earlier.

"I wonder if this is bringing back nightmares for Dmitry."

"If so, he need only consider his paycheck," Henri said. "Pierre's generous salaries are effective in helping people cope with personal issues."

Jake reflected on the accident twelve and a half years earlier on an American submarine after which his commanding officer, attempting to protect his career, had intentionally infected him with HIV. The act had instilled him with rage. The act had enticed Renard to recruit him. The act had transformed him.

"Yeah," he said. "He has a way with helping us forget stuff."

"You look tired. I can manage up here if you'd like to rest."

"You're sure you're okay?"

"I am," Henri said. "We're just driving in a slow straight line. Take six hours, longer if you need."

"You'd better not be exaggerating about your energy," Jake

said. "I'm willing and able to hibernate."

"I'll be fine. Get some sleep."

Jake crept along a passageway and turned into the scullery for a snack. As he unwrapped a protein bar, he saw a mix of French veterans and youngsters huddled around a dining table.

"You guys plotting a mutiny again?" he asked.

The wiry frame of his engineering officer twisted and exposed a cigarette dangling from the corner of a curled mouth. Jake also noticed him holding his Bible.

"We're using scripture to teach our young colleagues about the truth," LaFontaine said.

"Willingly, I trust?"

The toad-head of his sonar ace looked up.

"Of course, willingly," Remy said. "Bright minds like theirs are hungry to understand their place in the world, just like you. Would you care to join us?"

"I'm pretty sure I've read all the important parts at least three times by now."

"It's a document to be referred to daily in life's journey."

"No, thanks. Not now."

Jake bit off a piece of his snack and swallowed it while walking away. But after one step he felt guilty and stopped.

"Maybe later," he said. "In fact, I promise to join you for a study session before we get back to port."

"And I will hold you to it," Remy said. "For your sake."

Jake devoured his protein bar within several steps. After reaching his stateroom, he did a quick exercise routine of knee bends, pushups, and flutter kicks before crawling into his rack.

Sleep consumed him, and he slipped out of time and reality.

He awoke with a strange sense of refreshment. The silence surprised him. No alarm, no knocking at his door—just silence.

He read the time on a wall display, blinked, and checked again. Quick math made him panic.

After rushing through an abridged toilet routine, he hurried to the control room where Henri sat in the foldout captain's chair.

"Welcome back. You were serious about your hibernation."

"Was I really out for eleven hours?"

"You apparently needed your beauty sleep."

"Did it work?"

"I can't tell," Henri said. "You're so damned gorgeous that your beauty is beyond my ability to render judgment."

Jake snorted.

"The way you dress, I should be joking about your looks."

"It's my guilty pleasure," Henri said. "I've always enjoyed the finer fashions."

"Well, move aside, handsome. I look better than you in my chair. Thanks for keeping it warm."

As the Frenchman stood, Jake looked to the display and discovered the *Specter's* position dead in the water, loitering in wait of the *Goliath* and *Wraith*.

"Dang. You did a good job getting us here," Jake said.

"Right on station."

"You look tired," Jake said. "Can you keep going?"

"I'll stay here until Terry has us."

A half mile separated Jake's ship from the cargo vessel. Accounting for inaccuracies in the *Specter's* inertial guidance system and for Cahill's deviations from his predicted route, Jake knew the two ships could be far away or on top of each other.

"It shouldn't be long," he said.

"It's quite uneventful for us from now on."

"If all goes smoothly, we're passengers in our own submarine from here to Western Europe."

Since Jake had excused Remy to rest before the *Specter* became vulnerable during the loading process, his young bilingual understudy taken from the French Navy called out.

"I hear active sonar, very high frequency," Julien said. "The frequency correlates with the *Goliath's* scanning sonar."

"That's our ride," Jake said.

The French technician seemed eager.

"Should I send an active signal at the *Goliath*?" he asked.

"No, not yet. Let Terry get a little bit closer."

"Shall I verify that Antoine is awake?" Henri asked.

"Yeah, and also get the Aman guy. He'll want to talk with his buddies on the other ships once we have laser lock."

The Frenchman conducted his personnel search via sound-powered phone while his countryman who ran the sonar team in Remy's absence reported.

"I just heard the *Goliath's* trim pump. It cycled on and off. It's getting close."

"Very well," Jake said. "Now you can signal the *Goliath*. Highest frequency, ten percent power, twenty-degree beam."

The French technician tapped keys, and the submarine's sonar system whispered at the *Goliath*.

"I sent the signal."

The *Goliath's* lack of a bow-mounted array precluded its mimicked response. Jake instead expected to detect Cahill when he aimed his ship towards him and created an upward Doppler shift in the scanning sonar.

"Any Doppler shift yet?" he asked.

"Nothing," Julien said. "I lost it."

"Probably just bow nulls, assuming he turned towards us."

"I think so. We'll hear him as he gets closer."

"Signal him again, to be sure."

The technician obeyed, and two minutes later, he stirred.

"I have the *Goliath's* scanning sonar again on the towed array. Doppler shift above base frequency correlates to three knots."

"That's perfect. He's coming for us."

"I've got him on the bow array now."

"Good. Can you see a depression angle?"

"Minus twenty degrees. It'll get steeper as he drives in."

Jake expected the *Goliath* to be fifty meters below him, and the direction to its sounds needed to travel downward over time to comply with his expectation.

"Terry knows that we don't have steerageway, doesn't he?" Henri said. "We're drifting with the current and slipping southward of our eastward heading."

"Terry will adjust," Jake said.

As the *Goliath's* scanning sonar grew louder and walked under the *Specter*, Remy appeared in the control room and took over the listening duties.

"I don't suppose you'd hear it ahead of time if Terry's going to make a mistake?" Jake asked.

"I'm good, but nobody's that good," Remy said.

Jake accepted the guru's answer and waited. After several minutes of uneventful listening to the whir of cooling fans behind the Subtics tactical system consoles, he saw Henri look to him.

"Shall I energize the laser communication system?"

"Go ahead."

"The laser communication system is energized," Henri said. "No laser lock yet."

"Give it time. Terry must be delicate."

Thirty minutes later, Jake was reading a book on his phone while leaning his jaw against his palm. Doubts crept up his spine faster than the *Goliath* crept underneath him.

"I'm getting something," Henri said.

"Laser lock?"

"No. It's from Pierre's low-bandwidth feed. He's calling our attention to Israeli warships deploying from their ports."

"No kidding?"

Jake stood, stretched, and walked to the center charting table to see the overhead scene. Icons dotted the Israeli coast.

"Do you think we should abort our loading procedure?" Henri asked. "The last thing we need is all three ships tied together if the Israelis are seeking blood."

"No," Jake said. "Let's continue pulling all three teams together. Our plans should still be to head to the beach. Just because the Israelis are deploying doesn't necessarily mean anything for us."

Henri looked down to his console.

"There it is," he said. "Laser lock."

With the network of blue-green transceivers mounted over his submarine giving him secure communications with the *Go-*

liath, Jake returned to his seat and called the new feed to his screen. Cahill's face appeared.

"You found me," Jake said.

"I found you a long time ago," Cahill said. "I've been nudging meself into position under you for over an hour. Have a look. I'm sending you interesting camera angles."

Jake set the screens by his chair to receive the feeds from the *Goliath's* selected external cameras. One showed the tapering stern of his ship extending over the forward end of the cargo bed that spanned the centerline between the transport vessel's twin hulls.

"Why do I have to ride backwards?" he asked.

"Because Dmitry got here first. Those are the rules."

"Whose rules?"

"Mine."

"Bite me."

Cahill smiled but withheld further comment, and Jake looked to another screen.

The second view came from above and behind the *Specter's* conning tower and looked down upon the submarine. In the dim artificial lighting, Jake saw several hydraulic presses rotated to their middle positions between retracted and jammed against his hull.

"That view is coming from your rover?" he asked.

"Yeah, mate. Quite a helpful view it gives, letting us see things from above."

"Got it," Jake said. "But why do you have the presses partially deployed?"

"To nudge you back in case you drift side to side."

"Do I need to worry?"

"Not at all. It's just a precaution. I've got control over that with the outboard motors, and I've got range finders all along me hulls that measure how far away you are."

"Great. How long until you're carrying me?"

"About ten seconds ago. You're officially touching me cargo bed, and I've taken about two hundred tons of your weight."

"I didn't' feel anything."

"And now I'm closing the presses against your hull."

Jake watched the rams clamp downward with slow and powerful grace. When he realized he'd become a passenger, he sat back in his chair and took a cursory look at the final camera angle.

His bow faced its twin with a sliver of water between them.

"Holy cow," he said. "How close am I to Dmitry?"

"About half a meter."

"That's insane."

"That's how it has to work for you both to fit. And to keep it working, you need to pump water forward so that you don't flip backwards off me when we surface."

"Did Dmitry say anything when you loaded me?"

"He's been quiet. Want to talk to him?"

"Sure. Let's compare notes."

An image of the *Wraith's* control room wiped away an external camera view, and Volkov appeared with his English translator standing beside him. Jake thought the beard made his Russian colleague look distinguished.

"I guess I'm in charge until we're back in full communication with Pierre," Jake said.

The Russian and Australian conceded.

"Any opinions on the Israeli deployments?" Jake asked.

His two colleagues agreed the movements were innocuous until proven otherwise, and Renard's data lacked evidence of venomous intent.

"Then let's share tactical data recordings of all our encounters, study it, and compare notes in say, an hour?"

"Yes, I want the data," Volkov said.

"Did you just say that in English?" Jake asked.

"Yes. I practice," he said.

"Good job. Since Terry has the biggest computer, he'll download from both of us and then we'll download each other's data from him."

"Right, mate," Cahill said. "But we may want to let the Aman team have a chat before we clog up the bandwidth."

Jake picked up a headset, slid it over his ear, and lowered his voice.

"Should we give them privacy? I mean, without our Hebrew translators eavesdropping?"

A beautiful woman with athletic lines, fierce eyes, and an olive complexion stepped beside Cahill.

"I'm Major Ariella Dahan," she said. "I request privacy in talking to my team on the *Wraith* and the *Specter*. I haven't had secure communications with them since deploying with your fleet."

She seemed formal, strong, and feminine. Jake found himself unable to reject her.

"Of course, major. We're in no hurry. Take your time. I'll ask my guys to give you space to talk. They'll have to remain within range of hearing you, but I'd be impressed if any of us know two words of Hebrew."

"Thank you, Mister Slate."

Jake stepped toward the plotting table and gestured for his Aman officer to head to the conning platform.

As the conversation between the Israelis started, the French mechanic joined Jake by the chart.

"And if you'll excuse me, I'll rest my tired bones," Henri said. "I've moved the prescribed amount of water forward to distribute our weight properly, and I've called for my relief."

"Sure," Jake said. "Your relief won't have to do anything, unless something really terrible goes wrong."

"If something really terrible goes wrong, I don't think it will matter who's sitting in my chair."

"I can't argue that. Get some rest, my very old friend."

As Henri departed, the Aman officer waved to Jake.

"I'm having trouble."

Jake craned his neck at the frozen images on the monitors.

"Don't worry. They'll come back in a few seconds. The laser system is shifting frequency to penetrate whatever color of water we're moving through now. It happens once in a while."

The Aman officer turned back to his monitors, which came to life seconds later. He entered an animated discussion in a language that was unbreakable code to Jake, who called out to Remy in French.

"Do you hear anything out there?"

"No. Why are we speaking French?"

"Because it takes my mind off the fact that they're not speaking English."

"Okay. As you wish. It's quiet out there other than the usual merchant shipping noise. All my contacts are tracking at twelve knots or faster and at ten miles away or farther."

Jake pretended to study his chart while testing his patience against the duration of the lively discussion in Hebrew. As he thought about reneging on his promise of foregoing a deadline for the Israeli meeting, he heard the Aman officer's verbal volume drop as his conversation switched to English.

"We're finished, Jake. Major Dahan thanks you for the opportunity to let us speak together as a team."

"Do you have anything to report from your discussion?"

"Major Dahan will assess all the details with her team on the *Goliath* and will determine if there's any news worth sharing. She may also request to speak to her commander via radio link, if it can be made possible."

"So be it," Jake said.

He returned to his console and found Cahill and Volkov looking back at him on two of the monitors.

"Did they look agitated to you, mate?" Cahill asked.

Jake scanned the *Specter's* control room for his Aman officer and noticed his Israeli rider had departed. He turned his face back to the screens.

"Is the major still there?" he asked.

"She's gone. Just ran downstairs. Dmitry's rider is gone, too. It's like they're returning the favor of letting us speak in private."

"I agree," Jake said. "I don't know if they looked agitated or just looked Israeli."

"What do you think they were talking about?" Cahill asked.

"Probably the political outcome of our blockade run and any subsequent military actions."

"You think the naval vessels being deployed are relevant?"

"Hard to say," Jake said. "I'll go with a cautious hope that they aren't. Pierre told us to ignore them and to head home."

"It might be good to get a radio link with him," Cahill said.

Jake's mind filtered out the English-to-Russian translations running in the background of Volkov's audio while he recalled his employer's latest orders.

"Unless you picked up something else on the low-bandwidth feed, he didn't think it was urgent enough for us to risk exposure. We're apparently keeping the Aman people with us until we reach land, and he wants us to head back submerged and undetected."

"I've got nothing from Pierre to contradict that. But staying submerged kind of takes the fun out of me having loaded you."

"Even underwater, we still move all three ships faster together than separately."

"I know, mate. Supposedly twelve knots sustained, even with your heavy arses in me cargo bed. Let's give it a try then, stepping up in increments. Ready for four knots?"

"Yes," Jake said. "Let's leave Israel to its own fate. Unless something pops up to catch us by surprise, this mission is over."

CHAPTER 16

Cahill reclined in his rack reading a novel as he anticipated growing drowsy and drifting into a restful slumber. He entertained thoughts of waking to a quiet morning and a leisurely breakfast.

Then the awareness of a possible recurring nightmare chilled him, and he feared the crushing, drowning depths of sleep. He forced himself to start reading another chapter to delay the risk of a tormenting dream.

The knock at his stateroom door changed his plans.

"This is Major Dahan. I request to enter your quarters."

His heart jumped into hyper-drive, and his breathing accelerated. Rustling his blanket, his feet sought the floor.

"One moment please. I'm in me skivvies. Is it terribly urgent?"

"No."

He hated her brevity.

"Just a moment, then. Let me put on some clothes."

He wrestled into his chinos and tiptoed across the deck to his sink where he swished mouthwash and spat. He then angled to the door, stepped back, and opened it.

Her hair seemed impeccable and her subtle makeup unnoticeable but effective. Her eyes dazzled him with a natural brown glint, and her sharp features cast shadows that added mystery to her allure.

"What can I do for you, major?"

"I have news I wanted to give you myself. The prime minister is mobilizing his armored battalions in the Golan Heights. He means to extend his borders into Syria and defy the world to challenge him."

"How'd you learn about this?"

"It's in Pierre's latest data feed," she said. "I'm sure his source is satellite data, either American or European."

Cahill wondered why she alerted him before his crew did.

"I should've heard this from the watch section."

"My staff recognized the significance immediately," she said. "It's one of several scenarios we've been watching for. I had my sergeant ask your team to let me tell you about it first."

"Why?"

"You would have contacted me anyway. I wanted to tell you about it before you had a chance to speculate."

"Speculate about what?"

"About what we can do about it."

The maneuver irked him.

"You mean what I can do about it. Me and me ship. You can't do anything about it. Jake and Dmitry can't do anything about it. Only the cannons at the back of the *Goliath* can stop tanks."

Her defiant air evaporated, and her features softened as she appeared vulnerable. It intensified his desire.

"I know it's all about your cannons, and I know you're under no obligation. But the contract with Pierre is open-ended. If you can help convince him, he'll let you turn back and stop this madness."

"Jake's our leader at sea."

"Jake's too indebted to Pierre to defy him, but I've seen you stand up to him. You have the strongest voice with Pierre."

He questioned if she insinuated guilt as a motivator.

"Is this because of us running the blockade?" he asked.

"The prime minister has many motives, and we can't blame ourselves. If he wants to wage war now, it's on him, not on us."

"Did he state that it's in response to the blockade run?"

The hard shadow her brow cast over her eyes suggested he'd again provided her a clown show.

"Even if it were the truth, he's stating the opposite," she said. "He's been airing footage of the commandos commandeering our vessels and declaring his blockade impenetrable."

"Again, how do you know that?"

"That also came with Pierre's latest report."

"Did you bribe or threaten me crew into letting you carry all the latest news to me? I feel bad for Liam especially. He knows I'll clobber him if he withholds data from me."

"Your crew respects me. Liam knew you'd be okay with it."

He found her argument annoying but accurate.

"Fine. But what about this media skewing? The prime minister can pretend only for so long before the activists air videos of aid reaching the Gaza coast."

"It's already airing, but the prime minister is counting on conflicting stories to keep him looking strong while he earns internal support to extend his territory in the Golan Heights."

He inhaled to talk but she stopped him.

"And yes, that's also from Pierre's latest feed."

"I'm beginning to feel responsible for this. You make it sound like the blockade run pushed him over the edge of sanity."

"We can only guess if our work provided him a motive."

He ignored her counsel and internalized the blame.

"Bloody hell. This is what I do. This is what I signed up for. I defend a side that nobody else will because I know it's right. It just hurts to think me efforts could be backfiring."

"You fight for money."

He blushed. For once, he appreciated her brusqueness as it lifted him out of a skid towards self-pity.

"Yes, and the pay's good. Great, actually."

"I did this against my own country for a military salary. I suggest you stop the self-indulgent whining."

"Whining? I give you leeway when talking to me, but watch yourself. We're doling out the fates of hundreds of thousands, if not millions of people. Forgive me if I get a bit emotional."

Her voice rose a quarter octave for the first time since he'd heard her speak.

"Emotional? You're doing everything in your power to behave like a robot."

"I'm commanding a warship. You'll have to respect the...

the… Damn it, woman, you keep me off balance. You'll have to respect the… rigidity."

"The man I saw save his friend and lead his comrades through battle was anything but a robot. You did it with courage, intuition, and creativity that no robot could muster."

Her stare stymied him. Reading her was impossible.

"Thank you?"

"Don't ask me when you thank me. Just thank me. The commander of the *Goliath* doesn't ask. He just does it."

"Bloody hell, major, I can't figure you out. If I offend you, you'll snap me neck. If I ignore you, I'll hurt your feelings, if you actually have any. I can't win with you."

"I have feelings."

"What?"

"I said I have feelings."

His adrenaline subsided and let him recede into calmness.

"Of course, you do. I'm sorry. I didn't mean anything–"

"And there's nothing to win. You say you can't win with me. You pretend it's a competition, but we're on the same side."

"For the moment. But that could change day to day or even hour to hour. You're here to police me more than to help me, aren't you?"

"Don't be a bastard!"

"Can you deny it? I wish you would. I know you're trained to lie, but at least make the effort."

"Part of my job is policing you, but that's not the point."

"Then what is the point?"

"The point is that everything isn't an intelligence mission. Sometimes life happens, and it can't be planned out."

She was shaking.

"I didn't mean to make you mad," he said.

"I'm not mad."

"Dear God, woman. Why do you speak in tiny sentences? You try to behave like a man except that you can't be a man because you're a gorgeous Sheila."

She blushed, and her eyes glistened. As her helplessness explained her trembling, it melted him.

"So you're alone in your private quarters with a woman you think is gorgeous, and all you're doing is complaining?"

"You make me sound like a buffoon."

"Then stop thinking and do something about it."

"Will you... May I call you Ariella?"

The first smile she'd offered him illuminated her face.

"In private, as we are now."

"May I... kiss you?" he asked.

"Don't be an idiot. Just do it."

He swooped in and offered a gentle pressing of his lips against hers. After a few seconds of his body tingling and floating, he sought a gentleman's exit of a slow pulling away.

She refused.

Her tongue muscled its way into his mouth, and he melted into morass of oneness with her. Seconds slipped uncounted into timelessness, and he returned to reality where he was pushing her against the door as he gasped for breath.

Gentle afterglow kisses followed.

"Why did you ask to kiss me?"

"You mean after your sermon about me not needing to ask permission for anything?"

She nodded.

"If I surprised you, I risked a punch to me windpipe."

She laughed a gentle staccato.

"You're right."

"So, what now?" he asked.

"I don't know. I found you attractive in your dossier photographs, but I didn't plan a romance mission."

"I know you didn't. I guess you should start by calling me 'Terry', in private."

"'Terry', in private."

"We'll muddle through. No need to ruin this with rules."

"Okay."

He kissed her again before returning to thoughts of business.

"I suppose we should contact Pierre," he said.

"Yes," she said. "Ask him to use your cannons."

"Right. Follow me."

He stepped towards his door, stopped, and turned back to her. After stealing another kiss, he headed to the bridge.

With Dahan behind him, he paced forward, offering hurried greetings as he passed his staff. After he shut a watertight door and climbed stairs, darkness enshrouded the plexiglass hemisphere, and the space's solitary inhabitant rose from a seat.

"Welcome," Walker said. "I assume you've heard the news."

"Major Dahan told me everything, probably more than you can glean from Pierre's report. I'll take a look at it though."

He moved to a console and called a recent archive of his boss' messages. Everything aligned with Dahan's story.

"Let's get a satellite link to Pierre," he said.

"With two submarines in our cargo bed?" Walker asked.

"We'll have Jake raise his radio mast and feed us."

"Sounds good. See what he says about it."

Cahill tapped an icon to beget a gentle chime in the *Specter's* control room. Seconds later, Jake sat before the monitor.

"What's on your mind?" he asked.

"You've seen the latest updates from Pierre?"

"Yeah. I'm sure the media will eventually figure it out and let the world know that the Gaza blockade was broken. I'm not too worried about that. I don't know what to make of the tank movement, though. My Aman guy is playing dumb if he knows what it really means."

Sharing a new connection with his Israeli romantic interest, Cahill sensed her trepidation to talk. He recalled her discomfort during the crash dive and realized she struggled under the watery shroud of darkness.

He encouraged her.

"I would think your Aman man's silence is due to an order from his leadership," he said. "Am I correct, major?"

She cleared her throat and stepped forward.

"Yes. I ordered my team to remain silent about any scenarios that followed the blockade run."

Jake's face darkened.

"So you expected military responses to the blockade run."

"Expected? No. But my team considered and analyzed the possibilities, as a matter of prudence."

"But why make your men remain silent? I thought we were a team, working together to protect your country from itself."

She hesitated and swallowed.

"Dim the lights, Liam," Cahill said.

"Dim them? Why?"

"Just do it."

"Dimming the lights, sir."

Walker rotated a knob by his hip and the bridge's lighting softened, lessening the contrast with the dome's darkness.

"Better, major?"

She nodded, inhaled, and found her voice.

"I knew it was possible for the prime minister to become aggressive after the blockade, but I didn't want individual speculation by any of your fleet's commanders. If he did get aggressive, I wanted us all to discuss the matter together."

"Fair enough," Jake said. "I assume you didn't contact me to argue, though. I think I see where this is going."

"Renard," Cahill said. "We're wasting time speculating until we contact him."

"Okay," Jake said. "We'll stay submerged and undetected. We'll use my radio mast. You know the proper depth, right?"

"Sure do," Cahill said.

"We're rocking a bit," Jake said. "It might be choppy up there. You sure you can hold depth in the waves?"

"Not me, mate. The *Goliath*. It's easy in a big ship like this with huge automated pumps. I'll make it look like a slow dance."

Jake smirked.

"A hundred Euro says you'll lose depth control and break contact with Pierre."

"You're on, mate."

"What is happening?" Volkov asked.

"Good to see you," Cahill said. "Your English sounds pretty

good. Jake and I have decided to come shallow to get Pierre's opinion on the latest developments. I assume you read them?"

The Russian translator conveyed the message and then relayed Volkov's agreement with contacting Renard.

Five minutes of gentle ascent later, the deck bobbed and rocked under Cahill's feet. He held a railing and looked to Dahan to assess her comfort. Being shallower seemed to reduce her stress.

"I'm raising my radio mast," Jake said.

Seconds later, an unfamiliar person wearing a French naval officer's uniform appeared at Renard's chair. After a rapid exchange between Jake and the officer in the Romance language, the man departed.

"He's getting Pierre," Jake said.

A minute later, the boss appeared.

"Sorry to keep you waiting," Renard said. "I've been expecting your call, but I became distracted. I'll spare you the accusations and admit that I was smoking"

"That means you're stressed out," Jake said. "What's on your mind?"

"The tank movement, as well as the associated artillery and infantry support. The prime minister appears to be claiming the entire Golan Heights as his, and it's a matter of speculation how far into Syria he'll push. The Americans and Europeans are held helpless by diplomacy to stop him."

"But there's something we can do about it," Jake said.

"The *Goliath's* railguns with the satellite guidance I can acquire can turn back an entire tank battalion."

Cahill watched the American probe deeper.

"Then what's your concern?" Jake asked.

"I'm wrestling with the primary question. I have to ask myself if this is our problem to solve."

"The whole Israeli-Syrian border issue has been a mess since forever," Jake said. "The whole world condemns Israel's annexation of the Golan Heights but does jack shit about it, and now you think it's our job to keep it from getting messier?"

"That's what I'm considering," Renard said.

"Did you talk to Olivia?" Jake asked.

Cahill's urge to include Dahan in the team's history surprised him. Before he could consider appearances to his colleagues, he leaned into her ear and whispered.

"Olivia is Jake's old girlfriend. She was a CIA operative who seduced him to capture him about ten years ago, but then they grew close. Now she's in line for the Directorate of National Intelligence, and she supports our work in exchange for information and for serving as her private fleet from time to time."

"I didn't know," she said. "Thank you."

Her breath against his ear was scintillating.

"Terry, please," Renard said. "One conversation. Yes, I did talk to Olivia. Of course, she favors our intervention. Any Israeli offensive is a thorn in her side."

"Even into a terrorist country?" Jake asked.

"Syrians aren't all terrorists," Renard said. "And a unilateral land grab by Israel doesn't solve the problem of terrorists basing their operations within Syria. In fact, it accelerates the recruitment of disgruntled people into their ranks."

"So you've made your decision?" Jake asked.

"I'm not yet entirely sure. This isn't a democracy, but I trust you all know that I value your input."

"Forget it," Jake said. "I was okay helping people in the Gaza Strip because they were getting screwed. But my research tells me that people in the Golan Heights have pretty good lives under Israeli occupation. I say let it happen."

As the American's protest struck Cahill as Jake's first public dissention against their employer, his Russian colleague countered.

"No," Volkov said. "We do something."

As the *Wraith's* commander elaborated through his translator, Cahill recalled the strong diplomatic bond between the Russian and Syrian presidents.

"Our mission is to curtail unwarranted Israeli action," Volkov said. "We are in the business of countering despots in situations where nobody else can counter. This is why I joined this team. We must intervene."

"I have Jake's and Dmitry's positions," Renard said. "What do you say, Terry?"

Dahan cleared her throat, and the sound spurred him to lean into her again and whisper.

"Do you want to speak before I answer?" he asked.

"If I may."

"It's not like you to ask."

"It's not like your team to be divided," she said.

"Go ahead."

She stepped forward.

"Let me be candid that this is a matter of disagreement within multiple areas of the Israeli government and military forces."

Her discomfort under the hemisphere stalled her.

"Please, major, continue," Renard said.

"Aman's leadership believes, and I believe, that an offensive into Syria will beget the largest terrorist-led counterstrike into my nation of our entire history. The border skirmishes will be brutal and costly in terms of lives, and every sleeper cell will awake as an army of suicide bombers in our streets."

Again she paused.

"There's more, isn't there?" Renard asked.

"Yes. Arab nations will be pressured to join the fight with Syria, and there's a strong possibility that more than one of them will join. It could unravel decades of diplomacy."

"What say those who disagree with you?" Renard asked.

"They believe a show of force will silence all our enemies," she said. "I know the opposite to be true. Any idiot without an agenda knows it, but the prime minister is powerful."

"Let's do it," Cahill said.

The Frenchman's eyes shifted, and Cahill could tell he was looking at the American for a reaction.

"I must have a death wish," Jake said. "But I'd rather be taking questionable action with this team than skulking home to the beach alone. I don't think it'll make anything better, but I'll do it."

Renard seemed calmer.

"I appreciate your candor and your placing of the team ahead of your personal opinions," he said.

"Call it an exercise in trying to be less selfish," Jake said. "But for the record, I'm doing this despite my formal protest."

"I keep no record," Renard said. "But if you wish to file a grievance, I'll forward it to one of Dmitry's dolphins who I'm sure would be happy to address it."

"Bite me."

Renard frowned.

"I dislike your use of that idiom."

"Really?" Jake asked. "Bite me."

"I will not," Renard said. "But we are settled then, and this agreement begets a dangerous mission. The known risks are weighty, and when I consider the unknowns and the pressure of time, I grow concerned. Ergo, I would like to gather the most current detail from Aman."

"Can you connect me with my colonel via our secure network?" Dahan asked.

"Of course, major," Renard said. "I'll have my colleagues here in Toulon set up the link."

A swell lifted the transport ship's deck and then dropped it. Half a minute later, a middle-aged man with peppery hair wearing a green military top appeared on the screen. Israeli directness prevailed as the man skipped any pretense of pleasantries and began an earnest conversation with Dahan in Hebrew.

When she'd digested her fill, she looked to Cahill and switched to English.

"The *Crocodile* and the *Leviathan* will both deploy within six hours," she said. "The *Leviathan* was repaired with welded patches to the hull and with spare parts from the *Splendor*. It's limited in depth due to the emergency welding, but it's being declared battle ready."

"That's interesting," Cahill said. "But it doesn't get us closer to an answer on our next step."

As she looked at him, she seemed at ease, as if the barriers he'd broken with her offered her protection against the fear of the blackened dome.

"It gets more interesting," she said. "The prime minister has Israeli troops on merchant vessels with shoulder-launched weapons. He's also offered bounties for civilians who spot and report a submarine."

"That's bad news for us if we head back," Cahill said. "I can't think of a tactic to defend against soldiers with short-range weapons on ships too small to see and too silent to be heard."

She inhaled a deep breath and exhaled through her nose.

"I also have confirmation that the Israeli Navy did intercept a dolphin call and will rebroadcast it from drones and sonobuoys to confuse your dolphins."

"Dmitry's already dealt with that, but it's good to know he'll see it again."

"And you may see Seagulls again. The prime minister had the manufacturer dig into its prototype inventory. There'll be at least one pair per corvette again."

"These mongrels have no quit in them."

"But this is the last news we'll get from the navy. They suspect the rift within our military."

"It was only a matter of time," Cahill said.

"So they're minimizing their communications and are using new encryption schemes," she said. "All of Aman is now excluded from our legitimate updates, and we won't be stealing anymore encrypted tactical messages."

"At least you learned important facts before being shut out," Cahill said. "I'm curious, though. Why all this maritime effort?"

"To stop us. To stop you, specifically."

"Stop me from stopping the tanks?" Cahill asked. "We haven't even decided if we're going back."

"But the prime minister has," she said. "Apparently, your reputation proves that you will."

Renard's face reappeared in the monitor.

"That settles it then," he said. "If the prime minister already knows we're coming, we mustn't disappoint–"

The deck bounced, and the Frenchman's face froze in an unflattering silent, contorted mid-speech image.

"Pierre?" Cahill asked.

"Dang," Jake said. "That last swell swallowed my radio mast. Looks like you owe me a hundred Euro."

"No worries, mate," Cahill said. "We just picked up orders to earn ourselves a bigger bonus. We're hunting tanks."

Knowing his male comrades would believe his voiced courage, he pasted a grin on his face. But as he looked to the woman beside him expecting to feel desire, he instead felt the coldness of fear reflected in her caring eyes.

He could lie to his colleagues, and he could lie to himself. But she saw through his charade and exposed the secret lingering in his subconscious mind.

A resilient, augmented, and angered maritime force waited for him to expose himself while attacking the tanks, and despite two brilliant submarine commanders' protection, the *Goliath* would face its worst danger yet.

For a moment of his recurring nightmare, he was standing alone in a random compartment of his ship as the hull burst and the seas swallowed him.

Ariella Dahan's features bristled with concern as she mirrored his emotions, and her gaze ensnared him in the truth.

Cahill was afraid.

CHAPTER 17

Volkov stood in the *Wraith's* tactical control room, incredulous as the time lag with his translator tested his patience.

"Are you sure Jake's tried everything?"

"Yes," the translator said. "Well, no. I'm not sure, but Jake says he has. I can only be the messenger."

Volkov gritted his teeth.

"How long until I can speak for myself?"

"With my tutoring, the fastest would be eighteen months. But with the pace Pierre's placing on this fleet, you'll probably have three missions within that timeframe and be lucky to move at one quarter that speed."

"Ask again."

"I've asked twice already. Terry will surface and shoot holes in our hull if I ask again."

"I mean verify everything from beginning to end, including the alignment of the submarines if we actually try this."

The translator sighed and turned to the sour faces in the monitor. After catching a few words of English and reading body language, Volkov resigned himself to the task.

"I assume it's verified?" he asked.

"Yes," the translator said. "One of Jake's drones has a battery cell leak, and there's nothing he can do to fix it. Since you have three drones left compared to his one, he wants one of yours."

"And this is to be done underwater?"

The translator frowned.

"You would prefer to hand-carry the drone from your torpedo room to Jake's?"

"Don't be silly," Volkov said. "That would be ludicrous without cranes. It's just that I... well, I don't want to do this underwater either."

"Then may I conclude you don't want to do this at all?"

Volkov moaned.

"Let's get it over with," he said. "Are they ready?"

"Yes. The *Goliath's* rover will give you visual support, and Jake has his mirrored tube empty to receive."

"I suppose I should be grateful it's just a drone. Given the bravado of the American and his Australian friend, I wouldn't put it beyond them to try this with a heavyweight torpedo."

"Jake reminds you that we're deep and dead in the water, in the optimum position to attempt this."

"Did he use the word 'attempt'?"

"No, I filtered his words based upon my own doubts."

Volkov shook his head.

"I really need to learn English."

"French would be useful as well since Jake's entire crew is already fluent and it's Pierre's native language. I have some skill in the language, but English is best since Terry's shown no interest in learning French."

"I hate French," Volkov said. "It sounds so pretentious. I'll learn English. I swear to you I will."

"You're doing fine. You already have a three-hundred-word vocabulary, I'd guess. That's impressive for the time you've invested. You'll pick it up quickly."

"Perhaps some members of the crew should learn with me. We'll make it a team exercise, with friendly competition."

"Some of them are already trying. I could teach you all."

Jake's voice shot from the microphone. Volkov intuited the message and responded in English

"Yes, sorry," he said. "I start now."

As he glanced at a screen that showed the bulbous bow of his boat from the *Goliath's* rover, he switched to Russian and raised his voice to his sonar expert.

"Is drone one ready?"

"The drone is ready," Anatoly said. "Initial ordered speed will be one knot."

"Is our young drone driver ready?"

"He is. He says he'll make it look easy."

"I'll buy him a bottle of expensive vodka in our next port if he doesn't damage the drone or scrape any of the three ships."

Volkov heard whispering.

"What's the problem?" he asked.

"He says he doesn't like vodka."

"Then I'll buy him whatever he wants of equivalent value. And then I'll take him to a bar and teach him to drink vodka like a man, whether he likes it or not."

"Thank you, Dmitry. I agree," the young technician said.

"Open the outer door to tube three," Volkov said.

With a rare opportunity to view his ship from the rover, he watched the faired door slide sideways and reveal the torpedo tube's watertight muzzle door.

"The outer door is open to tube three," Anatoly said.

"Yes, I see—literally. I just watched it happen," Volkov said. "Launch drone one from tube three."

"Drone one is swimming out of tube three," Anatoly said.

"I don't see anything."

"One knot is very slow, Dmitry."

"This is testing my patience."

His anxiety growing, Volkov waited for his drone to emerge. Like a coy rigid eel, the plastic cylinder jutted its nose through the submarine's rounded bow.

"There it is," he said.

As he spoke, he glued his gaze to the screen showing the view from the camera. The angle became lower as the rover swam closer to the exchange, and Volkov saw his drone sliding towards the open outer door of the *Specter's* waiting tube.

"Drone one is clear of our hull, I mean just free of our muzzle door, rather," Anatoly said. "At this speed, I need to be specific. I know you can see it, but we have electrically confirmed wire connectivity and propulsion control."

"Yes, of course," Volkov said. "Just be careful."

"He's not doing anything, Dmitry. It's one knot, no steering.

There's no room to steer."

"No, I suppose not."

The drone bumped against the lip of the receiving tube's outer door but bounded inside the tubular conduit towards the muzzle door. The rover slid behind the moving cylinder's propeller and cast light into the tight space.

"Can he see anything?" Volkov asked.

"Yes," Anatoly said. "He's watching the same video you are, but with younger and better eyes. We should be done soon."

The propeller angled aside and ceased forward motion.

"What's going on?" Volkov asked.

"I think I'm stuck against the door lip," the young technician said. "Or maybe against the muzzle door."

"You don't sound distressed about it," Volkov said.

"Because I'm steering through it."

The drone's stern planes and rudder shifted through their extremes, but the vessel stayed stuck.

"Damn it," Volkov said. "Increase the drone's speed to two and a half knots."

The propeller twirled faster, and the drone jumped forward.

"Reverse!" Volkov said.

"I'm reversing!"

The translator called out for Volkov's attention and told him Jake's team heard the vessel bump against the breech door. The American then ordered the guidance wire severed.

"Cut the wire to drone one," Volkov said.

The cylinder became a dumb tool resting in a useless tube, and its guidance wire kept a muzzle door open on each ship. As Volkov turned to the screen, waiting for his teammates to act, he noticed the rover's camera pointing to the open hatches of its nest as it returned to the top of the *Goliath*.

The conversation in English was quick, and his depth gauge showed an upward crawl before his translator relayed the obvious.

"Jake ordered Terry to surface us. Jake's team will work on the drone while Terry carries us to the drop point."

"The speed will be nice," Volkov said. "But I don't like the exposure."

The *Wraith's* deck rocked as his gauge showed shallower depths. It then bobbed and rolled as the numbers reached zero. In the background behind Cahill's face he saw dawn's indigo piercing the distant horizon's blackness.

"Now we're at altitude," he said.

"Jake's team has pulled the drone and all the remaining wire into his torpedo room," the translator said. "He recommends shutting our muzzle door."

Volkov gave the order to his team to close the door, drain the tube, and reload it. When he turned his attention back to the screens by his chair, his employer's face appeared.

As the translator relayed the message, Volkov watched a circle of uncertainty rise from the Haifa coast on a display.

"Pierre says the *Crocodile* and *Leviathan* have deployed. Based upon their submerged speed limits and the time of their departures, the circle is the farthest extent of their location."

Finding the account self-explanatory, Volkov nodded. He filtered the translator's ongoing narrative of Renard's data feed as it showed the drop off point being ten miles from the future extreme reach of the Israeli submarines.

The velocity vector predicted the *Goliath* moving at twenty-nine knots, slower than its unencumbered maximum. Curious, Volkov toggled through screen views until he found a vantage from a camera atop the port weapons bay. Sea spray tickled the *Wraith's* dangling rudder as the laden transport ship held its cargo low in the water.

After seeing the extent of the added flow friction, he understood his team's speed limits. But the *Goliath*, serving its original function of a submarine transport vessel, was taking the *Wraith* faster into the combat theater than Volkov could take his submarine under its own power.

Moving two submarines with such speed despite the transport ship's stubby port bow impressed him with his fleet's abilities. Knowing the proper bow section would allow at least two more knots, he felt more empowered working for Renard than he had for the Russian Navy, and he appreciated his hand-picked key team members from his homeland–human and other.

But as the trainer entered the control room, the lithe man's demeanor concerned him, and the artificial light made the new arrival seem pale. With a lull in a conversation between the fleet's commanders, Volkov stepped away and met the dolphins' master beside a corner console.

"You look troubled, Vasily."

"Is it that obvious?"

"I don't know. I just happen to notice."

"I think you notice because we are indeed friends, Dmitry."

Volkov accepted the truth and nodded.

"Yes, we are. What's wrong?"

"I fear for Mikhail and Andrei."

"You fear for them frequently. Why now?"

"The Israelis know our return-to-ship order."

Volkov raised his finger.

"Yes, the Israelis have intercepted it, and they use it. But they don't know what it means. To them, it's just a wild hope of distracting your dolphins."

"But it's so dangerous."

"That's why we'll use a drone as a guide."

"I never trained them for this. We're making up lessons for them in combat. What if my babies get confused?"

"They've proven themselves. They know your voice, and they want to come home. They'll always come home to you."

"You can't promise that."

"No, my friend, I cannot. But I can promise you to treat them like my own. Have I not always done that?"

Color returned to the trainer's face.

"You have."

"Will you reassure them of this for me?"

"Yes, Dmitry. I will."

The mammals' master turned and headed to his dolphins, and Volkov returned to his seat.

New lines on his tactical display drew a quadrilateral over the Golan Heights and several four-sided shapes off the Israeli and Lebanese coasts.

He interpreted the smallest skewed box, farthest from the coast, as the *Goliath's* launch basket. From there, Cahill could fire his cannons and have them hit tanks anywhere within the larger form drawn over the Israeli-Syrian landmass.

Two larger waterborne boxes showed the areas he and Jake would patrol in protection of their comrade. As he questioned how they'd reach their defined areas, which intersected the hostile red arc representing the reach of the submerged Israeli submarines, the friendly boundaries disappeared and reappeared farther west in smaller formats outside the adversary's reach.

"This shows the drop off point, which you'll reach two hours from now," Renard said. "Terry will submerge there. From that point, Jake and Dmitry will take thirty-minute head starts and advance eastward while Terry remains dead in the water."

Volkov hung on his translator's words as Renard continued.

"The center of Terry's launch basket is defined in space and time with him making a speed of advance of eight knots from the drop off point. You can all see what that means in terms of your patrol areas. You'll need to keep moving forward with urgency."

Accounting for his half-hour head start, Volkov computed his speed needing to approach twelve knots to stay ahead of Cahill while conducting a back-and-forth zigzag search for submarines waiting to ambush him.

"Too fast," he said in Russian.

"Shall I translate that?"

"No. I can compensate by covering extra water with the dolphins. But the American cannot. Let's see if he protests."

"Merkava tanks provide low profiles," Renard said. "But Terry's rounds will come from the higher elevations of ballistic flight. He'll be targeting the engines in front, which should give large targets while placing the tank crews in minimal danger."

Volkov watched Jake for a reaction but saw none, and the con-

versation ended without dissent. He decided that his new teammates shared great confidence in their abilities, suffered from
group hubris, or both.

Cahill offered a warning that he'd be testing a new barrel
on a cannon, since repeated fire had worn the prior hardware.
Volkov passed the word to his crew, and then a solitary crack
rang.

To distract himself from the helplessness of being Cahill's passenger, he called his crew to their breakfast shifts and allowed a
leisurely eating pace.

Two hours later, the deck's rocking subsided, and he darted
to his seat on the conning platform. The waves behind Cahill's
image slowed to their natural wind-whipped speeds.

"Verify you're rigged to submerge, Dmitry," Cahill said.

Volkov looked to his veteran mechanic.

"We're still rigged for submergence," the gray beard said.

"I'm rigged for submergence," Volkov said.

"So am I," Jake said.

"Okay, gents. Any last words for Pierre?"

"No, thank you," Volkov said.

"None from me," Jake said. "I don't want to get him started, or
we could be here for hours before he finishes his next sermon."

"I resent that," Renard said. "As usual, I'd wish you all luck, but
I see no need. Prove to me again that you're all charmed."

"Submerging to thirty meters," Cahill said.

The concept of windows on a submarine disquieted Volkov as
indigo engulfed the dome behind Cahill and then became blackness. Gentle undulations replaced harsh rolling.

"We're at thirty meters," Cahill said. "I'm letting Jake go first
since he has a bit farther to travel. Are you ready, Jake?"

"Yes. I don't do anything except drive away when you signal
me, right?"

"Right. You haven't changed your trim much since we were
last under, did you?"

"No. I should still be heavy."

"Right. You'll have to pump overboard to rise. You'll lose laser lock quickly, but you won't be clear of Dmitry's tower until I can pull him under you. So be patient until I signal you with three bursts of scanning sonar. Ready?"

"I'm as ready as I'll ever be. Let me go."

Through an external camera feed, Volkov watched half the *Goliath's* presses roll back and release his ship's twin. Though free, the *Specter* remained in place.

"You're free, Jake. Start pumping overboard."

"I'm pumping overboard."

"You're a little heavy aft," Cahill said. "I see it on the cargo bed's pressure sensors."

"Got it. Pumping aft to forward," Jake said. "I see your pressure sensor readings, too. Now I look balanced. Pumping overboard from centerline again."

The submarine began to rise.

"I'm using the outboards to drive backwards and keep Dmitry out of your way," Cahill said. "You look clear."

Jake's image froze as his submarine floated from the *Goliath's* communications lasers. Volkov pressed a button to darken the screen.

"I'm taking us down another ten meters to be sure," Cahill said. "You're next, Dmitry."

As the *Goliath* settled deeper, Cahill sent three bursts of his scanning sonar outward, freeing Jake to drive away. Volkov looked to his sonar ace.

"Do you hear Jake's screws?"

"Yes," Anatoly said. "He's driving away."

"Same thing for you now. Are you ready?"

"Yes, I'm ready," Volkov said.

The presses released the *Wraith*, and after five minutes of pumping, the submarine started to float. Cahill's face froze with the loss of laser.

"Terry's going deeper now," Volkov said.

"I hear his pings," Anatoly said. "We're free."

Volkov looked to his gray-bearded veteran.

"Take us to five knots, course one-two-five, depth thirty-five meters, and get a neutral trim."

The deck rolled through the turn.

"The ship is at five knots, course one-two-five, depth thirty-five meters. I'm getting a neutral trim."

"Very well," Volkov said. "Tell the trainer to get his dolphins ready."

The gray beard lifted a sound-powered phone to his cheek.

"He's getting them loaded," the gray beard said.

Volkov glanced at a display showing his tubes. Since the dolphins preferred number three, he'd loaded drones in five and six.

"Anatoly, are my drones ready for launch?"

"Yes. One man each will control them, and Vasily can speak to his dolphins through either one, though we've set him up for tube five. Shall I launch the drones?"

"Not yet," Volkov said. "Let me see how Vasily's doing."

In the torpedo room, technicians guided a dolphin on a tarp towards a tube. By the animal's complacent nature, he assumed it was Andrei.

His hand on a dolphin, the trainer looked up from the tank.

"I don't think Mikhail will be so calm," he said.

"Maybe if you were calmer, Mikhail would be okay."

"Perhaps, Dmitry. You make it sound so easy, but I worry."

As the technicians wrestled the lead cetacean into the empty cylindrical space, a sound-powered phone chirped by the tube. One of them extended a free hand and answered.

"It's for you, Dmitry. It's Anatoly."

Volkov stepped and reached for the phone.

"This is Dmitry."

"I hear the *Leviathan*," Anatoly said.

Volkov sensed his breathing accelerate, and he forced himself to use his commanding voice.

"Already? You jest."

"I heard a fifty-hertz electric plant, and I wasn't sure, but then I heard a trim pump cycle."

"You mean we got lucky."

"Yes, Dmitry. I can't think of a better way to describe it."

"If we can hear our adversary, our adversary may hear us. Have the word passed silently to rig the ship for ultra-quiet operations. I'm heading to the control room."

Volkov looked at his trainer and his torpedo technicians.

"That means Andrei stays in his tube and Mikhail stays in his tank. We can't risk the noise of transferring either of them back and forth."

"Mikhail will worry if he's alone!" the trainer said.

"He'll be okay if you stay with him."

"Maybe, but this is unusual."

"So is finding an Israeli submarine with such little effort," Volkov said. "Gentlemen, be ready to launch weapons."

In the control room, Volkov darted to his sonar guru's shoulder. The raw sounds aligned with his expectations.

"Fifty-hertz electric bus," he said. "You weren't kidding. You've got it on the towed array but know it's from the south?"

"I heard the trim pump cycling on the hull and bow arrays. So that took care of any ambiguity of direction. And here's a fix on the *Leviathan* where the sounds crossed."

Anatoly slid his finger across an icon to shift the system's view of the engagement backwards in time. The distance between the towed hydrophones and those in the *Wraith's* bow allowed the crossing of the lines representing the incoming sounds, refining of a point in space.

"There's the *Leviathan* as of three minutes ago. Twelve miles away, at least as well as you can trust a fifty-hertz bearing. I assigned a speed of six knots, and the system is tracking."

"So it is," Volkov said. "Could this be a fake target?"

"It's possible, but I have no reason to suspect it. The sounds are clean to my ears."

"Then I need to pursue this."

"Orders to the helm, sir?" the gray beard asked.

"Come right to course one-seven-zero."

The deck tilted through the turn, and the *Wraith* aimed towards the southern end of its patrol boundary.

After forty minutes of pursuit, Volkov saw the frequency shift upwards as his sonar ace announced it.

"Target aspect change. Doppler shift upward. The *Leviathan* has turned towards us."

The frequency hit a maximum and then fell again.

"The *Leviathan* just gave us a bow aspect," Anatoly said. "Then it continued through the line of sight."

"This should tighten our solution."

"Give me a moment to analyze its new course."

"You have thirty seconds."

"The clock starts when you stop talking."

Volkov scoffed.

"I'm shooting in forty seconds whether you're comfortable or not. Open the outer door to tube two."

"The outer door is open."

"Well?" Volkov said.

"The solution is tracking. I recommend shooting."

Volkov suspected a trap, but he had to dismiss his doubts as paranoia. Luck played a role in submarine combat, and he had to capitalize on the opportunity.

"Very well," he said. "Shoot tube two."

CHAPTER 18

Stooping over the central table, Jake watched the toad-head turn.

"I hear diesels on too many vessels to count them all," Remy said. "I hear dirty screws, I hear chains on decks, I hear fake dolphin calls from three sonobuoys, but I don't hear any Seagulls."

"They're only fourteen miles away, according to Pierre."

"There are enough ships between us and them to mask the sounds of a symphony orchestra."

"I'm in Hell," Jake said. "We're in Hell."

"The Israelis have covered the water with floating distractions," Remy said. "Every ship in their merchant marine fleet is chasing around every ship in their fishing fleet to distract us."

"We shouldn't be here."

Jake pursed his lips, wishing to rescind his pessimism.

"At least it's equally hard for the *Crocodile* and *Leviathan* to hear us with all this noise," Remy said.

"Good point," he said. "So we'll stay focused on the Seagulls. We'll wait for our next update on them from Pierre and then listen down that bearing."

"Of course," Remy said.

As Renard's data trickled across the chart, Jake read a summary of Volkov's success.

"Incredible," he said. "Dmitry already took one out. Pierre says he has a satellite photo of the *Leviathan* on the surface."

"I'm reading it, too," Henri said. "It's good news, but there's a qualification. Keep reading."

Jake scrunched his eyebrows.

"Pierre says a skeleton Israeli crew abandoned ship to a nearby support vessel and then boarded their submarine again after Dmitry's weapon hit. There was also a tug boat nearby to tow the *Leviathan* back to port."

"Like it was a trap," Henri said. "A bizarre one indeed, but the behavior indicates premeditation."

"Yeah," Jake said. "What sort of trap involves letting the other guy torpedo your submarine?"

"A distraction."

Glaring at the geometry, Jake unraveled the Israeli tactics.

"Shit," he said. "The *Leviathan* wasn't battle ready. It was barely seaworthy and suckered Dmitry away from the real action. Now he's out of the fight, and we're by ourselves against the rest of the Israeli fleet."

"I think you've described the ruse accurately," Henri said. "And now we'll have to succeed alone against the world once again."

Having Volkov fooled away from his flank left Jake feeling vulnerable. Flustered, he valued his veteran Frenchman's faith.

"You sound like you enjoy having the odds against us."

"I believe I do," Henri said. "I may need psychological counseling, but this sort of challenge invigorates me."

"We all need psychological help for being out here."

"Not me," Remy said. "I trust my ears. And right now, they're telling me there's too much noise, too much activity."

"Nothing on the Seagulls yet?" Jake asked.

The toad head shook.

"Shit," Jake said. "Can you recommend a direction for me to drive bearing separation so you can hear them?"

"No. You can try whichever direction you'd like, but there's a surface ship making noise on every bearing around them."

Jake's head drooped and twisted towards Henri, who grasped his commander's body language and stepped to the table.

"I'm no expert in tactics, but I'm no dunce either. I recognize the difficulty."

"Is that your way of saying we're screwed?" Jake asked.

The French mechanic's tone became paternal.

"We've seen much worse situations, but this situation's frustrating because we're surrounded by things we can't shoot at. You're personally frustrated because you want to shoot your way out, but you can't."

The words stung and reinvigorated. Jake sneered.

"Your psychotherapy's gnat's-ass accurate as usual. It's a good point, but what do I do about it?"

"You use finesse over brute force," Henri said.

"I was actually considering using heavyweights against those damned Seagulls."

"Don't. You'd risk blowing up civilians."

Jake's first instinct to the Frenchman's warning was to voice a callous and uncaring opinion about strangers' lives, but he overrode his irritation with the forced virtue of compassion.

"You're right. That's the whole point of the slow-kills."

"You invented them to preserve human life," Henri said. "Don't deviate from your principles out of desperation."

"I don't like running face-first into this shit, but I have no choice. I need to clear the way for Terry."

"Then do what you must to clear the way for Terry."

Jake nodded and accepted the risks.

"Okay," he said. "We're going shallow. I'm going to use the periscope and the radio mast to get some tight data from Pierre–whatever it takes to make sense of this."

Henri returned to his control station.

"I understand. I'm ready."

"Make your depth thirty meters."

The deck rose as Henri compelled the *Specter* upward.

"Can you hear any better?" Jake asked.

"No," Remy said. "We didn't cross an acoustic layer. And I still hear too much and can't make out the Seagulls."

"I'm coming shallow, Antoine. Forget the Seagulls for a minute and make sure I don't run into anything. What's on the right moving left and vice versa?"

The toad-head twisted as the ace conversed with his sonar technician colleagues.

"We're tracking seven contacts with troublesome bearing

rates, but only two have sound power levels strong enough to be interferers. Triangulation supports only two of them being close."

Jake looked to his chart and saw two nearby vessels. Lines of bearing from the bow array and the towed array fixed them in space, but the steep angles created positioning inaccuracies. The contacts range estimates varied from two to five miles away.

"It's the best we're going to get. I'm taking my chances. Henri, get a message ready for Pierre giving him our location and requesting optimized data feeds for all warships within twenty miles and all other vessels within five miles."

The Frenchman tapped keys.

"Twenty miles and five miles. Got it," he said. "The message is ready in our transmission queue.

"Very well, take us to periscope depth."

After a gentle ascent, the deck rocked as Henri raised the radio mast.

"I've connected us with the satellite and have transmitted our message," he said. "Receipt is acknowledged."

"Very well," Jake said. "Pierre should be transmitting."

"Here it comes."

As the icons of the contacts around him shifted to their updated locations, Jake dedicated a side window in the central table for his boss' face. The Frenchman appeared but remained silent.

"Pierre's not talking," Jake said. "There's nothing for him to say unless we start talking to him. Lower the radio mast."

"Are you going to risk more transmissions?" Henri asked.

"Not in this environment. I don't want to guess how many ships out there have radio-sniffing equipment aimed at us."

Jake stepped to his seat on the conn as Renard's image disappeared, and he sent the periscope up for its panoramic sweep. As the optics descended, he looked at images spread across three screens showing the world above.

"Nothing within visible range," he said.

"The height of eye of the optics is too low," Henri said.

"That's fine," Jake said. "I've got what I need from Pierre. Take us back down to thirty meters."

The deck dipped and leveled.

"Steady on depth thirty meters," Henri said.

"Very well," Jake said. "I intend to shoot the nearest Seagulls. I need to take care of them now."

"With their high speeds and unknown patterns, they'll drive by at least three other vessels that may attract our weapon," Remy said. "Maybe more."

"That's why we have a wire. And if that fails, that's why I'm using a slow-kill. Two, actually. I need to sink both Seagulls. I'm not leaving one to hunt us."

Jake looked again at the tactical data.

"The other Seagull pairs are far enough away to ignore. Assign tubes one and two to the closest Seagull pair."

"The Seagulls are so close together that I have only one solution for the pair, and I still don't hear them. I'm using just Pierre's data," Remy said.

"I'll manage it with a staggered launches and wires."

The guru tapped keys.

"Tubes one and two are assigned to the Seagulls."

"Very well," Jake said. "Shoot tube one."

"Seriously?" Remy asked.

"Excuse me?" Jake asked.

"You don't sound serious."

Jake lifted his eyebrows and looked to Henri. The French mechanic shrugged.

"You do seem rather distant," Henri said. "Your command almost sounded like a question."

"Yeah, I get it. I'm shooting at robots I can't hear so that a bunch of other strange shit can happen. So forgive me if I seem a bit distracted. But, yes, I'm serious. Antoine, shoot tube one."

The soft whine and pressure change hit his ears as the *Specter* spat its torpedo. After the sonar ace verified control of the weapon, Jake crouched by his seat.

"Antoine, I'm still serious," he said. "Shoot tube two."

Jake saw the toad face blushing as the second abrupt baromet-ric shift impacted the compartment.

"I'm passing wire control of both weapons to my staff," Remy said. "I'll keep listening for the Seagulls."

Jake patted him on the back.

"Good idea. You do that."

Ten minutes later, Jake grew impatient with his guru's inabil-ity to hear the robotic hunters.

"Henri, take us to periscope depth."

As the floor leveled and bobbed, Jake ordered the radio mast upward. With the Subtics tactical system linked to Renard's up-date, the robots' new locations and speeds appeared.

"Lower the radio mast," Jake said.

"The radio mast is lowered," Henri said.

"You see the new Seagulls' locations, Antoine?" Jake asked.

"Got it. Listening. Yes, I'm listening down their updated bear-ing, and I finally hear their screws."

"I'm comparing them against our torpedoes," Jake said. "Give each weapon a twenty-degree steer to the left."

"The weapons have accepted the steers."

Jake watched the velocity vectors of his torpedoes shift to a new intercept course against the hunters. As he entertained thoughts of ridding himself of the robots and turning his atten-tion towards the *Crocodile*, he sent the periscope up for its pano-rama.

As the optics underwent their circular sweep, the toad-head whipped around, and Remy pointed towards the air.

"Missile!"

Jake cringed on his way to the deck and slapped his hands against the tiles. Expecting to see water inundating his ripped-open metallic coffin, he verified his safety with an upward glance. The *Specter's* hull had held.

Deafened, he recovered to a knee and made eye contact with the first person he saw. His buttocks balanced on his seat, Henri cramped his canted torso across the adjacent console.

"Henri."

The words were muffled murmurs in Jake's mind, and the mechanic mimicked a motionless mime.

"Henri!"

Nothing. Jake staggered to the Frenchman's station and reached for controls. He tapped the icon that signaled the engine room to accelerate to full speed, and then he tapped another image to rotate the stern planes to a full dive.

As the deck nosed downward, the mechanic straightened his back, studied his panel and looked to Jake.

"Emergency Deep!" Jake said.

Reading his lips, the Frenchman nodded and then reached to drive down the fairwater planes with one hand while flooding water into centerline trim tanks with the other.

Climbing against the *Specter's* descent, Jake walked sternward. His hearing began to return as he heard cooling fans and low-frequency electronic hums.

Sailors groped and gazed for awareness around him as he stepped to the conning platform and stood tall to give his crew an image of strength. He yawned to pop his ears, but sounds remained garbled.

The chaos of a missile attacking him receded as he counted the meters into the concealing depths. He assessed his status.

A small airborne warhead had wrecked his periscope, and his rudder, stabilizers, and the top of his propeller were offering his assailant his final vulnerable targets before he escaped below the waves.

He drew in a breath, counting the seconds until the water would swallow his ship into its safe confines.

When the second explosion rumbled in the distant rear of the submarine, Jake recognized the gravity, lowered his head, and sighed through his nostrils.

Another missile had struck, but this time, his enemy had hit something important.

CHAPTER 19

Jake lifted a sound-powered phone to his face and heard his engineer's harried voice.

"I shut down propulsion," LaFontaine said.

"What's going on back there?" Jake asked.

"The shaft started spinning erratically. I had to stop it."

"Understood. We took a hit in our screw, didn't we?"

"I'm afraid so. We probably lost a couple blades."

"But you could give me slow propulsion if I need it?"

During the silence, Jake thought he could hear LaFontaine's heart sinking.

"We'd be abnormally loud with whatever damage we've taken, and I wouldn't know your speed limit until I monitor the shaft under load. The uneven weight distribution and water resistance on the screw will create rapid and periodic shocks in shaft torque, radially and laterally. It's bad."

"I got it," Jake said. "Keep the shaft secured for now, but deploy the outboard motor. I have other business to deal with at the moment, but I'll be back there soon."

He jammed the receiver back into its cradle.

"Antoine, find me whoever shot us."

"I've narrowed it down to about ten degrees of bearing from the sounds of the incoming missiles," Remy said. "You could help me by giving me a limit of the range."

"Use three miles," Jake said. "Shoulder-launched missiles don't go very far."

"That narrows it down to two ships I'm tracking."

With tubes three and four dedicated to drones, Jake recalled having reloaded tubes five and six with torpedoes during his ride into battle aboard the *Goliath*.

"No time for guessing games," he said. "I'm taking out both contacts. Assign a slow-kill to each one, tubes five and six."

"I've assigned tube five and six to the potential vessels who shot us," Remy said.

"Shoot tube five."

Jake felt the pressure change.

"Tube five indicates normal launch," Remy said. "I have wire control. I hear its propeller."

"Shoot tube six."

"Tube six indicates normal launch. I have wire control, and I hear its propeller."

"Give me an update to all deployed assets."

"Weapon one is two minutes from the Seagulls with its active seeker on and should acquire its target any second," Remy said. "Weapon two is fifty seconds behind weapon one. Weapon five and six will go active in ninety seconds. Tubes three and four are guiding drones one and two."

Given his torpedoes' proximity to their targets, Jake relinquished his privilege of guiding his weapons.

"Henri, cut the wires to tubes one, two, five, and six," he said. "Reload tubes one, two, five, and six with slow-kills, and have them do it fast. Make all the noise that's needed."

"You're giving up your guidance wires?"

"Yes," Jake said. "Remember what you said about finesse?"

"Of course."

"Forget it. I need to be ready to start throwing punches in multiple directions."

The Frenchman relayed the order to the torpedo room.

"Get a hold of your relief and head back to the engine room," Jake said. "I'm sure Claude could use your help."

As the mechanic departed, Jake looked to the data feed trickling in from Renard over the low-frequency antenna his submarine trailed behind its stabilizer. He was relieved to see the communications connection had survived the blast.

The update identified the missile's shooter as a fishing trawler he correlated to the target of weapon six. With a silent and insincere apology to the target of weapon five, he continued reading his employer's feed.

As he expected, he found a recommendation to slip away unnoticed from the location of the attack and a request to send Renard his status.

"My status," he said. "My status is damned."

As Henri's understudy reached the control panel, Jake considered his options to communicate with Renard. Exposing his radio mast would offer his assailant another target, and he opted for patience.

"Weapon one has acquired a Seagull," Remy said.

"Still damned," Jake said. "But that should remove one major problem."

Renard's continuing feed showed the distant Seagull pairs turning towards Jake. With Volkov's *Wraith* to the south, the Israelis focused their complete visible undersea hunt on the known location of the *Specter*.

"Weapon one has detonated under a Seagull," Remy said. "Limpets are attaching–enough to sink it. Weapon two has acquired the sinking Seagull's partner."

"That's somewhat encouraging. Any sign of the *Crocodile*?"

"No. But weapons five and six have acquired the fishing ships."

"Let your young apprentices manage those weapons while you dedicate yourself to a search for the *Crocodile*."

"Of course," Remy said. "Do you have a preference for how I use the drones?"

"I deployed the drones to go hunting, but now we're the hunted, and I doubt we can move without being louder than a chainsaw. So we're in pure defensive mode now. Bring them back towards us and tighten your search radius to ten miles."

The technicians beside Remy stirred and murmured reports to their guru.

"Weapon six has deployed its limpets with most of them attaching," Remy said. "We're counting detonations."

"Keep listening. I want you to hear it sink."

At the ship's control station, Henri's understudy spoke with a thick accent.

"Would you like a message prepared?"

"Yes," Jake said. "Include our location, the sinking of the closest Seagulls, the sinking of the attacking fishing vessel, the loss of our periscope, and being stuck dead in the water while assessing damage to the propeller."

As the words swirled in his head, Jake sought his optimum tactical steps but conjured nothing to improve his lot.

"My team hears the fishing ship that attacked us taking on heavy flooding," Remy said. "Weapon five just detonated eighteen limpets against the other target, which is also flooding."

Having no time for pity, Jake consoled himself knowing his slow-kill weapon gave the innocent vessel's crew time to abandon their ship. He also distracted himself with thoughts of survival as he called up a chart showing currents in the Mediterranean Sea.

Paralleling the coast, a major current flowed north by northeast at a knot and a half, and Jake told Henri's understudy to align the ship with the current when he restored enough propulsion to allow steerageway. With a little luck, Jake could borrow a force of nature to help carry him from danger.

"Our attacker is sinking," Remy said.

"But not sunk yet?"

"I believe sections are still above the surface."

"I'll take my chances. They're too busy jumping overboard to shoot me again."

Jake stepped behind Henri's relief.

"Bring us to periscope depth real slow."

The Frenchman pressed icons to pump water, and the depth gauge showed a gentle ascent.

"While we're waiting, add a note to Pierre about us possibly driving out of here on the outboard motor with the current."

The replacement tapped keys on a keyboard, impressing Jake with a speed of typing that outpaced Henri's.

"Raise the radio mast," Jake said.

More tapping of icons.

"The mast is raised. No link yet."

"Wait for it."

The ship inched higher.

"There, we're linked, Jake."

"Transmit."

More tapping.

"Transmission receipt acknowledged."

"Lower the mast and get us back down to thirty meters."

Confident he'd done all he could in the control room, Jake headed aft to investigate the limits of his propulsion.

After passing through small berthing and dining areas, he entered the extra hull section that extended the *Specter's* length eight and a half meters but permitted air-independent propulsion through the ethanol-liquid oxygen MESMA plant. The familiar hiss of steam filled the section, and Jake felt heat waft over his body.

The air-independent power plant would bear the electrical loads and preserve his battery charge while he determined his next steps, giving him one less worry.

With cooler air than the MESMA plant, the quiet engine room seemed morbid. He walked its tapering length to the aftermost, tightest conical confines where he found a small crowd huddled around the propulsion motor and two young sailors standing over the controls of the lowered tiny outboard motor.

The wiry frame of his engineer wrapped around the shaft where it penetrated the hull through a circular bearing. Aiming a flashlight at the seals, the man greeted Jake from his contorted position.

"We were making turns for twenty-two knots when we took the damage," LaFontaine said. "That hurt."

"How bad?" Jake asked.

"The seals took a beating. They're holding now, but whatever mass was lost or deformed on the screw is causing the shaft to whip around abnormally during a good quarter of its rotation. That's wearing into the seals."

"But you shut it down before there was damage?"

"I did, but it's only a matter of time before you'll have bare metal against bare metal. You also need to consider the stresses on the bearings further aft that we can't see, and then you also need to consider the change to our lateral loads. That's putting a stress on the bearings and also on the motor."

"Call me crazy," Jake said. "What if we made flank turns and rode this thing until it seized or the first structural support broke? How long would we have?"

LaFontaine pushed on the shaft, wiggled his torso back over his knees, and looked up at Jake.

"You really want me to guess?"

"Yeah, give me your best guess."

"Five minutes for this bearing. Ten at most. The metal would heat up, the lubrication oil would break down, and at some point it would become a grinding operation. And God knows what would happen to the hidden bearings or the motor."

Having remained silent, Henri, who stood on the other side of the shaft, interjected.

"What about a very slow approach?" he asked. "Five knots or even three. That could be enough to allow our escape."

"It's the same problem scaled down," LaFontaine said. "But at low speed, it may delay the inevitable for hours or even days."

"The noise would still be harsh," Jake said.

"There's only one way to find out," Henri said.

"Right," Jake said. "Get Antoine on the phone for some diagnostic listening. We'll see what three knots sounds like."

"Shall I stay back here and coordinate activities while Claude focuses on the damage?" Henri asked.

Jake nodded and darted forward.

The toad-head turned as he entered the control room.

"You ready?" Jake asked.

"We all are."

Jake stepped to the conning platform and grabbed a sound-powered phone.

"Henri, this is Jake. Are you online?"

A deep, filtered voice came through the receiver.

"I'm online in the engine room. All is ready to make turns up to five knots."

"Make turns for three knots."

The toad-head shook before the speed gauge registered a knot, and Jake heard a nasty grinding whine echoing through the *Specter's* hull.

"Shit. Shut it down."

"Claude's shutting it down," Henri said.

"Is the outboard ready?"

"Yes."

"Give me all you've got on it."

The speed gauge showed the submarine moving at a knot and a quarter through the water. With the current, Jake estimated he approached three knots over ground, and his inertial navigation system confirmed it.

"Even the outboard is loud," Remy said.

"How bad?"

"It's like making ten knots normally."

"I'll take that for now."

"What's next, Jake?" Remy asked.

"Listen for the *Crocodile*. That's the major threat."

"We're listening, all of us. I'm listening for the *Crocodile* itself, and they're listening for its incoming torpedo."

Jake stared at Remy while digesting the pessimism, transforming it into realism, and accepting his guru's approach as wisdom. He was stranded, and the first sign of his enemy might be an incoming torpedo.

Seeking insights beyond his own, he called up Renard's data.

His boss had acknowledged receipt of his predicament and suggested surrendering as a viable option in which the Frenchman's negotiations would assure the safety of the *Specter* and its crew.

His employer had also deemed the anti-tank mission a failure and had ordered Cahill to abort the mission and turn back.

"Surrender?" Jake asked. "Defeated by a fishing boat."

Henri entered the room and joined Jake.

"I'm glad you're here. Take a look at Pierre's latest."

The mechanic's eyes moved across the screen.

"Logical," he said. "But it feels terrible when our boss sums up our problem so tersely and so desperately."

"Yeah," Jake said. "No rescue by Terry this time. I guess we're really screwed. I screwed this up."

"You didn't screw anything up," Henri said. "You had bad luck pushing into a dangerous situation. Keep your focus and shift your attention on surviving."

"We can take our chances sneaking away on the outboard."

The French mechanic frowned.

"You'd place our hopes on a tiny motor designed to maneuver us against a pier."

"The current will eventually carry us away."

"Away to where?"

"Away from Israel and its navy."

"And then what?"

Jake had to glance at a chart to grope for an answer.

"Then we can risk the noise and try using our shaft to make for friendly landfall. Turkish Cyprus, for example. Or have Terry come rescue us once we're out of the battle."

"That sounds desperate."

Jake let frustration overcome him, and he raised his voice.

"It is desperate!"

Wanting to apologize, he hesitated and let Henri speak.

"You're right. It is desperate. I shouldn't push you when you're under the stress of a command decision."

"My decision is to keep our hopes alive of evading," Jake said. "We'll use the outboard and the current, and I'll stake all our lives on Antoine's ability to hear any new danger with enough time to do something about it."

The Frenchman assumed the paternal tone that had given Jake confidence for years.

"Then your decision is made," Henri said. "We are stranded, but we're still a fighting warship. We're still quiet, and we can hear and shoot our adversary. Anyone who would brave attacking us must risk their own annihilation. All hope is not lost."

CHAPTER 20

Commander Levy burned his eyes on his low-frequency feed.

"Executive officer!"

The portly man looked up from across the table.

"Give me an optimum course and speed to put me six miles from the *Specter's* last known location as fast as possible."

"You mean the point of the missile attack?"

"Yes, you dimwit. Do you know a better location for the *Specter*?"

The man fell silent and began dragging lines on the capacitive screen.

"Fourteen knots, sir," he said. "Course two-four-two."

"Damn you," Levy said. "That can't be right."

"That's the solution, sir."

Levy glared at the geometry but found it flawless.

"How much battery charge are you calculating?"

"Thirty percent, sir. That's the standard–"

"I know the cursed standards. I said to get me there as fast as possible. I didn't say to adhere to any rules that slow me down. Recalculate with three percent battery remaining."

The officer drew new lines.

"Eighteen knots, sir. Same course. Two-four-two."

"That's better. Make it happen."

While the executive officer hailed the veteran mechanic to manipulate the *Crocodile's* dynamics, Levy turned to his sonar ace.

"I want all ears listening for the *Specter*."

"All ears, sir?" the supervisor asked.

"Everyone sitting at a sonar station listens for the *Specter*. I need to strike before this accursed mercenary ship finds a magical way out of this. This fleet's history is filled with fantastic escapes."

As Levy retreated to his chair on the conning platform, his self-assured sonar expert challenged him anew.

"The *Specter* will hear us at six miles, sir."

"With our bow-on aspect? I don't think so."

"At eighteen knots, the sound models support it."

"Then your sound models are wrong. Recalculate them."

"I'll recalculate, sir. Also, what do you want me to do with the drones?"

Levy realized his blood lust had blinded him to the complete tactical picture, and he'd ignored the speed limit of his roving sonar devices. He deflected with a platitude.

"I expect you to know how to handle such details," he said. "I await your recommendation."

"Drone two can reach the *Specter's* last known location a few minutes ahead of us and even reach a few miles farther south, if you want it to."

"Of course, I want it to."

"I'll have it sent ahead, then, sir."

Levy felt himself reasserting his authority.

"Very well."

"As for drone one, sir, it's lost unless you want to drag it behind us as a sea anchor."

Muted chuckles suggested his crew's fear of his positional power was waning. He saw the faces of those whose eyes dared express derision and flagged those men for disciplinary measures. Atop the list—his resilient sonar leader.

"Watch your tone with me, sailor."

"I apologize, sir," the supervisor said.

"That sounds insincere. Don't mock me."

"I was out of line, sir. I owe you better professionalism."

"That's better."

"I recommend cutting the wire to drone one, sir."

Levy barked at his senior veteran mechanic.

"Cut the wire to drone one, tube five. Reload tube five with a torpedo."

As the veteran acknowledged the order, Levy noticed his sonar ace standing and approaching him.

"You have some nerve the way you speak to me."

"That's why I'm making a peace offering, sir. I'm letting you know privately that the sound models support counter-detection from the *Specter* out to eight and a half miles at eighteen knots, even with our bow-on aspect. Consider this my real apology. You can now adjust your tactics with this private knowledge."

"You're still in my debt for your behavior, but I'll remember this gesture."

"I understand, sir."

"Back to your station."

"One more thing, sir, if I may?"

"Go ahead."

"We don't know if the *Specter* is crippled, barely scraped, or somewhere in between. I say we should roust it with the drone to figure it out."

The comment stimulated Levy.

"I see your point. The worst that could happen is I warn the *Specter's* crew that I'm coming, but they should already have deduced that."

"And if the ship is undamaged, sir, they've already driven away. You lose nothing by using the drone in that case."

"But the best case is that I could gather a targeting solution on a crippled target without having to risk a counter-attack."

"Precisely, sir. I recommend turning on the drone's active seeker in ten minutes."

The supervisor's abilities impressed Levy, and he decided to ally with him. After years learning to manipulate people, he knew a simple kind gesture would misdirect the man's suspicions long enough to suit his needs.

If he'd known how, he would have forced a smile, but he left that difficult trick to polished politicians.

"Thank you," he said. "I value your input, and I'll remember your contributions."

"It's my pleasure to help the team, sir."

The sonar expert returned to his chair.

Sprinting at eighteen knots with exclusive focus on the *Specter*, Levy stretched his legs and moved to the room's center. He hovered around the tactical chart awaiting news.

After eight minutes, impatience compelled him.

"Transmit active from the drone," he said. "Maximum power, twenty-degree search centered on the last known location of the *Specter*."

Ten minutes of the drone's active searching passed, raising Levy's blood pressure.

"Find me that damned submarine!"

"If it's there, we'll detect it, sir," the supervisor said.

"Of course, it's there! Find it!"

Before Levy's blood could return to normal, he heard the news he desired.

"Active return from the drone," the supervisor said. "Submerged contact, bearing two-seven-eight, range seven miles from the drone. Sending to the system."

The icon appeared less than a mile north of the *Specter's* last location.

"That's it!" Levy said. "That's my target."

"We're within weapons range, sir," the supervisor said.

"I know that."

The sonar expert turned his head and raised his eyebrows. Levy accepted the hint.

"Oh, yes," he said. "What does your revised sound model say about counter-detection range?"

"Eight and a half miles, sir. We're within nine and a half. I recommend slowing."

Levy heeded the advice and slowed the *Crocodile*. A second and third return from the mercenary submarine confirmed its hobbled status.

"The *Specter's* moving at barely more than a knot, sir," the supervisor said. "I think it's damaged."

"Can you hear it yet?"

"Not yet, sir."

"Keep listening. See if you can find a sign of damage. And assign tube two to the *Specter*."

The technician beside the sonar ace tapped keys.

"Tube two is assigned to the *Specter*, sir, but before you shoot, can I have a word?"

Annoyed, Levy reminded himself to use the man as a resource, despite his insolence. He gestured him to the plot.

The supervisor walked to him and leaned into a private conversation.

"Sir, I don't see any need to shoot at all."

"Explain yourself."

"You remember the cat-and-mouse games the Russians and Americans played during the Cold War?"

"Of course. They're required studies. The Americans usually enjoyed the role of the cat, but not always."

"Right, sir. But the unwritten rules were no launching of torpedoes. One commander outdid the other and announced the victory with a surprise sonar ping."

Levy leaned back and scoffed.

"I see your point, but I'm not playing a game. I'm protecting a tank battalion."

"It's not exactly cat-and-mouse, sir. It's actually cat-and-paralyzed-mouse."

"I don't follow."

"You've already won, sir. Send word to the task force and have them order the mercenaries to surrender."

Levy digested the concept but protested.

"The *Specter* can still hear me, and the *Goliath* can surface from wherever it's hiding and launch its rounds."

"Our task force has enough missiles to hold the *Goliath* underwater for hours, and the *Specter* is helpless."

"The *Specter* is motionless but not helpless. It can shoot torpedoes at me and Exocets at the task force."

"It doesn't carry enough Exocets to penetrate the task force's air defenses, sir, and it can't so much as twitch without us hearing it."

"I've given you enough leeway in your discussions with me, sailor," Levy said. "I'm going to simplify this and sink the damned *Specter*."

"Sir, these mercenaries... they're annoying, but they've gone out of their way to spare lives. Have you even heard of one man dying in this exchange yet?"

Levy knew every warrior had survived the mercenary fleet's attacks, defying the statistics of Renard's prior assaults.

"That's not the point."

"Then what's the point, sir?"

"Damn it! The point is that the decision is mine, and I've made it. Go to your station and obey my orders!"

"I'm a professional, sir, and I will obey your orders as long as they're lawful. I know you have the right to destroy the *Specter*, but the guilt will haunt your conscience. I wash my hands of this."

The supervisor walked away. In his mind, Levy spat the excuse of lacking the luxury of a humanitarian torpedo, but he refused to vocalize his feeling a need to mount a defense.

"Am I waiting for anything else to launch a weapon?"

The supervisor shook his head.

"No, sir. The weapon is ready."

"Very well, then. Shoot tube two."

The barometric change popped Levy's ears.

"Torpedo in the water, sir!"

"I know. I just shot one."

"No, sir. Hostile. Active seeker bearing one-nine-one."

"Impossible," Levy said. "Who shot at me?"

"The *Wraith*, sir. Who else could it be?"

"That's impossible. It can't be."

"You told us all to listen exclusively for the *Specter*, sir. You forgot to defend your flanks. None of us was listening for any threats, based upon your orders."

Levy looked to his chart, and a quick mental calculation supported the closure. Given the *Crocodile's* speed towards the *Specter* and assuming the *Wraith's* commander had risked a reckless all-out sprint, an incoming torpedo was possible.

And he'd let tunnel vision allow it.

"Time to impact?" he asked.

"Less than two minutes, sir. Closer to one minute. It was a well-placed passive shot and I have little history to track it."

"You should've heard it coming!"

"Do you really want to argue, sir? Or do you want to react?"

"Start listening for the *Wraith*, and inform me immediately if you hear anything. Prepare tubes three and four to go out on bearings ten degrees of either side of the incoming weapon."

Technicians tapped keys.

"Tubes three and four are ready," the supervisor said.

"Shoot tube three. Shoot tube four."

Levy knew the southern mercenary submarine had defeated him, but he consoled himself with his adversary's child-like weapons. He needed to only brace for impact, surface his ship, and continue his attack on the *Specter*.

"Do you want to try to evade, sir?"

"No, you've proved that it's pointless, and I want to keep my wires so that I can fight back," he said.

Levy raised his voice to fill the control room.

"I know their tactics. We're about to be attacked by limpet bombs. Prepare damage control parties for shoring, rig the ship for collision, and drive the ship to the surface smartly."

The veteran mechanic passed the word throughout the ship and tapped icons to raise the *Crocodile's* deck.

"Prepare a message for the task force with our location, our drone's location, our torpedo's data, the *Specter's* location and speed limit, and the data on the *Wraith's* incoming weapon."

The veteran tapped keys and dragged icons into each other.

"The message is ready, sir."

As the deck rolled, Levy ordered his radio mast raised and his message sent. After learning of his transmission's receipt, he took solace in knowing he'd claimed victory over the *Specter*.

No matter what the *Wraith* did to him, he'd silenced the invader.

Then he heard the *Wraith's* wrath as magnetic limpets clamped to his hull. Relieved that his adversary withheld the horrible surprise of a heavyweight torpedo, he braced for the impact of the bomblets and the crippling of his ship.

What he would do next depended on the extent of the damage, and he expected to know his fate within seconds–seconds that ticked in frozen time, like agony.

CHAPTER 21

Cahill roared.

"Holy Jesus! Dmitry's a bloody man-god!"

"How do you know it's him?" Dahan asked.

Cahill lifted his chin towards the console's microphone.

"How do I know it's him, sonar supervisor?"

Loudspeakers rendered the response.

"Jake didn't shoot it, and we're the only fleet on the planet that shoots limpet torpedoes."

"Are we close enough that we would've heard Jake if he'd shot?" Cahill asked.

"Yes, we are. Ten miles and listening on his bearing."

"There you have it, major. It was Dmitry."

"But you said he was too far away to intervene," she said.

"Only per the laws of prudent warfare," Cahill said. "But not per the laws of physics. I don't know how many risks he took or how many corvettes or sonobuoys he ran by, but he just raced from his attack on the *Leviathan* straight towards Jake–of his own volition, mind you."

Dahan frowned and pointed at icons.

"I see," she said. "Right here it looks like he actually hid in the wake of a corvette for ten miles."

"No shit. That bloody bastard. He's a man-god."

"I don't mean to piss on your parade, Terry, but there's work to be done," Walker said. "Dmitry put the *Crocodile* on the surface, but it still has a weapon heading for Jake."

"You're right, mate. We need to come shallow and communicate with Pierre."

"I'll take us up," Walker said.

"Please. I don't want to do it meself."

Dahan and Walker shot him ugly glances.

"Not like I'm a coward. I mean I'm afraid what Pierre's going to do when he realizes I turned back to help Jake against his orders."

"So, you are a coward," Dahan said. "Terrified of a French senior citizen."

He met her stare, but she broke, smiled, and looked away.

"That's okay," Walker said. "You're not alone. Dmitry may not have disobeyed direct orders, but he sure as hell acted against any intent Pierre could've had for the *Wraith*."

The *Goliath* rocked in the shallows.

"Raise the radio mast," Cahill said.

"Raising the radio mast," Walker said.

Videos came alive on two monitors as Volkov's translator and Renard were exchanging rapid sentences.

"Understood," Renard said. "I'll send word immediately to the squadron command at Haifa."

"Dmitry awaits your order or, God forbid, the *Crocodile's* weapon hitting Jake, to launch his heavyweight weapon."

"I've ordered Terry to come shallow."

"I'm shallow," Cahill said. "I'm here."

"Good," Renard said. "I want Dmitry to minimize his exposure since he's our final trump card. But you can take the risk of revealing your position by transmitting with high-frequency voice. I want your Aman officer to address the task force on an unencrypted line."

Dahan crowded Cahill's shoulder, and he welcomed the intrusion, wanting her warmth close to him.

"I can't reveal Aman's presence on your ships."

"You don't have to state your identity, major," Renard said. "You can claim to be a citizen activist if asked, but I assure you your navy has figured it out, or at the very least suspects your organization's involvement."

"If I agree, what would you have me do? Order the shutting down of the torpedo headed for Jake?"

"Precisely. Use the threat of the *Wraith* as leverage."

Cahill reviewed the geometry.

"It's a double threat," he said. "I'm in range of a credible torpedo shot now, too."

Renard's eyes aimed off the monitor, and his face flushed.

"I see you indeed are. Apparently, my orders have devolved into mere suggestions for my commanders."

"I sincerely apologize, Pierre. But you know I couldn't just turn me back on Jake."

"Have you no faith in my negotiating skills? I can talk us out of any surrender situation."

"Sorry, mate. Instincts."

"To be discussed later. We have more pressing matters."

Showing her compact strength, Dahan nudged Cahill aside.

"We're wasting Jake's time," she said. "I'll do it. Give me a microphone."

Walker extended a receiver. She grabbed it and started talking in her native language. While she spoke, the executive officer stepped around her and leaned into Cahill.

"We might need to start shooting to get the point across."

"Shooting what?" Cahill asked.

"The *Crocodile*. With the cannons. It's almost within phased array radar range if not already, and we could cripple its propulsion before anyone could place a Harpoon on us."

"I sure hope that's unnecessary."

An angry man spat Hebrew over the loudspeaker.

"He didn't sound cooperative," Cahill said.

"Actually, he was agreeing," Dahan said. "That was the task force commander. He understands the *Crocodile's* predicament."

"So he'll have Jake spared?"

"He's given the order. He's awaiting confirmation from the *Crocodile*."

"It could be a lie," Cahill said.

"It could be," she said. "But you have more than one way to call his bluff."

"Right. I've got four torpedoes left. Liam, assign tube three to the *Crocodile*."

"With pleasure... Tube three is assigned to the *Crocodile*."

"No confirmation yet," Dahan said.

Fear and frustration rose within Cahill.

"No confirmation, no compassion," he said. "Send that message as close to a literal translation as you can."

Her transmitted translation begat silence. Cahill's anger surged, and he growled at Dahan.

"Make this message very clear," he said. "If Jake dies, the *Crocodile* gets cut in half. Then, I'll see that Dmitry and I sink every bloody ship in this task force, and then after that, we'll go after the tanks. Make sure these mongrels understand me."

Her eyes wide, Dahan nodded and redoubled her zeal in the conversation. After she spurted words that sounded like venom, the task force commander's response arrived.

"The *Crocodile's* weapon is shut down," she said.

"Sonar supervisor?" Cahill asked.

Loudspeakers carried the response.

"I heard it shut down personally, Terry. It's true."

"Sorry, major," Cahill said. "I wanted to be sure, but I believe I cut you off."

"The task force commander reminds you, however, that he can still order the *Crocodile* to simply launch another weapon at the *Specter*, which presents an immobile and unmissable target."

"Does he think we're in a stalemate?" Cahill asked.

"I don't know," she said. "Would you like me to ask him?"

The boss interjected.

"No need," Renard said. "You've done your duty admirably, major, shortcutting the message to spare Jake, but the real negotiations are happening at higher paygrades as we speak."

"Dmitry reminds you that he needs to snorkel," the translator said. "He's critically low on battery charge."

"Wait," Renard said. "Have him run his hotel loads on the MESMA unit for just a bit longer."

Cahill considered taking a risk to help his team.

"Do you want me to raise me cannons and start shooting engine rooms?" he asked. "Or perhaps a demonstration of me reach against the tanks?"

"Not yet. I appreciate your vigor, but please wait. All of you. All Israeli naval assets are weapons tight while the senior Aman general states his case to the prime minister."

"And what about the tanks?" Cahill asked.

"There's nowhere they can reach beyond your range before these negotiations end," Renard said.

"I don't trust the speed of talking politicians," Cahill said. "The prime minister could be stalling."

"For what?" Renard asked.

"To rally his air forces? That's a possibility."

"I wouldn't worry about that. The senior Air Force general is joining the Aman general to lobby for peace."

"So he's finally chosen a side."

"I believe he chose his side long before our participation," Renard said. "Our efforts merely prompted him to voice his opinion. If nothing else, our mission portrayed the prime minister in his true light. It doesn't take a political strategist to see that his push into Syria is personally motivated."

"If you say so, but I still don't like waiting."

"You'll have your answer in half an hour. I promise."

Cahill frowned.

"How can you promise?"

"Because if you don't have your answer by then, you'll be sending ten rounds into the tank battalion. I see that your little stunt of heading back to help Jake placed you in your launch basket."

Volkov spoke in his crude English.

"Can I now snorkel?"

"Yes, Dmitry," Renard said. "I was awaiting the weapons tight confirmation from Aman, which I now have. Go ahead and snorkel."

"Since I gave you a little extra negotiating leverage by moving within range of the tanks, does this mean you forgive me for violating your order to leave the battle?" Cahill asked.

"No. I'm still docking your pay."

"How much?"

"I haven't decided. I'm not accustomed to my commanders disobeying me."

"How about ten percent, mate?"

"This isn't a negotiation. Have you forgotten that I'm your employer?"

"No. It just sounded fair."

Renard flicked his palm backwards.

"Very well, then. Ten percent it is. I actually can't tell if I should be punishing you or rewarding you. So we'll leave it at that until I've had time to reflect."

During a silence, Cahill leaned into Dahan's ear and spoke with a soft voice.

"You seem to be doing well under the bridge dome."

"There are so many thoughts in my mind that I'm ignoring it," she said. "I may be getting used to it, too."

"It's not natural for a human to be under the oceans, especially with windows as a constant reminder. But you can train your mind to get used to just about anything, I imagine."

"I don't know that I can get used to the idea of having to leave you in a matter of days."

Her words hurt like an inescapable truth. The mission's pending success would entail her departure.

"We'll worry about that after this mess is settled."

"I have news," Renard said. "The prime minister demands a demonstration."

"Like he thinks we're bluffing?" Cahill asked.

"Exactly like that."

"Did you agree to it?"

"I did. You'll take two shots, one from each cannon, at a Jeep being towed by a tank at its maximum speed. If you hit the Jeep, the prime minister will have to respect your reach."

"If you've got terminal guidance for me, it should be easy enough," Cahill said. "But are you sure you want to give in to his demand?"

The Frenchman's grin reminded Cahill of a mischievous cat.

"Call it a demonstration for future potential clients," Renard said. "In my line of work, I need to keep such an open mind. Several generals and members of the government will consider the naval battles as statistics over distant waters, but this demonstration will be a sight they'll remember."

"So be it. Can you send me target coordinates and launch timing?"

"I'm sending them now."

"I've got them," Walker said.

"Very well, Liam," Cahill said. "I'm bringing us to minimum cannon depth."

He tapped a key that set the *Goliath* into its routine of pumping water from its trim tanks to the sea. A depth gauge counted the ship's imperceptible rise while the deck tilted downward to raise the stern-mounted weapons bays above the waves.

"The weapons bays report being clear to raise the cannons," Walker said.

"Very well," Cahill said. "Raising the cannons."

He tapped two icons on his screen, ordering hydraulic fluid to lift the railguns above the waterline.

"Cannons are raised," Walker said.

"Prepare to shoot one penetrating round from each cannon at the assigned system coordinates."

Walker touched keys at his console.

"Each cannon is aimed at the assigned system coordinates, ready to fire."

"Fire."

The boom from the starboard railgun preceded the port weapon's supersonic crack.

Cahill tapped keys to submerge his weapons bays.

"Lowering the cannons and returning to snorkel depth," he said. "And now all we do is wait."

"I have tracking lock on the target," Renard said. "I have positive control of your rounds."

"No jamming?" Cahill asked.

The Frenchman sounded nonchalant.

"They may try jamming."

"You don't sound concerned about it," Cahill said.

"The jamming power levels would be small compared to those of naval ships, and the predictive algorithms that guide your rounds have shown good results against the reduction gears of destroyers, which are similar targets in terms of size and maneuverability."

"Time will tell. What if we miss?"

"Then you'll shoot ten splintering rounds and defy them to stop me from hitting with a constellation of buckshot."

"Sounds good, mate."

Cahill's mind drifted, and he found himself groping for a satisfying conversation to have with Dahan before her departure. He wanted to plan future time with her but needed the battle to end.

Renard's smug grin conveyed the victory.

"Not quite resounding," he said. "One round grazed the side of the hood, but the other hit left of center in the engine compartment—adequate to declare a mission kill. That would be one tank disabled per two shots, which is good enough."

"Good enough for what?" Cahill asked.

Renard sneered.

"To declare our mission accomplished. The prime minister has conceded that our demonstration is a success, and he'll pull his tanks back."

Cahill sensed a ruse.

"For how long, though?"

"Days. Weeks. Months. It's a matter of speculation. But at least we've weakened him politically. I pray that his regime crumbles from within."

Cahill glanced at Dahan, who shrugged.

"It's possible, but I don't have a crystal ball."

He wished she did and that she'd use it on their relationship.

"The Israeli task force will be ordered to disband and return home," Renard said. "We'll watch them, and once the entire task force is back within Israeli waters, you'll pick up Jake."

"Just Jake?"

"Yes. I don't trust all our ships geolocated so close to a still-angered prime minister who may forget his declaration of peace if tempted. Dmitry will remain submerged and undetected to protect your loading operation, and then you'll take Jake west fifty miles. Then you'll wait for Dmitry and load him."

Cahill felt his adrenaline subsiding.

"Can you connect me with my colonel?" Dahan asked.

"Of course, major," Renard said. "The link's already established. I'll connect him to the *Goliath*."

A middle-aged man with peppery hair wearing a green military top appeared and began talking with Dahan in Hebrew. After she received her update, she switched to English.

"The colonel confirms it," she said. "It's over."

Renard's face supplanted that of the Israeli officer.

"I'm sending rendezvous coordinates to Terry and Dmitry to pick up and protect Jake. I've sent word to Jake over the low-bandwidth link to shut down his outboard motor and wait for you."

An urge to be alone with Dahan overcame Cahill.

"Pierre, I need to debrief the major. Liam can handle things up here and take us to Jake."

He darted down the stairway, paused midway down, and looked up to verify she followed. At his beckoning, she came.

She trailed him through the control room where handshakes and congratulatory embraces slowed him, and then he continued to his stateroom. He heard her gentle steps three paces behind him.

"Join me, major. We need to debrief portions of the mission in private."

She entered the room, and he locked the door behind her. He moved to her, grabbed her waist, and pushed her against the bulkhead. His passion lifted her from her feet as he kissed her, but her response seemed rote.

"What's wrong?" he asked.

"This was only a dream. I couldn't tell you on the bridge, but my colonel is sending a helicopter tonight to retrieve all the Aman teams from your ships."

"Then I'll keep you as me prisoner."

"Terry!"

"I'm serious. I'll have Pierre make up an excuse that we need you aboard for a debriefing."

"We can debrief via satellite."

"Not if I need to be submerged at all."

"All this for what? A couple days together?"

"A chance to get to know each other. No combat stress. No subterfuge. Just us."

She shook her head.

"It can't work. I have my career in Israel. You have your career traveling the world, and in your free time you live on the other side of the planet."

"I have lots of free time, and I'll find me way to you."

"In case you haven't figured it out, you need to avoid Israel for a long time."

"Right. But there are plenty of ways we can make it work."

"When did you become an optimist?"

"It must've been the last time we were here and you let me believe we had chemistry together."

Inner conflict cast shadows on her face.

"You're just setting us both up for disappointment."

"Then I'll live every moment with you like it's me last."

She lowered her chin and looked away to hide a grin.

"Okay."

"Okay, what?"

"Okay, I'll stay as long as you and Pierre can keep me. I can't disobey orders. So I hope he's a good negotiator."

Cahill smiled.

"You have no idea."

He held her and kissed her for minutes that flowed like ages but receded into the memory of an ephemeral moment when he released her. Freeing her of his grasp, he ushered her ahead and waited several minutes before following.

While walking, he realized something about him had changed. A gap was filled. A vulnerability was removed.

He felt safe, and he questioned if he'd seen the last of his drowning nightmares.

When he reached the bridge, he saw Walker talking to the image of Jake's face.

"Look who's shallow and communicating," Cahill said.

"I just connected with him and let him know we're coming to pick him up," Walker said. "But that was hardly news since he had his low-bandwidth orders from Pierre."

Jake seemed distant. Cahill wondered if his being last in line for the news flow accounted for the phenomenon, of if he should credit his colleague's latest bout of mortal terror.

"I was just thanking Dmitry for saving my ass," Jake said. "I was getting ready to surface and jump into the water when he forced the Israelis to shut down their weapon."

"He says you would have done the same for him," the translator said.

"Hey, hold on," Jake said. "I'm safe, and that's great, but everyone looks so happy. Or at least relieved."

"Yeah. Isn't that a good thing?" Cahill asked.

"Well, sure, but clue me in. Something big happened while I was deep. What'd I miss?"

CHAPTER 22

Volkov liked Cahill's rule changes as he invented them, and he let his Australian colleague defend himself from the American as the screens portrayed the verbal exchange. His translator's intervention became a murmur feeding his subconscious mind.

"Last time, Dmitry got to ride forward because he got to you first," Jake said. "Now I'm here first, I have to ride fifty miles as your only passenger, and he still gets to ride facing forward?"

"Last time, I didn't have a guest of honor," Cahill said.

"Oh, that's nice. I'm not a guest, or I don't have honor?"

"You're a guest alright, mate. And you have honor. You're just not the guest of honor, as in, there's only one."

"All of a sudden, Dmitry's king of the world?"

"Let me review the scorecard. He defeated the *Splendor*, he defeated the *Revival*, he defeated the *Crocodile*, and he defeated the *Leviathan*–twice. In contrast, you ran from a bunch of robots before you lost to the *Crocodile*. Per my reckoning, that's five points for Dmitry and minus one for you, giving a net six-point advantage for our Russian friend."

The Australian's tally flattered Volkov, and he was unsure if he should interject. But as the realization that his troubled childhood and his alcohol-hazed adulthood had denied him any memory of someone he admired like Cahill praising him, he swallowed back the rising lump in his throat.

"The second *Leviathan* doesn't count!" Jake said. "That was a gift."

"A gift counts," Cahill said. "If I gave you a gift of money, wouldn't you spend it like your wages?"

"It's a moot question. You'd never give me money."

The Australian grinned.

"True."

"Well, technically, half his points should go to Mikhail and Andrei," Jake said. "And I didn't lose to the *Crocodile*. I was ambushed trying to clear the way for your backwards, backwoods, outback ass."

"Would you prefer that I give Dmitry two and a half points, the dolphins two and a half points, and stick you with minus one–which really should be minus two for getting crippled by rusted guppy chaser?"

The American rolled his eyes.

"Fine. Dmitry's the guest of honor. Just hurry up and lock him down so we can get out of here."

The Australian's eyes angled away from the monitor, and Volkov checked a view from an external camera to verify his connection to the *Goliath*.

"While you were complaining, Liam locked him in. Now that our successful submarine commander has arrived, we can go."

"Bite me," Jake said.

"And you can kiss me bare hairy arse."

Feeling free for the first time to poke fun at his colleagues, Volkov entered the verbal fray.

"It sounds like you two are getting romantic," he said.

The translator hesitated but then transformed the words into English.

"Well, shit, Dmitry," Jake said. "I think that's the first time you've insulted either one of us, and you got both of us with one insult. Welcome to the team."

Volkov exhaled, hoping he'd impressed his colleagues with the timing and content of his joke. He'd been afraid of offending them or worse, being ignored.

"Okay, enough games, mates. We need to surface as soon as Dmitry shifts his water. Go ahead Dmitry."

Volkov engaged his gray-bearded veteran in moving fluid throughout the *Wraith's* inner tanks. With Cahill's pressure sensors guiding the orchestra of water weight, the old mechanic made quick work of the rapid redistribution.

"You look good, Dmitry," Cahill said. "I've got you and Jake nestled in me cradle real nice. Let's get to the surface."

A gentle ascent brought the *Wraith's* depth gauge to its limit of zero before the *Goliath* lifted the submarine from the water. As the deck rocked below Volkov, his boss' image appeared on a monitor, and the aging Frenchman appeared rejuvenated.

"Can you hear me?" Renard asked.

"You sound and look great as usual," Jake said.

"Success is a panacea," Renard said. "I am energized."

"Great," Jake said. "Any news?"

"Nothing yet on the prime minister's fate. The only news I have pertains to our team. An oil tanker inbound for Haifa will rendezvous with you and transfer the Aman team from your ships via helicopter."

Volkov welcomed the removal of the foreign presence from his submarine, but the Australian seemed agitated.

"Any exceptions?" Cahill asked.

"Yes," Renard said. "Major Dahan will remain aboard the *Goliath* until you make landfall. I wanted the entire Aman team to stay for our debriefs, but I'm afraid I could only earn agreement for her to join us."

"Makes sense," Jake said. "I'm sure some factions in Israel consider them heroes but others consider them traitors."

"You assume that people know of their involvement with us at all," Renard said. "There are few who do, and it must be kept that way. Ergo, the team can't risk being seen with us, but since it's easier to hide one lady than her full team of men, we can keep Major Dahan."

The Australian seemed eager to change subjects.

"It's decided, then," Cahill said. "Send us the rendezvous coordinates and timing for the transfer."

"Of course," Renard said. "I'm having them sent now."

"We need to talk about something more important," Cahill said. "Where to park these ships. I'm thirsty for a coldie."

Volkov leaned into his translator.

"What's he thirsty for?"

"I believe he means a cold drink, like a beer."

Volkov had dreaded the prior mission's celebration for his sense of alienation. The language barrier and his newness to the team had made him uncomfortable.

The anxiety of another social gathering bothered him, and he tried to find reasons to feel accepted and comfortable. He'd proven his worth against the Israelis, and his Australian colleague had lauded it. He'd saved his American colleague, but he feared he'd embarrassed Jake.

As he attempted to excuse himself from the conversation, it drew him back in.

"Greece would be nice, but it's still too soon," Jake said.

"Agreed," Cahill said. "We could hang out in Turkey."

"Wrong direction, and it forces us to transit through Greek waters," Jake said.

The Frenchman interjected.

"Not necessarily the wrong direction," Renard said.

"What's going on?" Jake asked. "You've got that shit-eating aura like you're about to screw us."

"Not at all. There's a backlog in Toulon shipyards, and so I called my old friend, Admiral Khan, to arrange an earlier availability in Karachi. Since Terry's new bow is coming from Taiwan, I could have it diverted. And I can fly your new propeller and periscope from France on military transport."

"So we get to pick our repair yard?" Jake asked.

"You're surprised that I'm offering you a choice?"

The American's voice reached falsetto.

"Yes!"

"Agreed, it's unusual that I would do so, but tactically it makes no difference when looking at the cost and timing of handling the repairs and reaching our next client."

"You already know our next client?"

"I'm negotiating with my top choice, and there's no hurry as there's flexibility on the mission's timing."

"I don't suppose you'll tell us... never mind. Why would I bother to ask?"

"Indeed. I've never burdened you with such useless and dangerous a priori knowledge, despite your urchin-like curiosity."

The Australian interjected.

"I'm not curious about anything except me next drink," Cahill said. "We could head to Alexandria, if places in Egypt cater to beer drinkers."

"I think they do," Jake said.

"If not, then maybe Malta," Cahill said. "I've heard good things."

The American looked away from the screen.

"I'm checking the chart. I've heard good things about Malta, too. That would be fine, I guess. Or Sicily again."

"We could do both, if we want to make a vacation out of it," Cahill said.

The Frenchman redirected the conversation.

"Hold on," Renard said. "Don't become too liberal spending my money. Your fuel isn't free."

"Fine," Cahill said. "Since I'm declaring Dmitry as the superhero of this mission, I say he gets to pick."

As the translator finished the sentence, insecurity tightened Volkov's chest. He stammered through his first words, thankful for the translator's filtering of his fear.

He also pushed the terrible event far into the future.

"I would feel best if we put a lot of water between us and Israel," he said. "I'm also tired of France. Let's head towards Pakistan and put the major choke points behind us before we stop."

"That's what? Ten days? You're killing me, mate."

"No, he's onto something, Terry," Renard said. "Muscat, Oman is great for tourism. Sightseeing, fishing, snorkeling, and possible other distractions if I remember correctly."

"Could we charter a boat for a booze cruise?" Cahill asked.

"I'm sure I could arrange that," Renard said. "For those with more refined tastes, there's also a possible day trip to Dubai."

"I can be patient, then, I guess."

The Frenchman frowned.

"You sounded like you were near tears," Renard said.

"Well, you're keeping a thirsty sailor from his beer."

"Instead of making Terry cry, we'll head to Port Said to fix Jake's submarine. I can bribe our way into the yards for a couple weeks, and that will give us time to relax and unwind. Then we'll continue on to Karachi for the *Goliath's* new bow."

"Egypt could be cool," Jake said.

"I'll set up tours for Cairo, Alexandria, and the pyramids, but there will be free time," Renard said. "There will also be free time for men to travel home, if desired."

Smiles, affirmative murmurs, and nods followed the declaration.

"So be it, then," Renard said. "I'll make the arrangements."

Sensing a lull in the discussion, Volkov excused himself and sought solitude. Walking the quiet confines of the cramped corridors, he decided to distract himself with a snack.

Sailors filled the mess deck as his crew relaxed in front of computer screens, books, and each other. Even with men engaged in their own worlds, a solitary figure struck him as an outcast, distinct from the others and sitting alone.

Volkov skipped his snack and braved the greeting.

"May I sit, Vasily?"

The trainer looked up and smiled.

"Dmitry."

Volkov sat across the dining table and started with a topic he knew would beget a discussion.

"How are Mikhail and Andrei?"

The cetaceans' master assumed a quizzical expression.

"I am not entirely sure," he said. "But I think they're feeling ignored."

"You mean, they need more attention?"

"Oh, no. I give them plenty of love, and most crewmen visit them. It's more like they feel excluded or unimportant."

Volkov found the complexity of the mammalian emotions and a human's ability to detect them dubious, but if such a relationship could exist, he considered the trainer and his dolphins capable.

"Do you know why they feel… that way?"

"I think they sense their importance dwindling. They can sense the entire crew's tension, especially mine, and from that they can tell how intense our battles are. For the amount of activity we're seeing, they're spending too much time in their tank and too little time chasing submarines."

"Oh, I see. They feel unappreciated."

The trainer's eyes opened wide.

"Yes! That's the word. That's the sentiment."

"I suppose the only remedy is to make sure we find ways to make use of them."

"I'm afraid that may be difficult. What if they have no future? What if the Israeli tactics are the end for my babies?"

"We were caught by surprise when the Israelis intercepted the return-to-ship message and turned it against us. We have time to develop new tactics."

"But I don't know how to overcome fake messages. What if an intercepted message in our next mission sends them beyond our communications range?"

"It's a risk, but escorting them with a drone helped."

The lithe man showed tactical understanding.

"You can't waste resources like that. You wouldn't send two drones to the same location because it's wasteful. I'm sure similar logic applies for my babies and a drone."

"Similar, but not exact. A drone can't deploy explosive charges, for example."

"I guess not, but there's still a difficult challenge ahead."

"We have great minds on our team to help us. I beg you not to worry. We'll figure something out."

"I suppose we will. But you seemed worried."

"When?"

"When you joined me."

Volkov wanted to protest, but he knew the trainer would pierce the veil of such a charade. He conceded defeat.

"You know me well."

"Sometimes I need to study you, but this time it was so obvious that others may have noticed."

"I'm glad I found you. I can be honest with you."

"We're an odd combination, but that's a good recipe for friendship," the trainer said.

"Agreed. I don't know who else I could rely on. I need your help. We're going to be at our celebration dinner soon."

Dreading the ordeal, Volkov delayed in sharing the news with his crew.

"Is it already scheduled?"

"Yes. Port Said."

"Not France?"

"No, we're ultimately going back through the Suez Canal to Karachi for the *Goliath's* new bow section."

"Egypt should be nice."

"For everyone else, yes. But not me at the dinner. I was an outcast last time, and that's been an easy role for me to play. But this time, Jake and Terry will expect me to be more engaging. This is our second mission as a team, and I had a large impact on it."

The trainer's face became illuminated.

"Large? You were the hero. You saved Jake."

Volkov felt squeamish.

"That's the problem. I'm great in a submarine, but I'm terrible in social situations. Jake and Terry are masters of the waters, but they're also masters of men in any situation. I lack such charisma."

"Nonsense. Everyone on this ship trusts you with their life."

"This is an artificial world where I'm God."

The man's narrow shoulders rose towards his ears, and he tilted his head.

"Eh, you have a point."

"Outside of a command structure, I don't know who I am."

The trainer lowered his shoulders and gave a hard look.

"That's profound. Giving orders on a submarine has defined you, and you struggle for an identity outside the hull."

Volkov found the insight obvious, but sharing it in conversation with a trusted listener helped.

"I just pushed the limits of what any sane submarine commander should attempt, and I should feel like I've mastered my world. But instead, I'm afraid that I'm just a social buffoon the second I set foot off this vessel."

"It's poor self-esteem, but even if I concede for the sake of argument that you're socially awkward, you can't say that you're a complete social idiot. For example, I find our conversations stimulating."

"Yes, but you're an abnormal man."

The trainer laughed.

"I can't deny that. But I'm no idiot, and my opinion is valuable. You have social value. You just need to relax and have confidence."

"Perhaps. I don't know."

"At some point, you'll feel relaxed enough around Jake and Terry to joke with them."

Anxiety crept over Volkov.

"No, I am bad with jokes. I tried one with them earlier and almost died of fear."

"I can teach you. It's all about timing and knowing your audience. For example, when you called me abnormal a few moments ago, your timing was perfect."

"I wasn't trying to be funny!"

"But you can learn. For example, an insult can be humorous if given to someone you trust when they're expecting praise. Do you see why I thought calling me abnormal was funny? I'd just said something nice to you, and common courtesy would have you say something nice to me. But instead you called me abnormal. The contrast creates the humor."

"I guess so."

The trainer's eyes narrowed.

"You know I'll support you at the dinner in Muscat. I'll stay by your side, if it helps."

"Thank you, Vasily. That will help."

"I don't fit in with anyone else either. So you'll be helping me, too."

"If we're in agreement, why do you look so mischievous?"

"I have an idea to help you prepare for the dinner."

"Will you tell me what it is?"

"I prefer that you trust me."

Volkov retired to his stateroom and read a novel for hours until a sailor knocked on his door.

"Enter."

"Sir, Mister Renard is calling for all commanders."

Volkov arrived in the control room to see his boss, Jake, and Walker where he expected Cahill. He also lacked his translator, who showed up a minute later.

Walker explained he was waiting for Cahill, who was exercising on the far side of the huge ship.

"When did he start exercising?" Jake asked.

"The rumor mill says it's because he's trying to impress Major Dahan," Walker said. "I also noticed him eating more vegetables, too. It's the worst kept secret on the ship that they're getting romantic."

"Seriously?" Jake asked. "I didn't see this coming."

His French employer seemed unfazed, but the American's surprise in the burgeoning romance comforted Volkov in his ignorance of their fleet's love affair.

"Yes," Walker said. "Terry went mad about her when they met, but he must've found his nerve. At some point during this mission, he became a lot more sane around her."

"Very well," Renard said. "You can catch up Terry on events later. I have some insight into the effect of our mission, and I'm pleased to say it's positive. The impeachment process of the prime minister has begun."

"That's good," Jake said. "But does it really have any chance of sticking?"

"I can't say," Renard said. "But we've forced the issue, and that's all we could have done."

The next morning after breakfast, Volkov returned to his stateroom and read a book at his desk. Then the trainer stuck his head through the open door.

"I have a present for you, Dmitry."

"Really? What's the occasion?"

"Charisma."

He extended a folded piece of paper.

"What is it?"

"It's insight from Terry. I had the translator approach him for some ideas, and this is what he came up with."

Volkov wondered how much the trainer had shared that he'd considered private, but he excused his actions as those of a well-intended friend.

"That was sneaky of you."

"I thought Terry would be willing to help. He's more outgoing than Jake, but Terry assured me that Jake's fond of you and glad to have you on the team."

"Thank you."

"You're welcome. Remember to practice. The delivery is as important as the words."

Later that morning, Volkov returned to the screens showing his boss and the other commanders. A good night's sleep had given him a renewed perspective.

Jake seemed calmer than he'd remembered him, despite his recent dances with mortal terror. Cahill was invigorated, giving credence to the rumors of his new romantic life with the Israeli officer. Even Renard showed a renewed spirit, suggesting he could endure as the fleet's leader for years to come.

But among the commanding officers, Volkov grasped for his role.

Three ships, three commanders.

There must be three roles.

With tenure, Jake served as the leader. He had grown the fleet from nothing with Renard and had stolen the submarine that Volkov commanded. The American's lead position was secure.

With the most dynamic ship, Cahill changed roles as needed, serving the others with transport or rescue or taking the lead in railgun attacks. The Australian's self-assured ease let him shift between his roles like a chameleon changing colors.

But Volkov's role eluded him.

Since a third ship needed staffing, Renard had hired him for his abilities, despite suffering defeat against his future employer in the Black Sea.

He questioned if he served as a trophy. He wondered if he should see himself as a defeated citizen absorbed into the conquering forces.

Pursing his lips, he forced destructive thoughts from his mind, and he decided to let his success in the mission against Israel define him.

As he did, he enjoyed an epiphany.

"I'm the best commander in this fleet," he said. "I may be the best in the world."

"Excuse me?" the translator asked. "You don't want me to translate that, do you?"

"No, please don't. But I just realized it. Jake may think he's the best. Terry may think he's the best, but shame on me if I don't think I'm the best. After this week, who could argue?"

The translator shrugged and then translated a conversation as it started.

"So how's the romance?" Jake asked.

"We're going to give it a go," Cahill said. "There's going to be a lot of travel, but Pierre pays me well enough that we can afford first-class flights. Ariella's got some leave coming up, and we're going to try a vacation together."

"Where?"

"Far away. We're deciding tonight at dinner. You can help."

"Good," Jake said. "I can't wait to meet her in person."

"You will."

The conversation stalled, and then Cahill restarted it.

"You doing alright, mate?"

"Yeah, I guess," Jake said. "That was a rough mission for me, but I'm over it now. I've reviewed my tactics enough times to know that I made smart calls."

"I'm glad you see it that way," Cahill said. "You can't beat yourself up, even if you did make mistakes. But I didn't see any. You fought a great battle and just had bad luck."

"Thanks, Terry."

"Don't you think so, Dmitry?" Cahill asked.

A shyness crept over him, but he waited for it to disappear. When it did, Volkov surprised himself with the ease he found in expressing himself to his colleagues–his new extended family of heroes in whose ranks he'd etched a permanent belonging.

"You did indeed do an excellent job fighting in this mission. I couldn't have done better myself."

"I appreciate it, Dmitry," Jake said. "First, you came to my rescue. Now you're reminding me that I fought well."

"You did. You look like you're secure in knowing this."

"I am. I've put the negatives behind me."

Volkov considered Jake's confidence genuine and risked following the dolphin trainer's advice.

He switched to English and recalled the phrase the trainer had requested from Cahill.

Before Volkov got halfway through his recitation, the Australian turned red and made feeble gestures to suppress his laughter.

"But like Terry said, I scored five submarines to your negative one. That's a six-point difference, and that's just too huge to ignore. Therefore, when you see me next, you'll have to kiss my bare hairy ass and bite me."

THE END

About the Author

After graduating from the Naval Academy in 1991, John Monteith served on a nuclear ballistic missile submarine and as a top-rated instructor of combat tactics at the U.S. Naval Submarine School. He now works as an engineer when not writing.

Join the Rogue Submarine fleet to get news, freebies, discounts, and your FREE Rogue Avenger bonus chapter!

ROGUE SUBMARINE SERIES:

ROGUE AVENGER (2005)
ROGUE BETRAYER (2007)
ROGUE CRUSADER (2010)
ROGUE DEFENDER (2013)
ROGUE ENFORCER (2014)
ROGUE FORTRESS (2015)
ROGUE GOLIATH (2015)
ROGUE HUNTER (2016)
ROGUE INVADER (2017)
ROGUE JUSTICE (2017)
ROGUE KINGDOM (2018)

WRAITH HUNTER CHRONICLES:

PROPHECY OF ASHES (2018)
PROPHECY OF BLOOD (2018)

John Monteith recommends his talented colleagues:

Graham Brown, author of The Gods of War.

Jeff Edwards, author of Sword of Shiva.

Thomas Mays, author of A Sword into Darkness.

Kevin Miller, author of Raven One.

Ted Nulty, author of Gone Feral.

John R Monteith

ROGUE JUSTICE

Copyright © 2017 by John R. Monteith

Braveship Books

www.braveshipbooks.com

The tactics described in this book do not represent actual U.S. Navy or NATO tactics past or present. Also, many of the code words and some of the equipment have been altered to prevent unauthorized disclosure of classified material.

ISBN-13: 978-1-64062-008-7

Published in the United States of America

Made in United States
North Haven, CT
27 June 2022

20687400R00146